WELLSIDE

ROBIN SHORTT

Candlemark & Gleam

First edition published 2017

Copyright @ 2017 by Robin Shortt

For information, address
Athena Andreadis
Candlemark & Gleam LLC,
38 Rice Street #2, Cambridge, MA 02140
eloi@candlemarkandgleam.com

Library of Congress Cataloguing-in-Publication Data
In Progress

ISBN: 978-1-936460-77-9
eISBN: 978-1-936460-76-2

Cover design by Jenny Zemanek

Book design and composition by Athena Andreadis
Typeface: Calisto MT

Editors: Athena Andreadis and Kate Sullivan

Proofreader: Kelly Jennings

www.candlemarkandgleam.com

For Charlie

PART ONE

Chapter One

Essa Roth, alone at her table in the back of the cafeteria, was sketching again. Ben, also alone two tables away, kept glancing over to see what it was.

And maybe also to check out Essa Roth a little bit. But mostly to see what she was drawing.

His phone buzzed. His mum, with a calendar invite. *Meeting with lawyer.* She didn't say whether it was her lawyer (the divorce) or Ben's lawyer (the arrest) and he wasn't sure it mattered. He tapped *Accept* and watched his calendar shift itself around. Half a dozen alerts bloomed on the screen—conflicts with appointments his dad had sent him earlier.

He sighed and glanced at Essa again as she rolled her head back to ease her neck. She was wearing the same black blouse and jeans she wore every day—it was gearing up to be a brutal summer even for Queensland; it was barely noon and already the air tasted like it had been run through a clothes dryer, but she never even rolled her sleeves up. It wasn't that she didn't feel the heat, either. Her short dark hair (really short, just this side of a crew cut) was stiff with dried sweat. She was wearing her fingerless climbing gloves too, like she always did, even though it must have made it hard to draw. And also like always, she'd dusted her fingertips with gold glitter.

The glitter clashed with everything else about her, but then, that wasn't the weirdest thing about Essa. For a start, there was the whispering. She was doing it now, he could see her lips moving, forming those weird alien syllables like something played backwards as she bent over her sketchbook.

He looked back at his calendar. Every one of those conflicts was another argument waiting to happen—his mum pacing the kitchen, gripping her phone so hard the tendons stood out on her wrist, voice pitched low and full of venom, his dad's voice rising until Ben could hear it from across the room. He felt a headache ramping up, right at the base of his skull, as he started shifting stuff around on his calendar, getting rid of those conflicts. Proposed new times to his tutor, his Math Olympiad team, his online coding class. Watched his free time shrink to nothing. Played Tetris with his life.

He looked up again when Essa ripped the page she'd been working on out of her binder. She took a critical look at it before throwing it onto the table beside her, and Ben craned his neck to see.

It was upside down but he could tell it was a Librarian. She stood on a sandstone pinnacle barely large enough for her feet, robe blowing straight back in the wind. Librarians were a favourite of his, and he cautiously leaned back in his chair for a better view. He was careful not to cut his eyes to the right, where Ryan Bradman and his douchebag lackeys Nick and Troy had commandeered a table. Ryan was showing them something on his phone—something horrific and degrading, probably, from the way they were laughing. Nick had a fishing knife he was scratching something into the desk with.

It would be a spectacularly bad idea to make Ryan think Ben was looking at *him*. You never wanted to remind Ryan that you and he shared the same universe, because Ryan apparently had a grudge against everyone in it.

He didn't even know why any of them had shown up. It was Year

12, it was December, and he doubted Ryan was all that worried about his exams. Everyone was on edge as the year wound down. It was like the previously solid walls of Chifley High had grown thin, like a worn-out eggshell, and everyone was restless to break through and gulp air.

Or in Ben's case, depending on how the next week worked out, swap them for walls a whole lot thicker, and a tracksuit with CORRECTIONAL CENTRE ISSUE on it.

Essa sketched all the time. She always had her big binder out, or else a little leather-bound notebook she pulled out of her back pocket during any kind of downtime.

Ben had first gotten a look at her work one afternoon in the gym, while Essa was on the wall. You weren't supposed to be on the climbing wall without a teacher there, but then you weren't supposed to be in the gym anyway. A storm last spring had soaked all the ceiling tiles, and they weren't replacing them until after the school year. But you could fiddle the lock pretty easily, and it was the only way he could get any climbing time in.

Ben had been hitting the wall whenever he could lately, although not as much as Essa did. When he was solving a climbing problem, figuring out the route from *here* to *there*, he didn't have to think about his parents, or getting tried as an adult, or any of it. He climbed until his fingers buzzed and trembled so much he could barely type; he didn't know how Essa sketched like that after a session.

Essa was a phenomenal climber. She wasn't skinny like most climbers but she absolutely *swarmed* up and down that wall. She really lost herself in it—you just knew she had no idea she was smiling like that. It was the only time she ever smiled, and Ben loved to see it. Not that he saw it much. She usually came in, fiddling the lock without even breaking stride and dumping her stuff by the door, just as he was leaving. And one day he'd seen that her binder had dropped out of her bag and fallen open on a landscape, strange slumping spires like the dribble castles kids made on the beach, punctuated by hundreds of tiny windows. In one corner, in Essa's cramped handwriting, had been the caption *redsandcity*. Ben had googled it, and it'd turned out to be the name of Essa's deviantART account.

He'd spent almost a whole night going through the hundreds of images in her gallery and had come to school the next day sluggish and scratchy-eyed. She hadn't bothered sorting them into folders, but there were a few themes she kept coming back to, a few captions she used over and over:

Vats: a skinless, six-fingered hand (lots of detail to the musculature) holding a wicked-looking double-bladed scalpel, handle curved and recurved, its contours almost biological. A human face with a double row of black eyes like a spider's.

Cogs: an elbow joint with struts and cables of gleaming metal instead of muscle and bone. A guy in one of those tall Napoleonic soldier's hats, a cigar in his mouth and most of his face hidden by the smoke, so you could only see his muttonchop sideburns and the glass lenses he had for eyes.

And, of course, *Library*. Those figures in black cowls, faces hidden by shadow. Pages filled with complicated concentric patterns, like Buddhist sand paintings, in beautiful stippled pencil that must have taken her ages.

But all of those put together were outnumbered by the doors.

Essa loved drawing doors. All kinds of door—round metal hatches with wheel locks, giant granite slabs, wooden doors with slats and peeling paint. More than once she'd done the Mystery Door in the gym. She always drew it as slightly ajar, with darkness behind it.

That was a joke—that door had never worked; no one had been able to open it as long as Ben had been at the school.

Was she telling a story? Building a fantasy world? He had no idea, and she never explained anything on her dA page, never even replied to comments. Not that he'd left any. Anyway, she hadn't updated it in weeks.

He could have just asked her. He could have just asked her *out*. He'd definitely thought about it. But that wasn't going to happen.

He didn't have the time.

On cue, his phone chimed again. His dad this time, an extra appointment with his tutor. Getting back at his mum. The headache flared up, and he decided he didn't want to deal with any of it right now. He put his phone back in his pocket and leaned back a little further, getting a better angle on Essa's sketch.

Since Ben had been old enough to have a phone, his parents had been running his life through his calendar, scheduling it down to the minute. They'd always been in sync with each other, working around each other's appointments. Now that the divorce was finally going through, their schedules were drifting, like clocks at different speeds, getting further apart with time. Each of them had their own stuff they wanted him to do, and now every conflict was another choice he had to make, either his mum or his dad. He tried to keep them both happy—that was why he had two different math tutors—but he only had so much free time to give up.

Ben had tutors instead of doing regular math at school because he was "gifted," although he didn't think it was much of a gift. It was just a dumb trick, and not even the kind of dumb trick he could go viral with and make some ad money—he wasn't going to blow up Twitch doing linear algebra. It wasn't going to do much for him after school, either. He'd just be in a tiny office at some university, or maybe doing stats for a hedge fund. (Or tutoring his fellow prisoners for time off his sentence.) None of those options were exactly thrilling.

He bet Essa didn't have to deal with any of that. Not that he, or anyone, really knew anything about her. They'd both come to Chifley about a year ago: Ben from Melbourne, and Essa from somewhere in Canada, supposedly. Ben was hardly what you'd call outgoing, but even in that short time he'd picked up friends, guys who gave him crap and guys he gave crap to. He was part of the food chain, the Great Wheel of High School Karma. Even getting arrested hadn't really set him apart—you had to do a lot more than that when you were in the same year as a psychopath like Ryan.

Essa, though, had somehow stepped *off* that wheel, and no one knew what to do with her.

It wasn't like she was the only person at Chifley who acted like they were bored with everything. But with everyone else, you knew they were just being poseurs. It seemed to Ben that everyone was just poses on top of poses, and if you dug all the way down, who knew if there was a real person there at all. Writing everyone off like that was probably a pose too, of course, and the biggest poseurs were usually the ones who *called* everyone a poseur, but you could drive yourself crazy thinking like that.

"Quiet" was a word that came up on Ben's report cards a lot, and some teachers used it to mean "deep," but he wasn't. He just didn't want to say anything unless he was sure he meant it, so he didn't usually say anything at all.

Essa was no poseur, though. With Essa it was real, and bone-deep. She didn't seem depressed or sad, just absolutely weary of everything, like she'd seen it all before and it hadn't been any fun the first time either. She took an absolute blizzard of crap from everyone because of the glitter, and the whispering, and her unplaceable accent, and weird way of cursing, and everything else about her, but she just didn't care. Ben had no idea how she did it. In his year at Chifley High, Essa had become a…symbol, he guessed, of something that was, if not better, then at least *realer* than his own life. Like she was anchoring him to the world, which was weird because Essa herself didn't seem anchored to anything—

He leaned back just a little more, for a final look at the sketch, and realized he was tipping backwards a moment too late to do anything about it. The chair went out from under him and he landed flat on his back on the floor.

A couple of halfhearted snickers from the handful of people in the cafeteria. A loud snort of laughter from Ryan Bradman. Ben couldn't help raise his head a little to look at Essa, and of course she was looking right back at him. No mockery on her face, no contempt, just more weariness: *Will you look at who I'm stuck in this school with?* He'd have preferred laughter. A desolate future unfolded in his head, of getting that exact same look from Essa every time they crossed paths, of two more weeks of school that stretched out into infinity.

So he wasn't even thinking about what he was doing as he clambered to his feet and his gaze met Ryan's, and Ryan sneered a single word at him, and Ben said it right back.

The bell rang. If it'd happened two seconds earlier, it would've drowned out what Ben had said, but it didn't. Even with the deafening noise, the sound of Ryan's chair scraping across the floor as he stood up was crystal clear.

Ben grabbed his bag as he got to his feet. Before he turned to run he saw, very clearly, Ryan swipe Nick's fishing knife off the table.

Then he kicked his chair aside—it clipped some luckless guy in the head—and came after Ben, who was halfway to the cafeteria door.

Adrenaline obliterated thought, but a tiny dispassionate part of his brain noted that Nick and Troy *hadn't* gotten up. If this was just a bashing, they'd want to be in on it, but whatever they thought Ryan was going to do, they'd decided to sit it out. As Ben sprinted out of the cafeteria and into the hall, he speculated about what that meant. Like everyone else in Chifley, he'd been in denial about Ryan; the rumours, about what he'd done to that dog in fifth grade or what he'd done to that girl from Atherton High, were thin enough to ignore, especially if you were trying really hard to steer clear of the guy anyway. But he'd started to think that Ryan had no brakes at all. That he was capable of anything.

Right then it was looking like *anything* would be Ben.

No teachers outside the cafeteria, and the first couple of classrooms he passed were empty. He would have to run for the teacher's lounge, hang around outside until Ryan gave up. Undignified but safe. He hoped. He kept seeing Ryan grabbing that knife from Nick. He probably just wanted to wave it under Ben's nose, try and make him wet himself, but Ben wasn't taking chances.

The corridor was packed. They'd built it way too narrow and it was always a massive bottleneck, especially after lunch when everyone was heading to class. Like now. A double line of people ground past each other like tectonic plates, with the occasional shove or curse. Ben tried throwing himself into the crowd and pushing through. Someone jeered and pushed him back, hard. He gave up and headed for the main hall, hoping that whichever architect had designed that corridor had had a really crappy life.

His bag banged on his hip as he ran. It had his laptop in it, which he'd taken to school that day, against his better judgment, because his dad had signed him up for night LaTeX classes at the uni. The laptop was just a beat-up Dell with a shot battery, but he was pretty sure that if Ryan got his hands on it, he'd need to replace it, and he dreaded asking his parents for a new one. He'd end up with two, probably totally impractical seventeen-inch monsters that neither of them could really afford. Since his parents had gone to war with each other, Ben had spent most of his time trying to talk them *out* of buying him stuff. It was another battlefield for them, another chance to one-up each other. Like that first meeting with the lawyer after he'd been arrested—they'd blamed each other for the whole thing, and the idea that it was Ben's fault hardly came up, even though he was the one who had, you know, *done* it.

Right now, though, the divorce, and the arrest, and his laptop getting pissed on and chucked out of a window looked like they might be the least of his problems.

Halfway down the hall Ben took a hard right, his sneakers skidding on the laminate floor, and headed for the double doors of the gym. If he could fiddle the lock, get inside, and get the doors shut before Ryan reached them, he'd be safe. Assuming Ryan didn't know how to fiddle it too. If he'd been thinking clearly, he would have taken shelter in an empty classroom and hoped Ryan blew past him, then doubled back and lost himself in the crowds, but atavistic fear kept him running, the desperate need to put distance between him and his pursuer.

Ryan's boots squeaked on the floor somewhere behind him. Ben hadn't lost him, then, and the gym was his only hope. Not a sound from Ryan himself, no yelling or blustering, no putting on a show for the spectators in the hall, which was starting to scare Ben badly. He'd seen enough of Ryan to know there was really two of him. One was the standard-issue bully—loud threats, public humiliation, painful but ultimately trivial violence—and one was...the other Ryan. Who'd given Victor Jia a concussion that had kept him out of school for a week. Who'd done all that stuff that everyone tried not to think about. That other Ryan could show up without warning, for the smallest of reasons or no reason at all, and Ben was pretty sure that was the Ryan he was dealing with.

He put the brakes on as he approached the gym doors but still slammed into them hard enough for the *bang* to echo all the way down the hall.

He slid a trembling finger between the doors, looking for the latch. Pull it back as you lifted it, and it would—

The latch gave and the doors swung inward. He pushed through, turned and shoved them hard, sending them flying back at Ryan, who was still only halfway down the hall.

Sweet relief. For about a second and a half. Before he realized he'd forgotten to reset the latch. The doors banged shut, then slowly eased themselves open again, and he saw Ryan striding towards him, face bloodless and eyes wide.

Ben took half a step towards the doors, but he knew he didn't have time to close them. So he turned and ran into the gym, looking for an escape route that didn't exist.

The gym was in rough shape. The flood had soaked the ceiling tiles, and they were sporting a healthy crop of mould. The floor was a hillscape of warped boards. Little drifts of reddish dust had piled up in the corners that the janitors hadn't bothered sweeping up, since they were just going to rip everything out anyway.

At the far end was the Mystery Door. It wasn't really a mystery (it said right there on the door what was behind it, EQUIPMENT), but it just wouldn't open. They were supposed to be fixing that in the summer, too.

The gym's back doors were chained and padlocked. Ben headed for the climbing wall, because he didn't have a choice. If he climbed to the top then maybe he could yell for help. Maybe he could knock Ryan out with a thrown ceiling tile.

Or maybe he was screwed.

He passed the Mystery Door on his way to the wall, and with a new and gut-level understanding of the phrase "grasping at straws," he reached for the handle.

And it turned in his hand.

He let go of it like it was hot. It kept turning without him. A dull *click* from the latch, and the door swung out into the gym.

He should have been looking at a dusty collection of padded mats and medicine balls. Instead there was...darkness. Just darkness, and a faint, rich smell like rain-wet soil.

Something scraped the floor at his feet and he looked down.

There were hands down there, a pair of them, hanging onto the bottom of the doorframe. It was impossible—there was nothing to hang down *into*, the hands' owner should have been lying flat on the floor. The sallow fingers were obscenely long, their cracked yellow nails almost touching the toes of Ben's sneakers. Then another pair of hands appeared halfway up the doorway, and another close to the top, gripping the frame. Ben stepped back as something heaved its way up and into the gym.

It was bigger than the door, but it squeezed, *oozed* through, a lump of mottled flesh twice the size of a man. More of those long-fingered hands had appeared, connected to the waxy body by a multitude of arms. They were much, much longer than arms should be, and with way too many elbows that flexed with a sound like dry twigs snapping. A multitude of tiny mushrooms sprouted from the thing's back, casting a pale glow in the gloom of the gym. At the end of its long, wrinkled neck swayed a tiny head, features blurred and distorted but horribly human. A baby's face, eyeless, flesh sagging like half-melted wax. It opened its mouth and bleated.

Ben backed away. He bumped into something behind him and a hand grabbed his shoulder, and he lashed out without thinking. The hand let go and he turned and saw Ryan, who he'd completely forgotten about, bending double and wheezing. It seemed Ben had punched him in the balls. Touching the junk of the biggest homophobe at Chifley: Ryan was *definitely* going to kill him now, but the way things were going, it looked like Ryan could get in line.

He tripped on the uneven floor, fell on his butt, and scrambled backwards as Ryan, his face crimson, turned to look at him. He hadn't seen the thing looming silently behind him. It reared up and over Ryan on its eight spindly arms, and he had time to say "You're *dead*, you—" before the thing's belly split open to reveal a second mouth, a maw lined with tombstone teeth, that yawned wide as it fell on him.

Chapter Two

Rain dulls everything. It turns the grey flagstones almost black. The deep grooves in the stones have overflowed into puddles the girl has to work around with her chalk.

Drawing is difficult. The chalk clots and blurs, but the girl remains intent on her task. She's covered a fifth of the courtyard already, and it's not small.

The grooves in the flagstones form looping paths, complex interlocking circles. They track the stately dance of the three suns through the days and seasons, but right now, under the lowering sky, they might as well be random scribbling. The chalk patterns look random, too, but the girl's hand is assured and never hesitates.

Rain beads on the glossy black leaves of the vines that cover the courtyard's towering walls. It beads in the hair of the man who watches from the far side of the courtyard and settles on his coarse black robe. The man is tall but the Governess beside him is a head and a half taller. Her skin, stretched tight on her elongated skull, gleams a pearlescent white. Her high-collared dress doesn't hide how inhumanly spindly she is, and he wonders if she can even stand without her long steel cane. The dress, like her tightly braided hair, is a brilliant red, and even somewhat dulled from the rain, it's still the most vivid thing in the courtyard; he could almost hold his hands up to her for warmth.

She doesn't breathe through her bud-like lips but through the double row of holes marching up her long white throat. The sound puts the man in mind of an ocean, waves rising and falling.

He turns his attention back to the girl. Like the other children, she wears only a light shift and gooseflesh covers her bare arms. Her black hair straggles across her forehead. The blood leaking from her swollen nose mixes with the rain and drips from her chin.

"A dispute over the chalk." If the Governess's breath is the ocean, then her voice is the shore it breaks on, a million diamond pebbles chiming and clattering. With her cane she indicates another corner of the courtyard and the children clustered there, all about a season old, like the girl herself. One boy, much bigger than the others, is snivelling and nursing a bruised jaw. "He tried to take it from her. She objected."

"Antisocial?"

"She gets along fine with the others, for the most part. Once she's finished with her..." The cane indicates the chalk drawings.

The man walks along the wall for another angle on them. The Governess keeps up, cane tapping, steel on slate.

"Family?"

"If she had any family who cared, she wouldn't be here," she says in her lovely voice.

"Claims?"

"The Choir has formally denied her a part. The other Powers made their choices weeks ago; the children have already gone. We'd begun to think the Library was sitting this season out."

"We were busy."

"So I hear," says the Governess.

As they watch, the girl adds a final flourish and stands. She trudges across the courtyard to the snivelling boy and holds out the chalk. He slaps it out of her hand and looks away. The girl shrugs, goes back to her drawing, sits on the wet flagstones looking at it.

The man begins walking in her direction, the Governess keeping pace.

"What does it mean?" he asks.

"Whatever it means, it's to her alone."

"But there's a system?"

"Oh yes. She always begins with those spirals, then adds the angular things"—pointing with the cane—"then the connectors. Then elaborates from there. We assumed it was in the nature of an imaginary friend, only more...abstract. We were wrong?"

"You were exactly right. The symbols themselves don't matter. We're after a certain way of thinking...excuse me."

The Governess doesn't. Her cane blocks the man's path, striking the flagstones hard enough that a couple of the children look up. He looks up at her too.

"Will she be safe?"

"Will she be safe here?" he replies.

"The Exile left its scars on a hundred worlds. Your own most of all. If it were to happen again—"

"If it happens again," says the man, "no one's going to be safe."

He steps around the cane and the Governess doesn't stop him. She watches as he squats beside the girl. She can't hear what he says. The girl doesn't react. The man reaches into his robe, produces a worn leather pouch. He loosens the drawstring and spills a handful of red dust onto the flagstones. The Governess shivers.

He draws in the dust with a finger, and the dust stirs around him. He spreads his hands to invite the girl to do the same, but she's already copying the man's symbols, then after the briefest pause she elaborates on them, adds her own. The dust begins to dance. She's smiling.

"Poor child," murmurs the Governess.

CHAPTER THREE

en turned over and crawled, keeping his eyes on the floor. The buckled boards rose and fell under his hands and knees. He tuned out the thumping from behind him, the ripping and cracking and crunching.

He reached the open doors of the gym and stopped, staring at the scuffed sneakers in front of his nose.

He looked up at Essa, and Essa looked down at him. She gave him that weary look, opened her mouth to say something, and then she saw what was happening inside the gym, and all the blood drained from her face.

He glanced backwards himself, saw the spider-thing feasting with its belly-mouth, a spongy tongue soaking up the pool of blood on the floor while the swaying baby head mewed softly. He turned back to Essa and saw Mr. Barendrecht, the chem teacher, coming down the hall behind her. Maybe someone had told him Ryan was about to commit murder. A momentary surge of pathetic relief: Mr. B would take charge of the situation, and Ben and Essa could get the hell out of there.

Then Essa stepped *into* the gym, flipped the latch on the doors, and kicked them shut to lock with a *click*.

Had she snapped? She did look scared, but something told him that it wasn't of the bloody scene in front of her. She looked...

desperate. He'd seen that look plenty of times in the mirror lately. It was the look of someone who was running out of time.

Ben, without thinking at all about what he was doing, stood up and grabbed a broom that was leaning against the wall. He broke it over his knee—it took two tries—and clutching the splintered handle, he moved between Essa and the mushroom-thing. "Run," he said.

Instead, Essa dropped, sat crosslegged on the floor. "Ben," she said, "you're going to have to hold it off for a minute, can you do that?"

The doors rattled as Mr. Barendrecht tried the handles. "Hello?" he called.

No time to let him in: the mushroom-thing was rising from its meal and stalking across the uneven floor towards him. It had left no trace of Ryan at all. Ben looked back at Essa, who was stretching out her hands and doing something with her fingers, twisting them around like she was playing cat's-cradle without any string.

She *had* snapped. Ben wondered what he was going to do. Then, very clearly, he saw the blood-red sparks snapping between her fingers.

"*Ben*," snapped Essa. "I need a minute, all right? Go for the arms, they break easily." Her eyes bored into his, and that desperate need in them snapped him out of his daze.

Sometimes, when Ben's adrenaline was running high, when he was climbing and he missed a hold or he was tackling an exam question with a couple of minutes on the clock, the rest of the world just *went away*, leaving only him and whatever problem he was facing. It didn't always happen, but it was a rush when it did. He suspected it'd been that feeling he'd been chasing the night he broke into half a dozen corporate servers and gotten himself arrested.

He felt that rush now. The world became a problem to solve, and where the monster had come from and what Essa was doing were irrelevant to the problem and so they went away.

He took a deep breath and tightened his grip on the broom handle. Until Mr. B got the doors open and dragged Essa away, he wasn't letting this thing come anywhere near her. Anyway, if he got himself eaten saving her life, she might forget about his pratfall in the cafeteria.

The spider-thing reared up and one of the elongated arms came swinging at him. He met it with the broom handle and the impact of the blow almost knocked it out of his hands. The shock travelling up his arms dispelled any lingering idea he'd had that this was a nightmare: it was real, the spider-thing had killed Ryan and now it was going to kill *him*—

He yelled and swung at it. The broom handle smashed into its arm, which broke like rotten wood. He backed up a little, surprised, as the baby's face gurgled and the thing staggered, lopsided. Grey, spongy bone was sticking through its skin where he'd hit it, although there was no blood.

Ben spared a glance at Essa and his eyes widened. Her fingers were still twisting into strange configurations like those yoga gestures, mudra, and now streamers of red dust were rising from the corners of the gym and curling from between the floorboards, all of them snaking through the air towards her as she sat on the floor. They coalesced into a tiny crimson dust devil that swirled in front of her, tighter and tighter, flattening until it formed an almost solid-looking disc spinning in front of her chest. Her hands danced faster as she murmured rapidly.

The spider-thing must have seen it, too, because it moaned and lunged at her, moving fast despite its bulk and broken arm. Ben stepped forward to meet it, stabbing with the broken end of the handle; he heard Essa say "Ben, *no*—" right before it pierced the thing's skull, which burst. A cloud of black dust poured from its shattered head, filled the air like the time Helena Whatshername had dropped a toner cartridge in the PC lab, and before Ben could think not to, he'd inhaled.

His lungs started burning right away. His muscles turned to water and he fell to his knees. He managed to look up and saw the spider-thing looming over him, the mouth in its belly opening wide. The broken blade of Nick's fishing knife was lodged in its teeth.

Behind him Essa hissed a single strange syllable and a red flash blurred past his head. It tore through the spider-thing and cut it almost in half, sending it tumbling backwards through the gym. The monster staggered, managed somehow to right itself, and then collapsed.

"And *that*," said Essa, "is how we do that. Oh no. Ben! Door! Get the door, *get the door—*"

She almost sobbed it, and the naked desperation in her voice was what got him moving. He managed to lurch to his feet, although his legs didn't feel like they belonged to him and all kinds of weird zoom lens stuff was happening to his vision. He staggered across the floor towards the Mystery Door, which was slowly swinging shut. He tripped again and went down, but he scrabbled forward on hands and knees and just before the latch caught, he managed to get his fingers between it and the frame. It took him two tries to get a hold on the handle and ease it open. He really didn't feel so great.

Then Essa pushed him aside and swung the door all the way back, slamming it against its stopper. She looked at it for a moment, like she wasn't fully convinced it was still open, and then she grabbed him, hauled him to his feet, flung him back against it, and kissed him, hard.

It was over before he'd realized it was happening. She broke off the kiss and smiled at him, a grin that lit up her whole face, that managed to be sunny and ferocious at the same time. The smile was better than the kiss.

"Thank you," she said, and the feeling in her voice was better than the kiss and the smile put together.

Then the smile dropped away and she was all business. She reached into her jeans and took out a black rubber wedge, a doorstop. Why was she carrying that around? She dropped it on the floor and nudged it under the door with her sneaker. "Right," she said, "housekeeping," and turned to the dead spider-mushroom-baby-thing lying on the floor a few yards away in a cloud of red dust. Her hand made a couple more of those painful-looking gestures and the dust coalesced into a dozen paper-thin edges like knife blades that whipped through the creature's carcass again and again, carving it into chunks.

"Kick those through the door, will you, Ben?" she said, heading for the climbing wall now. She'd said more words to him in the last five minutes than in the previous year. "But don't fall in. And make sure it doesn't close."

He nodded. It seemed like the easiest thing to do.

"Ben? Say it."

"I won't let the door close," he said absently, most of his brain still lingering on the kiss.

She turned and went for the climbing wall. He'd thought she was fast before, but it turned out she'd just been dicking around those other times, because now she scaled the wall quicker than he could have walked along it if it'd been lying flat.

He eased himself off the door, making sure the wedge held it open. Gingerly, he hooked the bits and pieces of mushroom-thing with his feet, dribbled them to the door. He wasn't sure what Essa had meant about "falling in," but he wasn't in any hurry to get near that rectangle of darkness so he kicked the pieces through from a few feet away.

At the top of the wall Essa leaned out so far he thought she was going to fall, and pulled down one of the mouldy ceiling tiles. It hit the floor in an explosion of dust, making Ben jump as Essa hooked a hand up into the gap in the ceiling and pulled down a black knapsack.

She swung it over one arm and sailed down to the floor in what was less a descent and more a (barely) controlled fall.

Only a couple of chunks left to go. It wasn't as gross as he'd thought it would be: it really was more like mushroom flesh than meat. There was no sign of Ryan at all.

The hammering on the doors was louder now, Mr. B's voice raised indignantly, although Ben still couldn't make out what he was saying. Essa ignored the noise as she reached into her bag and pulled out a coil of bright orange climbing rope, knots spaced along it for handholds. Her other hand pulled out a length of black metal with a flat chisel-blade at one end, like a climbing piton. She threaded the rope through the loop at the end of the piton and tied it off with expert fingers, leaned through the Mystery Door and out into that darkness behind it, standing on tiptoe to stab it into something. She gave the rope a hard tug, testing it, then threw the rest of it through the door. If the world had made sense, it should have landed on the floor of the equipment room, but instead Ben saw it uncoil and hang taut, dangling down into an impossibility.

Essa pulled something else from the knapsack, a curved silver hip flask. Ever since she'd seen the monster, there hadn't been a single wasted motion about her, like she'd gone through this a hundred times in her mind before today. She unscrewed the lid of the flask and the cloud of red dust braided itself into a tight stream that flowed towards her, dived into the flask's open mouth, and disappeared. As she screwed the lid back on, she looked at him and her eyes widened. "Red Lady, Ben, are you all right?"

"I'm not sure," he said. The words hung in the air as he spoke them, he could see them curling and spreading like ink in water. "I don't think so."

Essa looked at him. For a long moment, Ben thought she was just going to leave him and head on out that door to…wherever. Then she sighed, looped the rope around the door handle to make sure it didn't close again, and helped him to his feet.

"The head's a decoy," she said, "it's full of spores. I *said* to go for the arms. Anyway, we'll need to get you looked at." She kicked the last still-twitching chunk of the spider-thing through the door and took Ben's arm, put it over her shoulder, maneuvered him carefully to stand in front of the doorway.

"They said you were from Canada," he said.

"Yes," said Essa.

"You're not from Canada."

"No. Now you need to focus, Ben." She pushed the rope into his hand. "You're going to have to climb, it'd take too long to lower you."

Ben took the rope; it didn't occur to him not to. "Lower me *where?*" he asked, looking through the doorway. He couldn't see anything but darkness. The darkness seemed to be oozing.

"One thing at a time," said Essa, glancing behind her. He heard the gym doors creak as they eased open. Evidently Mr. B or someone had found a key, and given what they must have been hearing from inside the gym, they were being cautious.

He tightened his grip on the rope and turned his back to the darkness. Leaning backwards, he could see Essa had driven the black metal spike into the top of the doorframe. He took a deep breath and reached down with a foot, probing until it met something flat and hard and vertical, flush with the doorway. A wall.

"That's it," said Essa, "no hurry," but she glanced again behind her, where a commotion was growing.

Okay. He could do this. Just like on the climbing wall. Except on the climbing wall he'd been able to feel his fingers.

The rope taut in his hands, Ben reached down with his other foot, took a step, then another, walking backwards down the wall. In the light from the doorway, he could see it was whitewashed brick, just like the walls of the school.

As soon as he was clear of the door, Essa swung out herself, one hand on the rope and the other holding the door handle. He could hear Mr. B up there, shouting something.

Essa cocked her head, listening, then nodded. "You know what, Mr. Barendrecht?" she said conversationally. "I used to spend nights, entire *nights* lying awake thinking of the last words I'd say to this *latrine* of a world. And now I find I can't remember a single one."

Mr. B huffed something Ben couldn't hear, but Essa just talked right over him. "And I don't care a bit," she said, and slammed the door.

Chapter Four

The last of the crystal girl's water ran out yesterday. She's pulled a button from her sleeve and sucks on it to encourage a little saliva. It's not really working.

She climbs.

The wind tugs at her robe, the cloth flapping monotonously. Sometimes she doesn't even hear the sound. Sometimes she's almost driven mad by it. Her name is Rachana, although at any given moment it's even money whether she remembers that or not.

The wall is packed red sand, has been ever since she started climbing, never changing. She focuses on the wall right in front of her. That was what the Librarians told them, in the camp at the foot of the wall. *Look up and you'll lose heart. Look down and you'll lose your mind.*

She reaches up and sketches three spirals in the sand of the wall with a finger. Her skin was colourless when she began the Climb, but the sand has nicked and scratched it until it's milky white, like an age-clouded eye. As she finishes the last spiral the sand loosens and streams away, leaving a hollow she can use as a handhold. Her bare toes cram themselves into a previous handhold, and she boosts herself up another couple of feet.

Then she does it again, and again, and again.

The wind gusts. It flattens her against the wall for a moment, plastering her robe to her body, and then it's pulling her away just as hard. She digs into the sand with raw fingers until she can move again.

Her hand begins to shake. The next symbols she draws are uneven, the resulting hollow shallow and misshapen. She can't do this anymore. Carefully she draws a longer set of symbols in the wall to her right. One minor avalanche later, a niche has opened, big enough to squeeze her body into.

She leans back and breathes deep, relishing the air in her lungs even though it's cold and thin and takes the moisture right out of her mouth. She runs a trembling hand through her white hair, shakes the red dust out of it. Movement not spent on the Climb feels almost decadent.

Others are out there too, climbing like her. She doesn't look up, or down, but fifty feet to her right someone's made a niche like hers; she can see their legs sticking out and dangling.

She forces herself to relax, let some strength flood back into her arms and legs and cramped fingers. Now that she's not keeping the fatigue at bay, it rushes over her like blood-warm water. She doesn't hear the gentle hiss from above until it's almost on top of her.

When she does, the shock wakes her all the way up. She swings herself out of the niche, fingertip already moving in the sand beside it. At the edges of her vision she sees other climbers scurrying like her. A Wave is coming, wiping the wall clean. They need to get out of the way.

The crystal girl carves out handhold after handhold, climbing not up but across the wall, while the hiss of the Wave bears down on her. It's getting closer.

She almost doesn't make it. When the ripple passes through the sand, a hundred feet wide, she's only inches from its edge. Her eyes are drawn to it, watching its passage down the wall. The figure she saw before is still in its niche; asleep maybe, or paralyzed with fear. With no fuss at all, the Wave smooths out the sand, wipes the hollow away, pushes the figure out and into the air. The wind is too loud for Rachana to hear anything as she watches it fall, robes fluttering. She follows it down with her eyes for just a little too long, long enough to take in Red Sand City stretching out beneath her, unimaginably tall spires unimaginably far below—

She doesn't know how long she hangs there, numb inside and out. What brings her back is the sound of falling sand. It's another Wave, she thinks, and she can't move, she *won't* move, she wants this to be *over*—

But it's not a Wave.

Sand rattles on her shoulders as the dark-haired girl slides down the wall from above, leaning out to look below her, one hand and both feet carving tracks in the sand as she descends. She stops beside the crystal girl, her finger already sketching. When she reaches out a sunburned hand, Rachana has just enough presence of mind to take it, let herself be drawn inside the hollow the other girl's created.

If she's older than four Wellside seasons—the earliest the Library lets anyone attempt the Climb—it's not by much. The shelter she's created is deep enough for them both to crawl into. Even when they're out of the wind, neither of them says anything. That awful numbness is fading, and what's replacing it is a curious mixture of gratitude and outrage. Rachana has fought for every inch she's climbed, and watching this girl skid down the wall like that is like watching someone throwing food away when you're starving.

"Where...you from?" says the dark-haired girl eventually, in a cracked whisper.

The crystal girl works to summon up enough spit to talk.

"Three Suns here," continues the girl, her voice returning. "Are you from the Bergs? I thought I saw you in the Bergs camp. I like your hair."

"What are you *doing?*" Rachana croaks. "They told us not to go back. Not for anything. That was the *first thing.*"

The dark-haired girl doesn't say anything right away, but she sets her jaw square. Finally she says, "That's why. The Library"—she points at the roof of the shelter—"wants to test me, fine. They want me to climb, I'll climb. But I'm not going to watch anyone else fall. I'm going to reach the top the same person I was at the bottom." She shrugs, suddenly uncomfortable. "Or the same person I thought I was."

Another silence.

"Rachana," says Rachana.

"Essa," says the other. "You ready? Let's go."

Chapter Five

The light from the gym cut out as Essa shut the door, leaving Ben hanging in darkness. He yelled in surprise, although it came out as an undignified squawk.

"Oh, teeth," said Essa, "sorry, Ben," and he heard her bag rustle as she rooted around in it. A burst of light sent his shadow dancing wildly across the wall beneath him.

It was the same whitewashed brick as the walls of the gym, but it extended out into the darkness on all sides. The door above him was the only feature he could see. Essa hung onto the rope next to the door with her feet braced against the wall and something black and slender in her free hand, a white glare sizzling at the end of it, magnesium-bright. A flare. She'd slung her knapsack over her shoulders. Ben realized he was still wearing the messenger bag with his laptop inside. He'd forgotten all about it.

"Where are we?" he managed to say.

"We are Wellside," said Essa. "We are *free*." She inhaled through her nose, a deep snort like the air was cocaine. "Lady's tongue, can you smell *that?*"

It smelled like the bottom of a log to Ben, but he wasn't sure he was an objective observer. Everything seemed to be rippling, like a sheet on a clothesline in the wind, only without moving.

He looked down. The flare's light showed the wall below him, his shadow sliding over it as he swayed on the rope. Beyond that the darkness took over.

"How high are we?" he asked. His voice cracked.

"No heights here," said Essa happily, "it's *depths* you need to worry about. Can you make it down?"

Down where? Ben thought, but he started walking down the wall anyway. The bricks scrolled past a foot from his eyes—the same whitewash, the same rough texture he'd idly run his hands over a million times as he walked from classroom to classroom. Except there shouldn't *be* a wall here—the gym was on the ground floor, and Chifley didn't have anything below that.

And as he descended further, the wall changed.

The colour began to fade, white turning to dull grey. The mortared gaps narrowed, lost their right angles, and then it wasn't brick at all but cracked concrete he was climbing down, beaded with moisture. One foot slipped a little and he tightened his grip on the line. His hands seemed very far away.

Essa's voice came from above him. "Ben, if I remember right there's a door just below us, can you see it?"

He did. It was set into the concrete wall, a rectangle of bare steel, scored with scratches. The rope dangled down beside it. "Do I—?"

"Straight on through," said Essa. She stopped a little way above, keeping the line steady for him.

Ben reached out for the handle, and as he did, his foot slipped on a slick patch of wall and shot to the side. He pitched forward, spinning around on the rope, and his back crashed into the door, knocking it open. He fell backwards through the doorway, only just remembering to let go of the line before he went sprawling on a dusty concrete floor.

"That sounded stylish," called Essa from above him. Then the rope sagged as her weight came off it. Ben sat bolt upright and scrambled to the door, expecting to see her plummet past the doorway, but leaning out and looking up he saw she'd half-dug that metal spike into the wall and was using it to slow her fall, leaving a long track of splintered concrete as she came down.

He fell back as she swung through the door, landing on her feet, already winding the loose rope around her forearm.

Ben sat up and looked around. They appeared to be in a cubicle, like the ones in his dad's office, with thin dividers separating it from its neighbours. It was larger than his dad's, though, and the dividers weren't made of plastic and synthetic fabric, but what appeared to be panels of dented steel. The door they'd come through was set into one of them.

No desk or filing cabinets in here either; instead, a tangle of twisted metal was heaped in one corner, shreds of fabric stapled to it here and there. In another corner was a pile of books, oversized fat paperbacks like old phone books. They'd gotten wet at some point and then dried out, leaving them wrinkled and swollen. Everything was covered in dust; it lay in a thick carpet on the floor. The ceiling, a couple of feet above the top of the divider, was cracked and filthy glass, barely letting any light through.

By the time he'd noticed the faint clatter coming from above the glass, it had built up to a roar. With a blast of displaced air that set the trash on top of the glass dancing frantically, something rushed past up there—and kept rushing, on and on, something like a cable car but *huge*. Each immense black car that whipped past had a row of narrow windows on its underside blasting actinic blue light.

It went on long enough that Ben stopped cowering. He managed to kneel, then stood, carefully, on tiptoe. His eyes just cleared the top of the divider, and the hellish light coming from above lit up the ceiling and showed him more cubicles, an infinity of them, receding to the vanishing point.

Then, just as quickly, the train-thing was gone, the hellish noise of it dropping in pitch as it receded, the vista falling back into gloomy half-light.

"*What* a dump," said Essa.

Ben looked back at the door. Above the lintel, he could see the next cubicle over, and the next after that. Below it, where he should have been seeing the same thing, the doorway opened onto darkness. His legs gave out again.

"Not a wonderful idea, Ben," said Essa, "not in your current state. Everyone thinks they'll be able to handle the spatial stuff, but usually they just faint. Or wet themselves. Just try not to look at it." She knelt and twisted the handle of the flare, which sprouted three stubby legs, then planted it on the floor. It was burning more gently now, and he could look at it without squinting. "What an *absolute* dump," she said, looking around.

"Where...?" said Ben.

Essa pulled a hoodie from her bag. "Just another world," she said from inside it as she shrugged it on.

When her head emerged, Ben said, "You're bleeding."

She sniffled and brushed a hand across her lip, wiping the bright blood from her nose. "Every bloody time," she said, wiping it on her jeans, and stuffed her hands into the pouch of her hoodie. It was bitterly cold, but in the state Ben was in, the sensation verged on the abstract.

"We're going to get you sorted out, Ben," she said. "I promise. And thank you. I absolutely cannot thank you enough." She looked suddenly uncomfortable. "Look...things might have gotten a bit weird back there."

"You think?" Ben asked. His lungs had been itching worse, and now they were starting to burn.

Essa persisted. "Well, yes, but that's not what I meant."

Ben waved a hand, which left a glittering trail. "It's fine," he said, staring at it. "We just nearly got eaten. I didn't mind, anyway." Some fragment of his sanity that had survived the last ten minutes started to protest. He ignored it. "It was nice."

Essa didn't comment on that last part. "Not just that. I wasn't expecting that Door to ripen for another week. If it ever ripened at all. Just bad luck the skulker came through...but if I'd seen it open and then it'd *closed* again..." She shuddered, then suddenly brightened. "But we made it, eh? Oh—come here, you'll want to see this." She was rummaging in her bag again.

Ben didn't think he was up to standing again, so he crawled to the door instead. That should have been embarrassing, but everything was a little too strange for that.

Essa produced another flare from her bag and Ben flinched as she struck it, a yellow light this time. How long had she had that bag stashed in the gym ceiling, while she waited for the door to open? (*Ripen*, she'd said, and what was that about?)

The flare's light seemed to rain down in droplets, a cascade of jewels. "Yellow for a cab," said Essa, "like in your New York—" and dropped it. It fell slowly, turning end over end, lighting up the wall. And the wall went on forever.

As the flare receded, it lit up another door below them, and another, and another. The light dwindled and the darkness crowded in again—but as Ben's eyes recovered from the glare he saw it *wasn't* darkness, not completely. There were more lights out there, very faint, twinkling like stars. The wall had a curve, picked out in lights, a very gentle one, bowing out and around them to either side. Suddenly everything came together for him—the wall was a circle, they were in a vast cylindrical pit.

"Are those...?" he said, pointing at the distant lights.

Essa nodded. "More Doors." He could hear the capital D. "More worlds."

"What is this place?"

"*This*," said Essa grandly, "is the Well." Capital W. "And isn't it the most beautiful thing you've ever seen?"

That wasn't the word Ben would have chosen. *Terrifying*, maybe. "Your drawings," said Ben.

Essa grinned.

"They're all real?"

"Real as I remember them, at any rate. How did you know about that?"

"Found your dA account."

"Stalker." She sounded amused. Ben shrugged, and his arm started to twitch. He had to hold onto it to stop it. "What's happening?" he asked. He sounded more scared than he'd meant to.

Essa's smile faded. She knelt beside him, put the back of her hand on his forehead. Her fingers were very cool and he leaned into them. "Spores," she said. "Looks like you got a double lungful. But help is on the way, fret not."

"Spores?" he managed to say.

"Skulkers are mould, basically," she said. Her voice seemed to be receding down a very long corridor. "We think they evolved here. They live Wellside, creep through any ripe Doors they find, eat someone, move on."

That was *way* too much for Ben to fit in his head right then, so he took the path of least resistance and just went away.

He drifted, he didn't know for how long. The world blew apart in a slow-motion explosion, all the connections between one thing and another gone—here were *hand* and *flare* and *ceiling* but they just didn't relate to each other.

It was more like dreaming than thinking, memories chasing each other through his head, around and around in ever-tightening circles like Essa's red whirlwind.

Over and over, he heard the lawyer his parents had hired. They'd only agreed on a lawyer after a long argument mediated by their own divorce lawyers, which had given Ben a hall-of-mirrors feeling which now came back, amplified nightmarishly by whatever was happening to him.

Be on time, said the lawyer. *Wear the suit. Don't give the judge any crap. Be on time.*

Stand up, read the statement—this statement, do not go off script—and sit down again. Got it?

Wear the suit. Be on time.

Be on time.

Each time, he got it into his head that the court date was *today*, he was missing it, and he jerked awake with his mouth paper-dry and his heart hammering on his ribcage. Then he remembered for the dozenth or hundredth time that it wasn't today, he didn't have to stand up in front of the judge in the suit the lawyer had picked out. He looked around the dusty cubicle in the unsteady light of the flare, saw Essa sitting in the doorway with her legs dangling out of the door into nothingness, and his heart started pounding again because even if he did have a few days, how the hell was he going to get back home? And the lawyer had been very clear on what would happen if he didn't make it. What would probably happen anyway, if the judge was feeling like a prick.

Tried as an adult. His mum had sobbed when the lawyer said that.

His thoughts would make it this far, or not, then he would lose his grip on them and they would start chasing each other around, and he would go through it all again, and again, and again.

Another voice cut through the lawyer's litany. Ben, it said. Ben. *Ben.*

Essa's hand on his shoulder, shaking him awake.

"Keep it together, Ben. Ride's here."

Something was climbing up into the flarelight on multiple spindly limbs. For a moment Ben saw another of those spider-monsters, skulkers, like the one that had eaten Ryan, and he shuddered and jerked backwards but Essa's hand was on his shoulder, squeezing—"Calm down. *Ben*. Calm down, it's all right"—and he paused long enough for his brain to process what he was really seeing.

It *was* a spider, but a mechanical one, all made of shining brass. Gears spun in its thorax as it moved jerkily up the Well. Its legs were slender metal rods, jointed like the spines of an umbrella, tipped with black claws that it speared into the concrete to pull itself upwards. Its flattened circular abdomen stuck straight out from its thorax into the void. It reminded Ben of something. The rhythmic, hammering clatter kept changing, more like music than a machine, and Ben became convinced it *was* music. The spider was singing, in a voice of metallic clangs and clashes.

Now the music slowed as the spider drew level with the door. It drove the black claws on its front pair of legs into the doorframe, deep enough that they should have been poking through into Ben and Essa's side, but of course they didn't. That disconnect between *here* and *there* still made Ben feel like throwing up.

The spider's gleaming head swung through the doorway and looked around the cubicle. Its eyes were clusters of tiny red lamps that clicked as they pivoted, taking in Essa, Ben, the guttering flare. Another run of metallic noise, no rhythm to it at all this time.

Essa stood, smiling politely, and responded, with more of those backwards-sounding syllables she'd whispered under her breath at Chifley.

The spider reared up, its body filling the doorway, head craning down to look at her. Essa wasn't tall to start with, and she looked very small as she stared up at it. Where a regular spider's mandibles would be was an array of steel shears, all different sizes, that clashed together a foot from Essa's nose, but her smile never wavered.

It clattered again. It was definitely talking, spinning flywheels and grinding gears adding up to sounds that were recognizably in the same language Essa was using. Essa replied, and this time she pointed at Ben. The spider turned its head slightly to bring more eyes to bear on him, and Ben saw the glass hemisphere at its crown. A human brain (or anyway it looked human) (or anyway it was about the right size) nestled in a cloud of snotty fluid in there, lit from within by a dull red glow.

Essa and the spider went back and forth. It sounded like they were arguing, or haggling. It didn't look like Essa was getting very far. She was ticking things off on her fingers, reasons for the spider to do…whatever. Give them a ride, she'd said. The spider responded to each point with the same set of sounds, clank-clash-clang. Shooting her down.

Its thorax whirred to life. It was going to leave.

"Lady's teeth," Essa said in English, under her breath, and held up a hand to stop it. Keeping it up, she tugged off her climbing glove. In the guttering light of the flare, Ben saw gold flashing on the back of her hand. More glitter? *Under* her glove?

The spider leaned forward again, bathing her hand in the blood-red glow of its eyes. A click and whirr, like an old-fashioned camera. A pause as it considered. Then another clattering phrase.

Essa nodded and stepped back. She turned to Ben where he sat on the floor, crouched next to him. "Its name's Lud, and it's thinking it over. How are you feeling?"

"All right." It was actually true. Ben was feeling more lucid than he had since he'd left Chifley through the impossible door, and he was hanging onto the feeling with both hands. "That's good, right?"

Essa sucked air through her teeth. "That's the false dawn you're feeling. It's working on you fast. But we'll be fine. We just need to get you to a..." She turned and rattled something off to the spider—*hurry up*. The spider responded with a single dismissive syllable.

Essa muttered a dismissive syllable of her own as she turned back to Ben. "Say something, Ben. Stay with me."

He tried to think of something. "What language was that?"

Essa said "Wellside Creole, heavy on the Cogs," exactly like it was supposed to mean something. Then she said something else, but he wasn't listening. He was staring at her hand.

It wasn't more glitter. He thought the golden lines and circles were tattoos, at first, but they looked like real metal, not ink. They covered the back of her hand, the pattern something like a printed circuit but all whorls and curlicues instead of a circuit board's straight lines and angles, flush with her skin and reaching all the way up until it disappeared into her sleeve. In the state Ben was in, it was unspeakably beautiful.

"The glitter," he managed to say.

Essa nodded and dusted some of it off her fingertips, showing the hair-thin metallic lines it had obscured. "Not my style at *all*, but I couldn't sketch in full gloves, and if I couldn't sketch I'd go mad—ah. Pardon me a moment."

The spider had extended a leg into the cubicle and was tapping its claw on the concrete floor to get Essa's attention. As she turned, it said something, grudgingly, and bowed, swinging out of the doorway and lowering its head and thorax to bring them level with the floor.

"*That's* the spirit," said Essa, in English again. She grinned at Ben. "Can you stand?"

With a *sproing* like an umbrella unfolding, a basket of gleaming brass struts sprang up around the rim of the spider's flat belly. It looked like the conical part of a shuttlecock, only without the feathers. Essa climbed over the spider's head, carrying their bags, hoisted herself nimbly over the railing and held out a hand for Ben. Ben was finding it difficult to stand up, but with Essa's help he managed to half-climb, half-pour himself after her without losing his footing and plunging into the darkness. One sneaker glanced off the spider's brain-case and it clattered something aggrieved at him.

He sank down onto the warm brass of the spider's abdomen, hugging his knees. His head spun and wouldn't stop. He was horribly aware of the nothingness beneath him, with only the metal spider's belly and the flimsy-looking basket between him and it. The spider shuddered, and his fingers scrabbled at the smooth brass in pure panic—but it was only getting underway, taking them up the wall. The clicking from its belly made everything vibrate, and Ben realised what it reminded him of.

It was an old-fashioned pocketwatch, a huge one. That deep clicking that shuddered through its frame must be coming from the mainspring inside.

The brass spider ran on clockwork.

Chapter Six

The Mandala chamber is a shallow circular pit with broad concentric steps leading down to the deeper pit at its centre. A group of Librarians sit on the outermost step, in front of Rachana and Essa. One of them is newly Bound, and it's not working out. His whole body shivers as the Wire overloads his nervous system. Drool soaks his chin. The others ignore him, just murmur to each other, too low for Rachana to overhear.

There are no formal divisions here, just those steps of packed red sand. Nevertheless, each Ism in the Library has claimed a wedge of the chamber as its own. In the centre, at the tip of each wedge, is the Mandala itself. The two girls can't see it from back here, but they can hear it hissing and surging. They stand, with all the other Servitors, against the chamber's circular wall.

The Bound Librarian tugs at his robe. His shaved scalp is a mass of bruises, the swollen flesh almost swallowing up his newly inlaid circuitry. It extends down his neck, gold gleaming in puffy flesh. He scratches at it, and a trickle of blood runs down his neck into his robe. His nails are caked with dried blood. The Librarian to his left— an older man with long and complexly braided hair—raises a hand, twitches it imperiously.

Rachana's eyes are on his neighbour's more spectacular twitching and she doesn't react for a moment. He has to repeat the gesture impatiently before she grabs the silver ewer and hustles to his side, fills his goblet with ice water. Then she hustles back to the alcove, stands at attention once more.

"*What* a waste of time," murmurs Essa beside her.

"Shh."

"You're blushing."

"*Shh.*" Rachana knows she is. Her skin has recovered from the Climb over the last year, regained its translucence, and the flare of violet blood in her cheeks must be obvious. *Like a tropical flower blooming*, Essa says. *Like a supernova.*

"They're not listening to us, Ra."

"*We* are supposed to be listening to *them*, Ess," says Rachana out of the corner of her mouth. "That is the point."

"Oh? That's easy, then." Essa's slippered foot moves in the sand at their feet, sketching out a skewed spiral. Immediately, the sand within it begins moving, forming symbols that march around the curving track, inside to out.

Rachana looks at the spiral, then at the Librarians in front of them. She can see their lips moving and hers move with them as she watches the symbols.

"How did you do that?" she hisses.

"Stones are good listeners, my Governess always said. So's sand."

"We're not supposed to *eavesdrop*—"

The Librarian with the braided hair shoots them an irritated glance. Rachana's blush deepens. Essa rolls her eyes, but when she resumes speaking her voice is lower.

"Do their research. Clean their rooms. Literally carry their literal water. For what? A mentorship we don't even need."

Rachana gives up. Servitors rotate through each of the major Isms in turn; currently they're with the Thousand Sails, and she doubts very much they'll find their mentors here. Or anywhere else, the way Essa is going. "If you want to face the Mandala instead, sure," she replies. "It'll eat your bones down to slivers, Ess."

"We'll see," says Essa.

"Anyway, it's not just that. If we want any influence here at all… look over there." She points, the sleeve of her robe falling from her arm. Henna creeps from her hands down her forearms like a slow-growing vine, each appointment with the Library's Binders adding a little more, picking out the paths where her golden circuitry will be inlaid once their Servitorship is over. Assuming it ever is.

Essa looks across the chamber to a knot of Librarians in the Heptacomb's section. They have a Servitor, too, but he's with them on the step, not standing against the wall, and they're all listening to whatever he's saying.

"*He's* not carrying any water, Ess. That's Gregor, he did the Climb before ours. He's already has the Heptacomb's ear…they say he'll climb the Spires before he's five Seasons old."

"Well, he's certainly in a hurry to get his hands dirty, Ra."

Rachana hasn't noticed the stirrings and mutterings around the chamber. Her gaze flicks from the spiral of sand to the Librarians.

…Plague…

…Contained worldside but sure to spread…

…Vats prepared to provide cure…

…Who's to bear the price?…

That she can't hear them makes the contrast all the more grotesque between their bored faces and the horrors they're proposing. A world behind a newly ripe Door is facing a pandemic and they're appealing to the Powers for aid. Today, at the Mandala, the Library is deciding its vote.

The Heptacomb is the first to send a Librarian down to the centre of the chamber to cast a formal ballot. They blithely resume their discussion. Only the Servitor Gregor is silent, seeming bowed by the weight of what they've done.

"They're letting a whole world die, Ra. And look at them, chatting away like nothing just happened." Essa's raised her voice, and she's attracted more than one glance from the Librarians in front of them. One squints at the sand at her feet and Essa's slipper casually erases the spiral.

"It's not just the Library's fault. The other Powers—"

Essa snorts. This time more heads turn her way. Even the Heptacomb Servitor, Gregor, raises his head. Essa sees him and gives him a cheery and insolent wave. His face clouds for a moment, then he looks away, ostentatiously dismissing her.

Then the Bound Librarian in front of them convulses so hard he breaks his collarbone, and they're sent to find help.

Rachana catches up with Essa on the broad red steps that spiral down to the studios of the Binders.

"That was not so clever, Ess," she says. "And I stuck my neck out to get you that Servitorship, if that makes a difference to you—"

"I didn't ask you to." Essa doesn't look at her as they both descend the steps.

"So it doesn't make a difference. Wonderful. What were you trying to prove?"

"I'm not trying to—"

"Oh, nonsense. And this is all *academic*. You're going to have to choose an Ism, throw in with a faction, get your *hands dirty*. If you want to stay in the Library, that is."

"We'll see," says Essa.

Chapter Seven

He had no idea how long the journey took. The spider rattled up the wall in a series of sharp jerks, each one making Ben shudder. The constant clattering of its mainspring didn't help; it felt like it was shaking up his brain as well as his body, everything spilling off the shelves in his mind and piling on the floor—

Was he saying any of this out loud? He clapped a hand over his mouth just in case. He wasn't sure Essa would have heard him anyway over the noise of the spider's clockwork and the rhythmic *thunks* as it drove its claws into the endless wall.

Now she craned her neck, peering at something above them, and without even looking at him, she nudged him in the side with her foot, harder than was probably necessary. *"Ben!* Get up! Take a look at this." She had to yell it.

Ben managed to get on his knees, get his head above the lip of the basket. He couldn't help looking down first, at the endless dark and the Doors twinkling like distant stars. The one to Chifley had long since been swallowed up by the darkness. The vast pit—the Well, Essa had called it—went down and down, the Doorlight merging into a dim glow at the vanishing point.

It was hard to tear his eyes from the void, but Ben managed finally to look up. The spider had a searchlight mounted on its thorax and the white ellipse was sweeping over the wall ahead, which wasn't concrete any more but smooth black glass. Was that what he was supposed to be looking at? But then he saw the glow spreading out above them and his eyes widened.

There were cables up there, huge lengths of braided steel with each end vanishing into a Door, strung along the Well's great arc like a geometry problem. They spread across one side of the Well, overlapping to make up an angular crescent-moon shape—

"*Deadbeat!*" Essa yelled in his ear. "*The town I mean! Not you of course!*"

It *was* a town, hanging from the cables, ramshackle buildings strung on a network of ropes and wooden walkways. Strings and clusters of flickering gas lights shone all over. Not just a town, though. Clusters of cogs, gears, pulleys, erupted from between the buildings, like a clock's innards blown up to an absurd size, so dense in places it was like the town was jammed into the machinery and not the other way around.

Huge pendulums swung beneath the workings of the town, several smaller ones and one immense brass lyre, four or five stories long with a bob on the end the size of an SUV, sweeping back and forth with terrifying momentum.

Ben gaped. He turned to look at Essa, who was resting her elbows on the rail, chin on her hands, looking for all the world like someone lovestruck.

Ben stared as the town, Deadbeat, descended over them. The spider's path curved to the left to avoid one of those immense pendulums, then straight up into a mass of netting, layers of it, wire and rope and plastic mesh stretched over poles hammered into the immense curved wall. Stuff was caught in it, splinters of wood and lumps of stone and heavier things that dimpled the nets' taut surface. He didn't know if they had fallen from the town or from even further up. They passed a battered grandfather clock, hanging half out of the netting and close enough to touch, with more than the usual amount of numbers on the face and way more than the usual number of hands.

Before Ben could focus on any of it, the spider—Lud, that was its name—was marching up into the town itself, blocking the rest of the Well from view. Wooden buildings and boardwalks and bridges loomed up and over him, tangles of rusty pipes clinging to their underside. Dim light glowered behind lace-curtained windows.

They passed part of Deadbeat's rigging, a colossal trunk of steel made of thick cables twisted together. Smaller cables had been strung from it, and then ropes strung from the cables in a confusing snarl that held the buildings up. Now he could see people moving around, crossing rope bridges and climbing the winding stairways, all silhouetted against the flickering lights.

The Well here was jagged blocks of stone. Up ahead it turned to smooth glazed tiles, with a giant set of double Doors. Things were crawling in and out of them, too far away for Ben to see clearly, some like Lud and others even more outlandish. They followed paths picked out in luminous mushrooms, radiating out from the Doors, waved along by flags wielded by skeletal metal arms emerging from other Doors. It was an airport, a parking garage, a stable.

Abruptly Lud veered off course, heading into a part of the town built close to the wall. Essa raised her head at this, looking at the spider curiously. It was headed for a rickety wooden Door, with a platform of the same splintered wood extending out into the Well. A figure stood there, dressed from head to toe in a bright yellow robe that bulged oddly. The bulges seemed to be moving, undulating slowly. A bone-white, spindly arm emerged from the yellow cloth and pulled the Door open; a shaft of yellow light, like sunlight through bushfire smoke, shone through it into the Well.

Lud crawled up onto the platform and shuddered to a halt, its mainspring slowing until it was barely ticking over. Ben's ears rang in the sudden quiet.

Essa helped him over the edge of the basket, holding his arm as he stepped shakily onto the platform. After the constant motion of the ascent it felt weird to be standing on solid ground. Relatively solid, anyway—Ben could see the gaps between the planks under his feet, and beyond them there was nothing but darkness.

Behind him, the basket flattened itself against Lud's abdomen with a *clang* that made him flinch. The robed figure motioned to the Door with that skeletal arm, and the spider clattered to life again, climbing through. It blocked Ben's view for a moment, and then he was looking into another world.

The spider stalked away across a barren rocky plain the colour of old newspaper, towards a row of low buildings. Beyond the stables, the plain extended to a distant horizon and mountains like broken teeth.

There were things in the stables—skulkers, like the one that had eaten Ryan—feeding at a low stone trough. Ben shuddered and backed up.

"No," said Essa, hanging on to his hand to stop him bolting, "they're tame. We need to go."

The spider clattered something from the plain behind the Door, and the peremptory tone made its meaning clear—*wait*. It still crawled across the barren plain, but now something detached itself from its head, scurried back over the thorax and slid off the abdomen to the ground. The spider just kept on marching stiffly towards the buildings while the smaller thing scuttled back to them, winding its way through the rocks. It was Lud's brain, mounted in something like a horseshoe crab, the crystal case flush with its rounded shell. The spider was only a vehicle, then, something for the brain-crab to ride around.

Ben felt a tug on his T-shirt. Essa was backing up across the platform and dragging him with her. "Come on, Ben. Places to be."

He let her pull him to the edge of the platform, where a flight of rickety wooden stairs descended into the lower levels of the town. "Are we fare-dodging?"

"Not quite. He's got my ID." She held up her hand, turning it to show off the golden tracery flush with her skin. "Every Librarian's is different."

Librarian?

"And we really, really need to get you looked at, so come *on*, Ben, while you can still walk."

Ben's throat closed as nausea swept over him without warning. Whatever was wrong with him, it was getting a lot worse. That was when he switched from passively afraid to really, actively scared. If he kept getting sicker at this rate...

The door was level with Ben's head now, as he descended the stairs, and he could see the spider's brain clambering over the threshold of the Door on half a dozen pairs of articulated legs. Like a horseshoe crab, it had a long and weaponish-looking spike of a tail, which twitched as it called out something to Essa. Then they'd left it behind.

Ben couldn't walk straight. He veered left and right on the boardwalk in a wobbling path that Essa, her hand on his shoulder, was doing her best to control.

They were in a narrow wooden canyon, structures built up on either side of them, no two alike. Lanterns dangled from ropes that zig-zagged between the buildings above them.

"Where is everyone?" he asked through lips he couldn't feel.

"The Cogs run Deadbeat," Essa replied, "and they roll up the footpath early. Not much for nightlife, Cogs." There were wooden signs hanging on chains from beams above their heads, symbols carved into them, and Essa was peering up at each one they passed. "Come on," she muttered, "come *on...*"

The world was going seriously wrong. The woodgrain of the walls shimmered and twisted in the corners of his eyes. He turned as something came rolling through the intersection behind them on twin metal treads like a tank. It looked like a tank, too, although it was only the size of a Doberman, a box of thick riveted steel with long slot-like windows in its sides. Heat rippled from those narrow windows—he could feel it from here—and their thick smoked glass did little to dim the white-orange glow inside. A shadow swam up to the window, and Ben thought he saw it look at him. He paused, but Essa yanked him away.

He didn't feel like walking any more. He wanted to stop, and sit down, and melt into a puddle and drip through the cracks between the boards.

"Do you even know where we're going?" he asked, and was appalled by how slurry and strange he was sounding.

"I haven't been here in a year, Ben. But I think...oh. Go away."

She wasn't talking to him. They'd turned a corner and a swarm of...things...had instantly mobbed them. Ben stared. They were the height of a small child, and consisted of one arm, one leg, and that was it. Elbow and knee were joined by a short length of flesh that could have been biceps or thigh. One of them hopped next to Ben, plucking at his T-shirt with its lone hand.

He squeaked.

"It's fine, Ben. They're just beggars. *Shoo*, I said. But it means we're heading in the right—ah *ha*," she finished triumphantly, and he looked up at the building that had just come into view.

The possibility had occurred more than once to Ben that everything that had happened since the skulker's head had burst had been a hallucination, the black spores rampaging through his brain. He didn't really believe that, but it was a comforting thought (although not *very* comforting, since it implied the skulker itself, and the Door it had come through, had still been real). Now, looking up at the building looming over them, he clung to that thought really hard.

There wasn't a right angle in the whole thing. Everything about it was slumped and rounded, like melted wax. The windows and tall narrow door were black holes within their sagging frames. Worse, the building appeared to have skin. Worse than that, the skin was moving, subtly inflating and deflating like the whole structure was breathing. The skin was translucent, and lit from within by an unwholesome green glow. Shadows rippled across it as things moved inside.

Music oozed out through the door and windows. It sounded like breathing, like a huge animal with a lung infection, topped by a high thin theremin whine.

"We're not going in there," he said, without even thinking about it.

"Red-Eyed Lady, no," said Essa with feeling. "That's the House of Green Lights. Vats build them all over the Well. Like Starbucks, only more eldritch. It's Vats territory, they don't answer to anyone, and you absolutely do not want to go in there in your current state. Or ever. But where there's a House…"

She was leading him across the boardwalk to a small self-contained building that made Ben think of a food truck, a shack with a big window cut into the front where something hunched over a counter. The thing unfolded itself, stretching up and over them as they approached, and Ben wanted badly to back up again but that would have brought him closer to the big building with skin and he didn't know which was worse.

Its impossibly long arms were little more than bone shrink-wrapped in blue-tinged skin, and its fingers had more knuckles than they should have. It only had one eye, covered by a monocle of black glass that appeared to be riveted to its eyesocket. The other socket was eyeless, and something sprouted from it, a slender twig with a pale flower like an orchid at the end. It bobbed as the thing moved its head. It was wearing something like high-collared surgical scrubs made of white plastic.

"Apothecary," said Essa, and she stepped up to the counter and spoke to it.

It grinned at her, revealing a double row of needle-sharp teeth and a long forked tongue that unrolled to its chin. It spoke back, a series of liquid consonants and moaning vowels. It seemed to Ben to be a different language than the clockwork spider had used, but that didn't slow Essa down at all; she replied right away in the same greasy tongue, like she had a mouthful of phlegm. She pointed to Ben.

The thing said something else.

Essa pointed at Ben again, this time flourishing her hands like a model at a car show.

Ben decided that whatever was going on, he didn't like it. He liked it even less when the thing reached behind its back—its limbs bent in places they absolutely shouldn't have, like it had whipcord for bones—and produced a glass syringe with something blue roiling inside, tipped with an enormous needle of gleaming steel.

"Wait a minute," said Ben, then "What the *hell*—" as it *licked* the needle up and down with its glistening tongue.

"Calm down," said Essa, squeezing his shoulder.

"No! What the *hell!*" repeated Ben, his eyes glued to the syringe.

"He's sterilizing it, that's how they do it, it's in the saliva. Relax. He's just going to take a little blood, and—"

"*Blood?* No!"

"Well, it's absolutely your choice, Ben." Essa's voice was tense. "Your *other* choice is to sit there tripping until your brains drip out of your ears. But you don't have a great deal of time to decide, so—"

Ben swallowed and stepped up to the counter, not quite believing he was doing it. The tall thing loomed over him as it brought the syringe to bear. The bore was so huge he could see right down it, a pitch-black tunnel and he was rushing into it, the circle of darkness growing until darkness was all there was.

Chapter Eight

Essa sits on a bench outside the Mandala chamber, baggy-eyed and greasy-haired, chewing cheap Vats speed. She catches her fingers digging into her forearms and deliberately places her hands on the bench either side of her, palms flat on the packed red sand. Her arms are black with bruises and raw, skinned flesh. She's in the worst shape of anyone here. The others waited until they'd recovered from taking the Wire, but Essa is in a hurry.

She tries a couple of finger exercises and winces as fresh blood trickles from under her newly laid circuitry. She'll have to save it for the Mandala.

The others are Servitors too, all waiting their turn to face the Mandala. There are barely a dozen of them. Most in Essa and Rachana's tranche found sponsors among the factions of the Library, dedicated themselves to an Ism in a private ceremony. Like Rachana.

The ones that are left are the freaks, the outsiders, the ones who've alienated every faction and the ones with something to prove. Like Essa.

They space themselves well apart on the benches, look away sharply whenever their gazes accidentally meet. All of them are whispering to themselves, running through the Chants and Taxonomies they've crammed into their brains over the last month.

Essa should be doing the same, but she can't. She tries again, running through the Outermost Paths, the litany every Servitor learns almost from the moment they end their Climb.

Copy the sixth—the summit—the eight the quadrant over the ninth plus eighty—coward—coward—

She jerks on the bench, shakes her head, plunges back into the Paths.

Four circles—weave the eighty and call the fourth copy coward liar psycho—

Again.

Enter nine—seven by seven a seven the seven call seven and seven liar liar liar liar—

She can't straighten her thoughts; they always twist back around to the fight with Rachana the night before. She's picked over every word, wrung half a dozen meanings out of each of them, built and discarded a dozen exegeses for every glare and turn of the head. And they all end up in the same place.

Liar, Rachana sobs.

Coward, Essa spits.

Madwoman, Rachana shrieks, and she starts to say something else but Essa is already leaving to bury herself in the Stacks, delude herself she's doing final research when all she's doing is staring at the sand until sunrise, trembling and bleeding.

She gives up on the Path and leans back against the red wall, letting her thoughts scatter. The fight falls through her mind again, each word a shard of glass.

You need to play it safe, Ess. Any Ism would be glad to have you, they'll smooth the path if you let them. But you have to let them.

Let them get their hooks in me.

So their hooks are in me, then? Gregor's hooks? Can you see them, is that why you've been looking at me like that?

Like what?

Don't you—if you face the Mandala alone, either you'll find an Ism anyway, just like the rest of us, or you won't and you'll die there. People have died there.

Well, thank you for treating me like a child—

You promised me you wouldn't do this. You—

Don't manage me. Just because you let them manage you—

You promised. You liar.

Coward.

Madwoman.

The Librarian at the chamber door calls her name. He's called it before, she realizes, but she couldn't say how many times.

"Let's have an end to it, then," she mutters. She stands, pushing off the bench with her hands, feeling the fresh rivulets of blood under her sleeves.

She's seen the Mandala up close before, during her Servitorship, but she's never stood on the floor. The outermost rings are only inches from her slippered toes. It doesn't look all that different from the Mirrors you see in the Stacks, but look at it longer than a moment and you see the detail of it, the meaning in each grain of endlessly shifting sand. She's on her third day without sleep, and Library days are long. She has to squeeze her eyes shut and take a harsh breath to centre herself.

None of the Librarians behind the parapet around the Mandala notice this. They look down at her with half-lidded eyes. They've been here all day pulling Invigilator duty and they're bored. They know she'll be like all the other candidates—stepping through the Outermost, navigating the safest circles for a moment before they choose an Ism they could have been mentored into anyway, just for the bragging rights.

We'll see, thinks Essa.

Almost before she realizes she's done it, she's stepped over the outer rim and into the pulsing circles of sand. Her eyes track the patterns and she takes another step, then another. The sand smooths itself out in calm circles around her, each marked with a single symbol—here the sigil of the Slow Walker, there the Thousand Sails, across from her the Inverted Spire. And others, all the major Isms. She only needs to step into one. The Heptacomb's sigil appears—Rachana's Ism now. Just a step away.

She ignores them all and steps forward instead. She whispers Chants in a never-ending stream as her fingers twist and claw at the air, blood dripping from her nails, instantly swallowed by the sand.

A couple of the Librarians notice her, bestir themselves, nudge their neighbours.

The still circles are fewer now. Between them, the Mandala turns faster. She's entering the uncharted areas of the Library, where no Isms have calmed and sorted the sands.

To her right, a tiny dust devil springs up. She pauses, lets it cross her path, then takes another step forward. Another. She's not even sure she has a plan anymore, or if she's trusting to blind luck.

Another dust devil, and another. A lull…and then a yard to her left, the sand erupts in a bone-stripping tornado, wind whipping at her robe and almost wrong-footing her.

The Librarians are looking at each other with incomprehension, then irritation, then concern. No one's gone this far today. No one's dared. Invigilation is a chore, but a dead Servitor is an embarrassment. One of them stands, gripping the parapet, and others follow suit.

The sand is rushing like whitewater. More of those whirlwinds slice through the circle. Essa takes another step. Another. The last one puts her right in the path of a whirlwind, and she stops. The whirlwind moves closer. She can feel the edge of it score her cheek, embedding sand in her skin, drawing blood. She clenches her fists.

And it all goes away.

The whirlwinds collapse into the Mandala, which smooths itself out perfectly flat. In front of Essa, a tiny raised circle appears and leaps into the air as a cloud of dust. It hovers, formless, then tentatively rearranges itself into a few simple polyhedra. Essa raises a bloody hand, and it sends out probing tendrils that gently brush her fingertips.

The Librarians collapse back into their seats. "Silly child," one of them mutters as she blots the sweat from her forehead with her sleeve.

Essa isn't listening. She's staring at the fragile little dust cloud, her face rapt. Her fingers ripple through a quick pattern and the dust follows suit, shivering in a way that brings to mind a laugh.

Essa laughs too, or maybe she sobs. "Hey, you," she whispers.

CHAPTER NINE

Ben woke from a dream of earthquakes. He had a pounding headache, but otherwise he felt more like himself than he had since he'd seen Ryan get eaten.

He'd been sleeping sitting up and his head had lolled onto his shoulder. He lifted it and hissed at the bolt of pain through his stiff neck. A voice said "Mmph."

His eyes snapped open. Essa was sitting beside him, her head on his other shoulder. Carefully, he disengaged from her without waking her up and slowly stood, wincing as the blood surged through his legs.

The boards trembled under his feet, and he remembered his dream. A deep bass note thrummed through the whole town, and he thought of the masses of machinery between the buildings, those huge pendulums swinging below. He was inside a clock, and it was ticking.

They'd been sleeping on a long wooden bench, like you'd see on a proper boardwalk facing the ocean, although all this one faced was the Well's vast wall across fifty feet of empty space. The boardwalk was empty, the buildings behind them shuttered and dark. He stretched, and a distant flare of pain in his shoulder reminded him his messenger bag wasn't there. A rush of panic—and then he saw it, stuffed under the bench with Essa's knapsack.

His skull throbbed. He walked up to the boardwalk's balustrade and looked out at the Well, or at the patch of it he could see with all of Deadbeat's hanging buildings crowding around. If that really was the town's name, anyway. The infinite wall was bare red brick here, soot-stained and crumbling, and someone was clinging to it.

They weren't moving, just hanging there spreadeagled. A girl, he thought, with a thick braid of iron-grey hair, wearing a black jacket and leggings. The hair said *old*, but nothing else about her did; she was hanging onto the bricks with her fingers crimped in shallow depressions in the mortar. Her grip strength must be incredible.

She erupted into motion.

She didn't climb so much as *run* across the sheer brick, out to her right at first and then pushing off with a foot to effortlessly reverse her momentum. Up, down, sideways, never missing a foot- or hand-hold; Ben had seen a ton of amazing climbers on YouTube, but none of them could have done what this girl was doing. Maybe Ashima Shiraishi could. Then he saw her striking out, hitting the air with elbow, knee, fist: vertical kata. Finally, the girl extended herself perpendicular to the Well and hung there in space, horizontal, her palms flat against the brick. How was she doing that?

Then she let go, and dropped out of sight.

Ben leaned out further, putting more weight on the balustrade, which wobbled a little. The girl came back into view as she fell across a rope stretched between two buildings and hooked her feet over it to check her fall. The rope bowed out, deeper than it should have for such a tiny figure, and then she was swinging around it. As she came up, she let go and flew, tucking and somersaulting through the air. Ben had to stand on the lower rung of the balustrade, gripping the edge of the nearest building's tin roof, to see her.

"Ben?" he heard, and turned. Essa was standing beside the bench, running her hand through her hair.

Ben held out his hand. "Can you hold on? Then I can lean out more. I can't see her."

"Perhaps," said Essa carefully, "you should get down instead."

"Why?" said Ben. "I don't—"

He looked down. And down. And down, through the layers of the town, the dark bulk of one of those massive pendulums swinging, and the empty darkness below it, Doorlight in the void like dim jewels. He reeled and Essa grabbed his hand before he could overbalance, then planted her feet and yanked him backwards. The railing shook as he fell. He sat up and scooted away until his back slammed into the bench, his heart hammering. He was covered in slick sweat. He looked up at Essa, unable to speak.

"It's the shot," said Essa. "One of the things it does is sort out any fear of heights you might have, but your brain chemistry's going to"—she mimed a pair of scales tipping one way and the other before resting level—"for a little while before it settles down. Try to err on the side of caution, all right?"

Ben looked down at the wooden floor of the balcony. The cracks were full of darkness and he quickly looked away again. "Where are we?" he asked. "What is this place?"

"Well," said Essa, crouching in front of him, "there's one thing we need to get out of the way first." She took something from her back pocket, that little leather-bound sketchbook with the pencil jammed in the spine. "I apologize in advance, by the way," she said, quickly jotting something down on the page.

"What now?" said Ben.

"Once again," said Essa, "sorry," and she held up the book, showing him the complicated symbol on it.

Ben opened his mouth to ask her what it meant, then clamped his lips together. He scrambled on all fours to the balustrade and stuck his head through. He only just made it in time.

Essa gave him a moment. "Well," she said, "better above than below. Is what they say here."

"What—*urk*." Ben grabbed his head with both hands. "What—" He swallowed hard, then paused. "Wait." He turned to Essa, hoping his chin was puke-free. "Say that again."

"Better above than below," said Essa again, carefully. She said it in that backwards-talking Wellside Creole, not English, but the words *changed* in Ben's mind, he could almost feel them squirming and twisting in his brain. He resisted the urge to scrabble at his temples, claw them out of his skull.

"I *did* say sorry."

"*What the hell kind of drawing was that?*"

She closed the sketchbook. He caught a final glimpse of the symbol and his mind shivered as she stuffed it in her pocket. "The drawing was just the trigger. It was really in the shot."

"The—oh man." He flexed his shoulder, felt a distant twinge. "It really jabbed me with that thing? That blue stuff?" His mouth felt furry from throwing up. His tongue felt weird.

"Yes, you probably don't remember. Along with the heights thing, and killing off the skulker spores, of course, it gave you Creole."

"How can a *shot*—" He very suddenly realized that the reason his mouth felt funny was because *he was speaking it, too*. He clamped his lips together.

"The shot had tiny...things in it. I'm no biologist, I'm afraid. They made their way into your brain, electrified your synapses, set up a self-propagating pattern...again, I'm no biologist. Oh, and you've got a full set of antibodies now, too. All kinds of worlds out here where a faceful of sneeze would kill you stone dead, otherwise. If you ever go home, you'll never have a cold again."

"What was that thing? With the syringe?" said Ben. He said it in English, very carefully, and was a little relieved to find he still could.

"Empty Ones. 'Empties' if you like. From the Vats. Oh!" She dug in her pocket again and produced something that she slapped into Ben's hand. "Your fee."

At first he thought it was a tiny copper cog, a disc with teeth all around the sides and a design stamped on the face, three stylized interlocking gears. A coin? He turned it over in his hand. On the other side was a pattern of raised dots in neat rows. It looked a bit like an old-school programming punch card. "Wait a minute," he said, "why did *he* pay *me*?"

"The Vats are all about collecting genomes," said Essa. "You're a virgin."

"I am *not*," said Ben, accidentally speaking Creole again. It made his lips tingle.

"Don't be vulgar, Ben. It means you've never been collected before, and that's worth money. You signed over your rights."

"I don't remember signing anything."

"I'm not surprised, the state you were in. Anyway, they've got your DNA now, they get to make whatever kind of horrible thing they want out of it, and you get paid. Less a nominal finder's fee." She shook her hand in her pocket and Ben heard it jingle. "Win-win."

Essa was talking a mile a minute, animated, eyes sparkling, the weary loner of Chifley High almost unrecognizable. It made her beautiful, but with it came a brittleness, a fragility, that Ben didn't like. Considering she was his only link to home.

"What's this worth, anyway?" he asked, running his thumb over the coin's teeth.

"Not a room for the night," said Essa, "as you probably guessed. But I think it'll cover breakfast. We'd better get going if we want to beat the—"

Another of those deep bass thrums, no different from the others, but this time all the doors on the buildings opened crisply and suddenly the boardwalk was full of people, marching along in two neat rows.

"—rush," finished Essa.

The stall was in a gap between two buildings, with just enough frontage for a bar and three stools. There wasn't even enough room for the cook, a tiny wrinkled creature, sexless, legless. It sat in a swing that hung from a pole braced between the buildings, dangling over nothing. What looked like bunches of dried grass dangled around it.

Ben and Essa stood in line, waiting for a stool. Everyone seemed to be getting their breakfast to go, and the line moved fast. On the boardwalk, that double line of pedestrians filed smoothly past each other, everyone keeping to the right and advancing at a measured pace. People stepped in and out of doorways without breaking the flow, slotting neatly into gaps in the traffic. They weren't marching— they weren't even keeping step—but somehow they were all in sync. Ben thought of those times when he'd tried to get around a stranger on the street and they'd both sidestepped the same way, kept blocking each other over and over. This was the opposite of that.

It was more than just the way they moved, too. There was a *sameness* to them he couldn't pin down. It wasn't that they looked alike, they were all different shapes and sizes, genders and ages—a wider range of shapes and sizes than he was used to, actually; there were quite a few people that had to be over eight feet tall, and quite a few less than four. They all wore the same thing, though, buckle shoes and breeches, cravats and long coats, all of plain black cloth. In the distance he could see a couple of tall black hats, like soldiers used to wear a couple hundred years ago, bobbing above the crowd, although he couldn't see who was wearing them.

"What's up with everyone?" he asked, in English in case anyone was listening.

Essa shrugged. "That's the Cogs for you. They like things neat and tidy."

"And the Cogs are…"

"Another world with a Door to the Well. One of the Powers, actually. The most boring one. Very punctual, though. They've had a couple of holy wars over what time it was."

Another of those subtle vibrations ran through everything, another tick of Deadbeat's huge machinery. The ticking made it impossible not to think of how much time was passing. He didn't even want to look at his phone, see all those notifications, the missed appointments piling up. "So Essa," he said, "about going home—"

"You just got here," she said, and then they were at the head of the line. She slid a couple of coins across the counter and the cook slid a couple of shallow cups back at them. It pushed off a wall, swung over to one of those bunches of grass, and cut the dried little nubbins off the ends of the stalks with a tiny curved knife. Its backswing took it to the opposite wall and a shelf with a kettle steaming over a tiny coal stove. It flicked the kettle once, twice, and Ben nearly fell backwards off his stool as a splash of boiling water flew towards him, but it landed neatly in his cup, followed by the dried thing, which absorbed the water instantly, blooming into a strange-looking flower.

Essa was already plucking a fleshy petal off hers and chewing it. Ben followed suit. He was ravenously hungry, and he'd eaten half of it before the taste even registered. Not bad.

"So the Well—" Ben said when he was half done.

"Or the Pit," said Essa, looking up again. "Some people call it the Shaft—and no jokes, I've heard them all."

"How big is it?"

Her eyes narrowed. "Was that a joke?"

"*No*," he snapped, without meaning to. He realized his heart was racing. He didn't even know what day it was, how much time had passed in the Well's endless dark. How long he had to get home. This place put him on edge: something about that neat double row of people pacing past, everyone in sync but him.

Essa shrugged and held her hands up, palms facing each other in a vague impression of size. "A few miles wide? Ish?"

"And how deep?"

"No idea," said Essa. "No one's ever found a bottom. Or a top for that matter."

"So where *is* it?"

Essa smiled, extended her arms like wings, to take it all in, Deadbeat and the immense wall and the Well rising up above them. "It's everywhere," she said, "or rather, it *leads* everywhere. All those Doors open on all kinds of different worlds, maybe all the worlds there are."

Ben focused on his breakfast, took a deep, shaky breath, felt himself relaxing a little. "But how?"

"Excellent question. The big theory at the moment—or it was the last time I checked, I've been out of the loop for a while—is that someone took a core sample. A biopsy of reality. And the Well's what's left behind."

That about hit Ben's limit for epic weirdness right then. He took his phone out of his pocket and looked at it, the gesture reflexive, normal, comforting. No signal, which was less so. "I'm guessing I can't call home."

Essa shook her head. "No Vine to your world. And your phone won't work—nothing like that works in the Well, no wifi, no radio, no nothing. You'd have to find your Door again, but if you want my advice, you're better off just walking away. I mean, what will you tell your people back there? What could you possibly tell them, what can you say that'll stop them worrying while you're gone?"

"'Gone'? So I'm staying here?" said Ben.

Essa looked at him like he was insane. "Why would you *not?*" That mad sparkle was back in her eye. Ben thought about his court date and his chest tightened up all over again.

"I have to get back, Essa," he said. "I have a…thing. In five—shit." He looked at the date on his phone. "Four days' time."

Essa relented a little. "Look, Ben," she said, "even if you absolutely have to go back, don't you have a couple of days to see the sights? Whisper and I are heading downWell to the Library—you could make it there and back in four days, with a bit of luck. Are you telling me you don't want to see the Library?"

"Who's Whisper?"

"Who's—oh, you haven't been introduced." Essa slid that silver hip flask from a back pocket. It was *old*, dulled and worn from years of handling, more years than he or Essa had been alive. She'd tied a loop of braided leather around the neck and fastened the other end to her belt. Now she unscrewed the cap and softly whispered something, not in English or Creole, a dry hiss like sand falling.

A thin stream of red dust rose from the mouth of the flask, curling in the air like smoke. Essa, he noticed, was careful to keep it under the countertop, her body shielding it from the boardwalk and the eyes of everyone but Ben. She gestured with her hand, and the dust congealed into a thin and sinuous shape like a tiny snake. It twined around her hand, racing through her fingers in complex patterns, flicking its crimson tail, then began to chase itself around her wrist, like a bracelet. Tiny red sparks crackled inside it, pricked Essa's circuitry-inlaid hand.

"She's an Ism," said Essa—it rhymed with *prism*—"from the Library. Just a baby one. I was showing her around when we got stuck in your world. But we're going home now, aren't we, Whisper?" A twitch, like a shrug, shivered through the cloud of dust as it ducked back into Essa's flask. "The Well doesn't agree with her," said Essa, "but she'll be worldside soon."

Ben persisted. "And you're sure I can get home in time? It's important."

"It *must* be pretty bloody important, to turn your back on all this."

"It kind of is." He hoped Essa wouldn't press him for details, but as it turned out she wasn't interested.

"Fine then. We'll get going as soon as I can wire myself some cash. You *need* to see the Library." She nodded to herself. "Someone from your world needs to see it. I want at least one person from that poky little self-important backwater to have an idea of the *scale* of things."

Her voice was shot through with bitterness, and Ben was worried all over again for her. And for himself. He ducked his head and ate his flower.

They descended through Deadbeat, down twisting, switchbacking stairs, lower and lower until they were at the very bottom of the town, near the anchor point of one of the huge pendulums.

Something hugged the Well's vast wall down there, something like a cable, or a climbing plant, he wasn't sure which. It emerged from the darkness below Deadbeat, thick as a tree. Tendrils split off from the main trunk here and there and anchored themselves to the Well. The end of the thing climbed up and through a tiny wooden Door, and that was where they were headed.

"The Vine," said Essa. "First big collaboration between the Powers. Between the Vats and the Library, anyway. Vats grew the cable, Library handles the software. Cogs don't care, they have their semaphore for talking to each other, which is why it's stuck down here in the back alleys." Ben was just letting it wash over him when Essa said things like that. They weren't explanations, they just left him more confused, and he was beginning to think that was at least partly her intention. It was starting to piss him off, and also he needed to use the bathroom.

The Well here was crooked planks, knotted and splintery, studded with rusty nails. Essa was already hammering on the rickety wooden Door. It was made of vaguely parallel planks, big gaps between them, with another Z of planking holding it together. Dim light shone through, soft like daylight through curtains.

Essa kept hammering on the door, cursing under her breath. Ben, having nothing better to do, stepped up and looked between those loose planks.

Something on the other side was looking back at him.

It was a black faceted crystal in a brass mount like a telescope, that just as quickly whisked upward and vanished. Then there came a high-pitched screeching and wheezing from behind the Door and something yanked it open.

The thing behind the Door was a machine like Lud, but it wasn't shaped like a crab, or spider, or any other animal Ben had seen. The closest he could think of was a sea urchin. It was a knot of gears and springs the size of a soccer ball from which radiated a haphazard assortment of slender metal arms, and it moved by tumbling over itself, supporting itself with skeletal brass hands. Black rags were tied to it at various points to hang over its frame, approximating a robe.

Its name was 黃銅鐘. It pronounced it carefully for Ben but the best he could manage was 黃銅蟲, which resulted in a hurt silence from 鐘 and an amused snort from Essa. Ben clenched his teeth and didn't try again. It didn't look like he was going to be much of a part of the conversation anyway.

It didn't look like anyone would, for that matter, beside 鐘 itself. The Vine, which he gathered was a kind of Internet-analogue for the Well, wasn't that popular among the Cogs. So 鐘 didn't see too many people, and now that it had, it absolutely would not shut up.

The Door belonged to a tiny one-room wooden shack, and that odd organic cable had ramified through the whole place, hanging in loops and tangling in knots like the world's worst-organized server room. Glowing screens nestled here and there in the mess.

鐘 was a Librarian like Essa, apparently, and as soon as it caught a glimpse of the golden circuitry in Essa's hands it had immediately started talking shop. Essa had mostly answered with shrugs and grunts, and she never once—had never once, since she and Ben had left his world—given her name. Assuming 'Essa' even was her name.

"Field agent? Grand Tour?" said the Librarian.

Essa shrugged, grunted.

"Which Ism?" said the Librarian. "Canted Plane? Heptacomb?"

"Does it matter?" said Essa. "We just—"

But 鐘 just went on talking, about the City, and the High Gardens, and the West Face Observatory, and the Mandala, looking for gossip. Essa was getting increasingly uncomfortable. She pushed a few of those hanging cable-fronds out of the way and sat at one of the terminals, where she paused, clearly not wanting the clockwork ball to look over her shoulder.

Ben had needed to go to the bathroom for a while now. He hovered, waiting for a break in the clockwork Librarian's uninterrupted stream of chatter, and finally just spoke right over the top of it. "Excuse me."

The Librarian broke off, swiveled to bring more eyes to bear on him.

"Where's the toilet?" Ben asked, feeling self-conscious.

"The privy?" said the Librarian, and one spindly arm tipped with an unidentifiable tool waved at the shack's second door opposite the Door.

Ben looked at it. "It's out there?"

"'Out there'," the librarian said, "is 'it.' Go anywhere you like."

Ben had no idea what that meant, but he wasn't about to hang around and argue. He grabbed his bag and swung the door open.

He stepped out into bright sunlight. It was a shock to his much-abused circadian clock, and a wave of unreality washed over him as he looked out onto endless rolling grassland studded with colossal boulders.

He was standing on a gentle rise, one of many that undulated away to the horizon like a frozen ocean. It felt like he could see forever. There were clouds overhead, and he could see their shadows clearly drifting across the plain. Huge ripples flowed through the grass from the wind.

The boulders were granite, and enormous; some of them were hundreds of feet long, lying half-buried in the soft ground. Smaller (but still huge) rocks lay scattered at their feet, and he made for the nearest one, for some privacy.

He trudged back to the shack the Vine was in, watching the wind thrill through the grass. Halfway to the horizon was a cluster of those boulders, or at least he thought it was until he saw one move. Another rolled over lazily. A herd of something, sunning themselves. It was hard to judge scale on the vast plain, but they must have been *huge*.

He checked the laptop in his messenger bag. He didn't want to turn it on; he was going home as soon as all this was over with, which according to Essa was imminently, but the thing's battery was ancient and he didn't want to run it down any more than he had to.

As he made his way to the shack, he looked around again at the rock-studded plain. Another world. It still didn't quite fit inside his head.

Including his own and the one with the endless cubicles, and the Well itself if that counted, it was the fourth world he'd been to. As far as he knew, no one else back home had been to more than one. Although maybe they had; maybe others had wandered through a Door they thought was a door, and ended up in the Well. He hadn't heard of any, though, which didn't make him feel any better about his prospects of getting back home.

He tried to make himself feel that sense of wonder, or pioneer spirit, or whatever it was he should be feeling right now. Instead, contemplating the Well, all he felt was unease shading into outright terror. All those Doors, all those infinite possibilities. How would you choose?

And Essa was yanking him from one mind-blowing sight to the next…why? Just so she could show him how small he and his whole world were?

But with all the weird stuff he'd seen, what he kept coming back to was how *off* Essa was acting. Her being wound-up like this was understandable. For whatever reason, she'd been trapped in his world for the last year, and now she was free, and Ben could guess how that felt. He'd dreamed a dozen times since he'd been arrested that all of it was somehow magically over, that he didn't have his court date and trial and sentencing hanging over his head anymore. Waking up, feeling that relief slip away, had been like dying.

But relief didn't explain why Essa was so tense. It was like something was still hanging over her head, and she was trying to ignore it and failing.

He gave the endless grassland a final look and returned to the darkness of the shack.

The terminal Essa was using didn't have any keyboard, just that curved glass screen nestled among the Vine cables. Close-up, Ben could see the cables were pulsing, ripples travelling through them like they were digesting something. Blood-red patterns of concentric circles pulsed on the black screen in time with the cables' twitching. Whisper was out of its flask and dancing in front of the screen in its own patterns. Essa's hands danced with it, fingers and wrists twisting in smooth circles.

"Better?" she asked, without looking over her shoulder at him.

Ben wedged himself into a gap between two thick cable-buds. "Much. What are you doing?"

"Waiting, mostly. This is the frontier up here, they don't get the best service."

Symbols chased each other around the patterns on the screen. He waited for them to turn into English in his head, but they didn't. Essa saw him looking and shook her head. "That's Library flatscript. No shot for that, you learn it the hard way."

"Was there a shot for English?"

She shook her head.

"You speak it pretty well."

"The Governess at the Choir tithe-house I grew up in always said: a language is an instrument. Even if you don't like it, even if you're being forced to play it, you owe it to the instrument itself to keep it in tune." She smiled, a little sadly. "Anyway. Once I get in touch with the Library I can sort out a line of credit, and we can get moving."

"About that," he said. "Thanks for the offer. I mean it. Also for saving my life."

Essa waved a circuitry-inscribed hand magnanimously. "We saved each other's. Whisper and I were growing that Door for a year. I don't know what I would have done if it had closed again. It was a one-shot deal."

Ben's stomach lurched. "What? It won't open again?"

"No, it'll open just fine from Wellside. Worldside's tricky, though. It has to do with—"

"I just want to go home," Ben said. Blurted, really. "Forget the tour. Just send me home." He wondered if he was whining.

"You're really serious." She shook her head. "You want to go *back*."

"You really didn't like it there, did you?" asked Ben.

She looked at him, appalled. "Did *you?*"

He thought of Chifley High. "Well, no, but—"

"I hated your world, Ben. I hated it *so much*, I mean no offence but...I was stacking shelves at *Woolworths*, did you know that? Living in a shelter. Whisper was working on the Door—you saw her, she was spread through the gym, too attenuated to even have a conversation with. So *every day* I waited by that Door *alone* in that shitty school while all those bullying bitches who ran the place just—I mean, just thinking about them, that insane amount of power they had to make people's lives miserable...

"I wanted to say to them—have you ever seen a city, a million people in it, wading across the ocean on legs five miles long? Or a city made of sand castles that change every night, where you can go to sleep in a hovel and wake up in a palace, or the other way around, and you never know which? I've seen the flesh-forests in the Vats. I've seen the sun hit the Nine-Heaven Ossuaries as it came over the Granite Curtain. And *I'm* getting picked on? By *you?* I am a *Librarian* of *Red Sand City*"— she drew herself up on the stool, overenunciating words she'd clearly run through by herself a few times, or a few dozen—"two-one in the Climb and wired for the Mandala—but oh, wait, *you* have a boyfriend with a beach house? You got hammered on Bailey's and fingerbanged in a toilet by some nonentity whose daddy bought him a Subaru? Well, you *win*, your Majesty, allow me to peel you a *grape*."

She waved her hand at the Door and the Well beyond it. "There's a Door out there somewhere and behind it there's a world where the serfs have their tongues cut out at birth, and anyone who sees a nobleman's face loses his eyes. And I think Chifley was worse. And that's what you want to go back to."

Ben had never been that enthused about the state of his world, but suddenly he felt like defending it. "It's not like there's nothing to see in my world. Maybe not as incredible as the Library or the Ossuaries or whatever—although I don't know how you even measure that—but there's enough stuff to see that you could spend your whole life—I mean, I've never been to Africa, I've never been to—and we have problems too, sure, poverty and climate change and whatever, but how is running away to the Well going to solve them?"

The hand pointed at the Door clenched. Essa's eyes glinted dangerously. "Small problems, Ben. In the scheme of things."

"Not if it's *my* world, they're not. Like, you think we don't know the universe is *big*? You can't just hide away and—"

"You're not going to change anything, Ben. Same people running your world that run your school. Same small-minded—but forget it. Forget it. They can do what they want. *You* can do what you want. Go to all the parties you want, tweet *all you want*, screw whoever you want, and why stop there, you can go be some high-powered corporate dickhead or Prime Minister or the head of the World Bank if you want but guess what? All you'll ever *really* be is another Door I go past on my way to somewhere *interesting*—"

The terminal gave a harsh buzz and she half-turned to glance at it. And froze.

"Essa?"

Essa didn't turn back to him, didn't complete her turn to face the monitor. Didn't move at all. In front of her Whisper was cycling rapidly between two different patterns, like a stuck CD.

"Essa?" He tentatively put a hand on her shoulder. She didn't react. Under her hoodie, her muscles were rock-hard and trembling. Had the screen done something to her? Before he could think not to, he'd glanced at it himself, but he didn't feel a thing.

New symbols had appeared at the top and bottom of the screen, and they must have been Creole because Ben could read them. Sort of. Looking at them gave him real empathy for the dyslexics at Chifley. The characters squirmed in his head, changed into English while somehow keeping their original shape at the same time. They scrolled by like the ticker on a news show, and he only caught scattered words (or meanings, or sense-impacts). Words like *non grata.*

Hazard.

Revoked.

Expelled.

Apprehend.

"Oh dear," said a metallic voice in his ear. 鐘 was looking over his shoulder. "Irregular."

"What's going on?" asked Ben. "Can you stop it? Can you help her?"

"Why in the Well—no, I can't 'stop it'," said 鐘. "And we can help her best, I think, by leaving her to the authorities." The ball of clockwork rattled as it shook from side to side.

"Authorities?" Ben stood and looked behind the screen. One of those living cables fed into the back of it.

"The authorities here will detain her until a Library representative arrives. This is very serious. Only the Spires can order a Lacuna."

"Is it hurting her?"

"Well, depending on how long they take to get here, some... degradation in capacity will be unavoidable—"

Ben had heard enough. He reached for the cable, then gasped in pain as one of 鐘's multiple hands closed on his elbow.

"You realize," it said, "that if I let you do that, they'll never let me out of here?" Its grip tightened, grinding the bones of Ben's arm against each other. "I'll be stuck in this empty world in this vile little town until my mainspring's worn through? I have *not*—"

Ben lunged for the cable, managed to curl his fingers around it. 鐘, preoccupied with its rant, reacted in exactly the wrong way, yanking Ben's arm back, and the cable came with it. Clear fluid dribbled from its severed end, and the image on the screen shivered and died. Instantly, Essa slumped forward. Her forehead struck the top of the screen and she slid bonelessly to the ground.

Every cable in the shack was squirming violently. 鐘 squawked and whirled, hurling Ben into a nest of pale tubes that writhed against him, curling around his arms. The Librarian advanced on Essa.

"*Whisper!*" bellowed Ben. Cutting off the screen had freed Essa's red dust, but it seemed only semi-conscious, hanging in the air in a formless twitching cloud. Now, hearing Ben's voice, a ripple went through it like a dog shaking itself and it swept out a razor-edged tendril, severing three of 鐘's limbs. 鐘 crashed to the ground in a shower of sparks.

Ben freed himself from the knot of cables and went to Essa. She'd managed to prop herself up on her elbows, muttering nonsense to herself.

"We're leaving, Essa," said Ben, putting one of her arms over his neck, grabbing her waist, and lifting her with a grunt.

"Gregor," Essa muttered. "Gregor."

"That's great," said Ben, "but we have to get moving." Something warm dripped on his shoulder. He turned and saw Essa was bleeding freely from her ear. "Shit."

Whisper zigzagged through the air around them like an agitated housefly as Ben maneuvered Essa through the Door. 鐘 clacked something in its own language as they made it through. Ben swung the Door shut behind them, cutting it off.

"Gregor," Essa whispered, almost too low to hear, then said it again, spat it like it was a mouthful of venom.

"Absolutely, let's go see Gregor," said Ben. "But right now I think we need to lie low for a bit, so if you have any suggestions...?" He trailed off hopefully, but Essa was shaking her head. Her legs gave out and he nearly dropped her on the stairs.

The Door behind them rattled. Ben looked around for something to bar it with, then gave up. Anyway, 鐘 had said the Cogs authorities were already coming. They needed to get off the street. Somewhere no one would come after them until Essa could recover. Somewhere no one went...

He almost missed the flash of green light coming down a side street. When he realized what he'd seen, he backed up and looked again. Along with the light he could hear something, a sound like a chorus of musical saws.

He hesitated, not wanting to get any closer, but a rhythmic stomping was approaching, the sound of boots marching in step, and he muttered "Shit," and started hauling Essa along the street, Whisper dancing around them.

Chapter Ten

Essa sits at the side of the bridge, forehead leaning on the black iron railing, legs dangling into nothing. The railings have been wrought into complex patterns and Whisper streams around and through them, splitting and coalescing, chasing her tail.

A sullen red glow lights Essa's face from below, bathes her gold-inlaid arms. The glow intensifies, and Essa's eyes track the lantern as it rises up past the bridge and over her head. It's an icosahedron of crimson Thorn silk, the heat from the candle inside sending it sailing upWell. It bobs in a random breeze from a Door.

Other lanterns rise in the distance, hundreds of them, thousands, constellations of red stars lighting up the Well.

There are others on the bridge watching the display, but Essa has a couple feet of clear space either side. They're giving the Librarian and her Ism a wide berth, as most do Wellside, ever since the Exile and especially today.

The bridge extends right across the Well, curving slightly so it can line up properly with the Doors at either of its ends. On one side the immense bronze Doors of the Thorn; on the other, the Bergs, their Door a single slab of polished ice, so pure and glassy you can see the reflection of each point of lantern-light.

At the Thorn end is a station of the funicular that zigzags down the side of the Well. The Library station is just downWell, or was. If Essa leans to the side she can see the twisted tangle of black iron where the tracks cut off a few hundred yards from the Library Door. She can see the scars too, the long twisting paths that splinter the surface of the Well itself, like the crisscrossing welts on a lashed back—

"There you are." Essa tightens her grip on the railings as Rachana strolls along the bridge in the lantern-light. She's on the arm of a tall Librarian in a ceremonial robe, his hood up.

"There I am," murmurs Essa, looking at the lanterns again. Rachana and the other one watch them with her.

"There's a bag of your things in my room," says Rachana. "When are you getting it?"

"Don't need it."

"I didn't even say what was in it." Rachana is already exasperated.

"I don't need it. Throw it off the Spires."

"Throw it yourself—" snaps Rachana, and the tall Librarian steps up between them, pushing his hood back from his fine-boned face. His sleeves fall to his elbows as he does it, revealing the dense circuitry in his pale forearms. Circuitry circles his brow, too, and the front of his head is shaved, henna staining the skin, marking where the Binders will put in more. Essa can't help raising an eyebrow.

"Essa, Gregor," says Rachana.

Essa is inspecting Gregor's circuitry. He catches her eye and she returns his gaze unabashed.

"The Thousand Sails," he says, pointing to the golden lines on his scalp. He holds up an arm. "The Heptacomb, of course. The Shells. The Heavy Boughs."

"And the Spirals." Rachana is looking at Essa as she says it.

He touches his stained skin. "Not yet."

"Gregor's the youngest to be wired for five Isms," says Rachana. "Ever."

A lantern has been bobbing under the bridge and now it frees itself, rising past the railings. Essa reaches out and brushes it with a finger. "Hard on the old central nervous system," she observes.

Gregor shrugs. "Rewarding, though. There aren't enough of us doing this. It lets me be a connection between Isms." He knocks a fist against the black iron railing. "A bridge."

"Or play one side against another while you feather your own nest," says Essa. "If you wanted to, I mean."

Rachana groans. "Not tonight, Essa, all right?" Through her crystal skin, Essa can see her blood fluorescing. She's on something. "Gregor, just tell her and let's go."

Gregor nods. "To the point, then. I've been putting together a sort of ad-hoc…research institute, I suppose, although that's rather too grand a name. We just call it the Group—"

"I know this part," says Essa.

"So you did receive my invitation."

"Not technically. It chased me across half the walls in the Stacks but I managed to shake it off."

Rachana presses her lips together. She struggles to stay quiet and fails. "The Group hasn't even gotten started yet, and we've already registered half a dozen Proofs. Everyone keeps the rights to their own work, none of the Isms are involved…no reason for you to moan and bitch about getting your *hands dirty*."

A balloon is rising past the bridge a few hundred yards away. On the ornate gondola they can just see a Vats party, Empties in white plastic robes surrounding the immense flabby shape of a Luminary taking up half the deck, coloured mists roiling around it. A peal of whining music sets Essa's teeth on edge. She makes a circle with her thumb and ring finger, and Whisper leaves the railing and begins to circle her wrist. "But there *would* be an Ism involved. If I joined. Correct?"

Gregor's easy expression doesn't change. "It'd be a coup, I'm not denying it. Bonding with a brand-new Ism, your first outing in the Mandala? We could learn a great deal from your little friend." He extends a hand towards Whisper, fingers already curling in a petitioning mudra. "May I?"

"You may not."

"Oh for—it's Victory Day, Essa," Rachana snaps. "Lighten up."

"Betrayal Day. Saving-Our-Own-Skin Day."

"Do you really think of it that way? A betrayal?" Gregor sounds more interested than offended. He raises his arms, taking in all the lanterns. "One for every one we lost. We didn't escape unscathed."

Essa narrows her eyes. "In an absolute sense, no. In a relative sense?"

Rachana rolls her eyes, another psychedelic ripple passing through her flesh as whatever drug she's on does its work.

Essa abruptly stands, drawing Whisper out into a lens aimed downWell. They can see the huge iron Door down there in the light of a cluster of lanterns. It's the same black iron as all the construction Wellside, but this Door is streaked and spotted with dull rust. Every other Door, bridge, platform in the Well has a cluster of people watching the lanterns ascend, but not this one.

Except now Essa magnifies the view, and there *are* people down there, a small knot of black-clad figures, some tiny, some the size of a small building. Clinging to the Well. Watching.

"They come here every year. Fewer all the time. Watching everyone throw a party." Essa raps the railing with knuckles in a not particularly kind impression of Gregor. "They gave us the Well, and we slammed their Door on them and left them to die, and now we celebrate it."

"And if we were in their place?" says Gregor.

"If we were in their place, we'd deserve to be cut off," says Essa bitterly.

"Because we don't face consequences? Take responsibility? Such as, for example, picking up a bag of your underthings from your ex's rooms?"

"Wow," says Essa brightly, "you really like being a jerk, don't you?"

Gregor holds up a placating hand. "I'm not saying it's not an interesting discussion—"

"She's not interesting." Rachana spits into the Well. "She's not political. She's just sanctimonious. And contrary." She shakes her head. "I've had enough." She heads back down the bridge, tottering a little.

"My invitation stands," says Gregor quietly. "I'd urge you to reconsider." Essa turns away, looking fiercely at the lanterns, and when she risks a sideways glance Gregor has gone too.

Chapter Eleven

A flock of those arm/leg things hopped around them as they walked down the green-lit street, plucking at their clothes. Essa didn't seem to notice. Ben tried to shoo them away like Essa had, but it didn't work. Then he kicked one in the shin, which did.

He felt a little bad about it as the flock hopped away, but he was starting to get seriously pissed off. And scared. What were they doing? What was *he* doing? What if, instead of giving Essa time to recover, he was just letting whatever was wrong with her get worse? Why had it even happened, her paralysis on the Vine? If she was a fugitive, on the run from the Library (whatever that was), shouldn't he be turning her in anyway? Maybe if he did, whoever was in charge in Deadbeat would let him go home.

Essa was dragging her feet, stumbling against him every other step, but thankfully she was moving under her own power. She was still muttering under her breath, nothing he could understand. Whisper, at least, had disappeared into Essa's hip flask, letting them at least try to keep a low profile.

They were almost at the building with skin, the House of Green Lights, when a dozen of those soldiers in black with the tall hats trooped past at the end of the street. A couple of them seemed to be missing arms and legs, with prosthetics made of gleaming steel.

Ben ducked into an alley beside the House and waited beside a line of puckered scar tissue that disfigured the wall. The House's skin stretched, extruding a lumpy limb that probed at him, and he decided that the coast was as clear as it was going to get.

The apothecary across the street was shuttered and there was no sign of the thing with the syringe. Ben cursed. He'd been hoping they'd be able to fix Essa. He still needed to get off the street before more soldiers showed up, so he took a deep breath and led Essa into the House of Green Lights. He hesitated on the threshold, then held Essa tighter and forged inside.

The only light in the tiny foyer was a green glow coming through a curtain hanging opposite the door. The curtain rippled aside as they approached it, and Ben saw it was made of the same fleshy substance as the building's walls. Beyond the curtain was a long room bathed in dim light from bulbous lamps hanging from the ceiling. No, not lamps—they were alive, tiny insectile bodies with claws that gripped the ceiling and huge, pendulous bioluminescent abdomens that flared and dimmed in a slow rhythm.

Thick and spongy moss covered the floor and crept halfway up the walls. The air was thick and humid, like they'd stepped into a greenhouse or a rainforest. Curtained alcoves lined the walls, snatches of conversation and puffs of smoke emerging from them at intervals.

Two people glided up to Ben and Essa. One was short and thin, the other tall and broad shouldered—he couldn't tell any more about them, because their necks and heads were covered with a riot of shaggy growths, green and fleshy with more of those flowers sprouting from them, like the apothecary creature had. They were wearing the same thing as the apothecary creature too, white plastic high-collared gowns that went all the way down to the floor.

Ben held up two fingers. The smaller one drifted away, and he thought he'd screwed up, but then the taller one turned and retreated further into the room, beckoning slowly over its shoulder. It led them to a booth in an alcove in the wall and left them.

"I hope I wasn't supposed to tip him," said Ben.

"You weren't."

Essa looked terrible. Her eyes were so bloodshot he could barely see any white at all, a thick crust of dried blood trailed from her ear down the side of her jaw, and she hunched over the table with her palms pressed to her temples like her head would burst if she let go. But she was alive, and awake, and he let out a shuddering breath he didn't know he'd been holding. "What are they?" he asked, hoping that if she kept talking, she'd stay with him. "You called them 'Empty.' What's wrong with them?"

"There's nothing wrong with them." She talked in a monotone, her eyes fixed on the surface of the table in front of her. "There's no 'them' for there to be anything wrong with. They're empty. Their skulls are empty. They weren't even born, the House grew them. That's what the House does."

"No way," said Ben, "look at them. They're awake, they're—"

"No. When they get decanted, the House plants a seed in their head. Those flowers. The plant's a parasite, it latches onto the top of their spine and works them like a puppet. It's about as smart as a really dumb rat, and the House teaches it to sit up, and beg, and do weird stuff for money."

Ben stared at the retreating figure. "That's sick," he said. "That's so *sick*." He spoke quickly. The longer his mouth was open, the more likely he would throw up.

"Thank you, Ben," said Essa quietly. "For getting us out of there. Even if it's not going to make any difference."

"Don't talk like that," he said.

"I need to run now, Ben." She sounded so tired. "You need to go to the Cogs, tell them about me. Give me a head start if you want, but just get it over with."

"Tell them what? Maybe if you told me—" He broke off, because Essa was weeping, long silent sobs that shook her shoulders. Her tears were tinged pink with blood.

"Ra." Ben didn't know what it meant but Essa's voice was thick with tears. "Oh, Ra." She wilted, fell slowly forward until her forehead was touching the table.

"Essa?"

She didn't respond.

The big Empty drifted up to their table again, deposited two glasses of water, drifted away. That was what waiters did. That was normal. Ben hung on to that, because nothing else in the House of Green Lights was.

No Cogs in here, at least. Most of the people he could see, at the tables in the centre of the room and the booths that weren't curtained, looked pretty much human. Were they? Were the worlds behind all those doors alternate Earths? Another question to add to the pile.

Not everything looked human, though. He saw something tall and skeletal, amygdaloid skull like an African mask, its limbs wrapped in red bandages, and over there someone or -thing that was pure and total black, a silhouette that swallowed all light like a hole cut out of the crowded bar, slumped in its chair with a drink in its hand. In a booth on the opposite wall, a cluster of balloons bobbed near the ceiling, except each balloon was just a blob of water with nothing apparently holding it together. Shoals of tiny silver things flashed and whirled inside each blob, and a tendril led down from each one to where they were bunched in the hand of something like a mudskipper in a suit.

A group of people, just dim shapes in the half-light, clustered around a table at the back of the room. They parted for a moment and he thought he saw that girl again, the one doing that martial arts display on the Well that morning. Grey hair, skin dead white like a Butoh dancer's, great dark eyes. Across the table from her was something huge, naked to the waist, with a physique that wasn't even vaguely human—muscles on top of muscles like a badly drawn superhero. They rippled obscenely as the thing put its arm on the table. The girl held out her own, her hand almost disappearing in the thing's meaty paw. They were arm-wrestling.

Ben winced, waiting for the girl's arm to break off at the elbow, but then he saw she was holding her own. The huge thing's bald head sagged with rolls of fat, a grotesque contrast with its ripped body, and its piggy eyes narrowed as it applied more pressure. The crowd was chanting something softly. The monster's arm was trembling. The girl's wasn't, but something was rising from her hand and arm and curling in the air—steam, he thought, or—was that *smoke*? Then the crowd drew closer and he couldn't see.

He leaned back in the booth and sipped from his glass. It wasn't water, but it tasted fine. Essa was slumped over their table, and when Ben shifted to give her some room, something pricked his thigh. He took the toothed metal coin out of his pocket. The Empty drifted up again, and Ben had an idea.

He slid the coin across the table. "This is all I have," he said. The phrase in Creole made his teeth buzz. "If it's more than the drinks are worth...is there someone heading out of here? With a vehicle? That isn't, you know, going to ask questions..."

Nice. Smooth.

The Empty reached out and palmed the coin, then departed once more. Ben thought it'd probably go straight to who- or whatever ran the House and get them arrested, but he didn't know what else to do.

He sipped his drink and waited.

Whatever was in those glasses, it definitely got you drunk. The high had a mellow edge like pot, and like alcohol with pot, Ben suspected you could get seriously messed up on it if you tried. He pushed the glass away and rubbed his eyes.

He'd half-expected the Empty to come back with soldiers in tow, but it didn't come back at all. Instead the girl he'd seen at the end of the room stepped lightly up to his table and stood there, shoulders hunched, arms folded.

Even up close, he wasn't any wiser about the girl's age. From her face she looked about as old as Ben, although the grey hair looked real, too. This close, he could see strands of white in it. He glanced at the table he'd seen the girl at. The crowd had dissipated, and the only one left at the table was the muscle-bound thing. It was cradling its elbow in its other hand.

Then she turned on her heel, jerked her head once—*follow me*—and stalked across the corner of the room to a curtained booth. She didn't check whether he was actually following her.

Ben left Essa where she was, her open flask beside her. He hoped Whisper was keeping an eye on her.

The girl dropped herself into a chair at a table a few yards out from the booth. The chair protested with a groan.

Cautiously, Ben drew the curtain aside, then blinked. "Oh. Hi. Lud, right?"

It was the spider, or rather the little crab-thing that housed its brain. It reclined on a cushion inside the booth in a cloud of smoke. Ben could see its underside and its complicated arrangement of articulated brass legs. Also in the booth was an Empty, his face distorted by the roots twisting under his skin, who stared right through them.

"Ah," said the crab, not entirely enthusiastically. "Excuse me for a moment." It was the first words that Lud had spoken that Ben understood.

The crab gestured to the Empty with one spindly limb, and the Empty reached into an open tub near the cushion, emerged with a handful of grease that he plunged into the crab's clockwork guts. The crab shuddered. Ben wasn't sure what he was watching, but it was definitely weird and possibly gross.

"Lovely," said Lud when the shuddering stopped. "My bill?" The Empty nodded and glided off.

"Okay," Ben began, "so I don't know how you and Essa left things, but we kind of need your help."

"So my associate tells me," said Lud in its clattering voice. "You've met Winter?"

"'Lo," said the girl at the table without looking at him. Her voice was a squeaking drawl, like a rusted hinge, no emotion in it at all.

"Hi," said Ben.

"And you ain't got nothing to worry about there," said Lud, waving a pincer in the air magnanimously. "Let's get you where you're going, then we can worry about settling up. Now: where is it you're going, exactly?"

"Thanks," said Ben, relieved. "We're going downWell, I guess. You know where you picked us up?"

He didn't think Essa would be thrilled to find herself in Chifley again, but he reckoned if she was on her feet by then, they could drop her off at the world of cubicles. Anyway, he couldn't think of a better plan.

"Of course. Brilliant," Lud was saying. One of his eyes was twitching, tracking something behind Ben. He turned to look.

There were three of them, standing at the door and surveying the room. All of them were in those black soldiers' uniforms and tall hats—the hats were called shakos, he thought. A tall woman and slightly taller man in front and an even taller and wider man bringing up the rear.

The man in front wore glasses of some kind, lenses gleaming green. They settled on the booth with Essa in it. Why hadn't he drawn the curtain? He said something to the woman, who pointed at the booth, and the huge one started lumbering in that direction.

"Shit," said Ben. "Shit. That Empty sold us out."

Lud said nothing.

"What," said a tired voice, "is all this, then?"

The other two soldiers had strolled up to Lud's booth. There was something wrong with each of them: the woman's nose was brass, shiny scar tissue surrounding it where it met her flesh. Her sidekick's glasses weren't glasses at all, but lenses in brass mounts that protruded directly from his eye sockets. Behind them, the scattered customers of the House of Green Lights were fading out the door, faces held carefully away from the big soldier as he stomped towards Essa's table. He encouraged a few of them with a shove that sent them stumbling. The hand that did the shoving was made of steel, and his whole lower jaw was brass.

It was the woman who'd spoken. She wore a single epaulette with silver braid. She pointed at Lud with a gloved finger. "Apostate," she said.

"That," said Lud, "is uncalled for."

"You are the one who contacted us?"

"Oh. Oh, you little turd," said Ben.

The spider held up a placating pincer. "Now then—sorry, I never got your name—"

"You little *turd*," said Ben, clenching his fists. He took a step towards Lud, and a rusty cough from behind him made him turn. Winter had slid her chair very slightly back from her table. Her slouching posture hadn't changed.

"Look, what was I supposed to do? Soon as I ran her pattern, L'Armée twigged. Might as well cooperate, yeah?"

"Shut up," snapped Ben, trying to think.

"*You're* not wanted, far as I know," said Lud. "I might even see my way to giving you a cut of the reward, if you—"

"Shut *up*. Hey! *Hey!*" Ben yelled at the big soldier, who'd grabbed Essa by her arm and dragged her out of the booth. She stumbled along with him, barely conscious, on autopilot. "Leave her alone!"

"*Everyone* shut up," said the woman wearily. "Hektor?"

The big one let Essa go as he saluted. "*Foutue,*" he said. "*La Bibliothèque l'a...*" He tapped his temple.

Essa swayed and Ben took her arm to hold her up. She mumbled something inaudible. He didn't think she was going to be much help.

The one with no eyes reached up to adjust his lenses. They clicked as he manipulated them. He turned to Essa. "Your hand, please?"

Essa didn't seem to have heard, but then she slowly held up her hand, the circuitry giving off a ghostly glimmer in the unnatural light.

Click click click, went the lenses. He looked at nothing, but intently, like he was reading something that wasn't there. He turned to the one with the braid. "It's her."

"Right," said the woman. "I am *Chef de Bataillon* Henriette-Marie Poinkaré of *L'Armée du Puits*. This is *Adjudant-Chef* Houellebek." The one with the lenses half raised his hand in greeting, then realized what he was doing and dropped it. "We are here for the Librarian. Everyone else is free to go, and I *strongly* encourage you to do so at once." She paused expectantly.

"My friend—" said Ben.

"My reward—" said Lud at the same time.

Poinkaré gripped the bridge of her metal nose. "Houellebek?"

Houellebek stepped forward. Lud's spike of a tail plunged into the cushion and it flipped over like a pole vaulter. It scuttled to the edge of the booth and reared up, its tiny glowing red eyes boring into Houellebek's. "The Committee will contact you regarding any remuneration," he said to it. To Ben he said, "You and the Librarian are associates?"

"Well, yeah," said Ben. "But—"

"Take him too," said Poinkaré. "Put them both in a cell. I want to go home."

Lud jabbed a pincer at Houellebek. "You're blowing me off, is what this is. Discriminatory, is what this is. I'm no apostate, first thing, and second thing, Deadbeat is ecumenical ground. I want my money—"

"Wait," said Ben. "Wait." Something Essa had said, when they'd arrived in Deadbeat... "You're Cogs, right?"

Poinkaré turned to Houellebek. "Is he touched?" she demanded.

"You're Cogs. And Essa's from the...from the Library. Right? And this is Vats territory," he said, gaining steam. "Do you even have jurisdiction here?"

The two soldiers looked at each other.

"You don't, do you?" asked Ben, starting to smile. "You were going to hustle us out of here and arrest us out there. Well, we're staying. We want, I don't know, diplomatic immunity—"

"From the *Vats?*" said Houellebek, looking at Ben like he'd sprouted an extra head.

"Well, at least get someone out here so we can—"

"*You.*" Everyone turned to look at Hektor, who was advancing on the table where the grey-haired girl, Winter, was sitting. He loomed over her, pointing, but she just stared at the table. Not like she was lost in thought. Like thinking, or anything else, was just too much effort.

"A problem, Hektor?" called Poinkaré.

"This one," growled the big man through his brass teeth. "I know her."

Houellebek's lenses clicked.

"You," the big soldier growled again. "You were warned."

No reaction from the girl.

"Houellebek?" said Poinkaré. She sounded tired.

The one with the lenses turned to his captain. "Itinerant. Cited for vagrancy twice. Official order to vacate Deadbeat with all speed."

"And still here." Poinkaré rubbed her temples. Ben thought she was maybe working off a hangover. Finally she sighed. "Just get her out of here, Hektor." She pointed at Essa, then Ben, then Lud. "Take her to the Committee. Her lawyer friend as well. And the heretic."

"Why *me*?" demanded Lud, outraged, but Hektor's rumbling voice ran right over his.

"You were warned," he repeated to the girl. "Now I'm giving you a choice. You can choose right now to leave. UpWell or down, it's your choice. You don't choose? Then you still leave, downWell, in a hurry. Terminal velocity."

The girl hadn't moved at all. She stared at a spot on the table between her elbows.

"DownWell it is," said Hektor cheerfully, and reached out for her. The girl's arm blurred, then she was clasping his. Ben hadn't seen her move. She held their hands up, like she was still arm wrestling and Hektor was her new opponent.

"What do you—" Hektor began, and then, as fast as she'd grabbed his hand, the girl twisted it, slamming it down on the table and shearing it off at the elbow.

Hektor shouted, but the girl was already airborne. Leaping over the table, she hooked an arm around his neck and swung her whole body around his, taking him down to the floor. Her arm tightened its grasp, Hektor wheezing and his face above his brass jaw turning purple, then grey.

Muttering a curse under her breath, Poinkaré drew a long pistol from her belt, stepped up to the prone figures and placed the barrel against the back of the girl's head. Ben drew breath, meaning to shout something although he didn't know what, then Poinkaré pulled the trigger and the girl's skull disappeared in a burst of gunpowder smoke as the detonation rang around the room.

They made their way down the boardwalk with Poinkaré and Houellebek ahead of them and Hektor limping behind, Lud scuttling along at their feet. The streets were full of Cogs, but as the soldiers approached, they moved smoothly out of the way and fell back into step behind them, giving them a moving clearing to walk in.

Essa was walking under her own power, stumbling along with her shoulders hunched and her head lowered, and even without seeing her face Ben could tell she was *royally* pissed off. He was getting that way himself. Getting dragged around like this was really beginning to grate, and the air in the Well was damp and cold. He'd come here straight from high summer in nothing but a T-shirt and jeans, his teeth were chattering and he could really have done with a change of socks.

This part of Deadbeat was all fresh timber, some of it still oozing sap. Everything was right angles and arrow-straight avenues, unlike the meandering boardwalks of the older part of town, and all of it was freshly swept and spotless. Even the ropes and cables that crisscrossed the air seemed neater, laid out according to an actual plan instead of haphazard additions to stop a building falling into the void.

The wire netting above his head gave a deep bass twang as something thumped into it from above. He ducked, covering his head. Essa didn't even break stride, just said "Oh, don't be a *tourist*, Ben," and kept limping down the boardwalk. He looked up at a lump of stone caught in the netting right above his head. It was the head of a statue, wind-worn and noseless, purple lichen like a bruise over one eye. He looked past it into the darkness, wondering what world it had come from. The Well soared up endlessly, studded with Doors. The vast curved wall had its own traffic, a steady stream heading up and down. Some of them rode living mounts, like the skulker from the school gym—the memory still made him shudder—and others mechanical things, some like Lud's spider-harness and others with chugging diesel engines or boilers hissing steam, all with legs that they drove into the Well one after another to keep from falling. Many of the ones heading down into Deadbeat were laden with crates and sacks and nets bulging with all kinds of stuff. He assumed it had been scavenged or stolen from the countless worlds up there, behind all those Doors, and brought to Deadbeat to barter or sell.

"Incredible," he said.

"Told you," said Essa, a small smile interrupting her scowl like a ray of sunlight through lowering clouds.

"What's going to happen to us?"

"You're going home, Ben. They're just being tedious. As a matter of fact, the whole place seems a bit...on edge."

Ben looked around at the placid faces of the Cogs strolling along the boardwalk in their neat double line. "Seriously?"

"Well. For Cogs, anyway. I'm betting it has to do with *that*." She nodded upWell, just above Deadbeat, where a wooden scaffold led up to an enormous Door that loomed over the town. Or half a Door. It seemed more like a carving in low relief, set into a part of the Well that was solid, lichen-covered rock.

"Going to ripen in a week, tops," said Essa.

"Ripen?"

"Really stable Doors are rare. Most come and go with the seasons—one season Wellside is around...four years your time? This one's about to open, and the Cogs are going to tear up the world behind it, chop everything down and strip-mine it, like Cogs do. That's why they're expanding the town." She hawked and spat a bloody wad of phlegm.

"Are you all right?"

"Bit my tongue when they put the Lacuna on me. Anyway the Cogs don't want anyone swooping in before they can claim it, so they're keeping a lid on any ruckus in Deadbeat, that's all this is. They'll probably deport you back worldside. You'll be fine."

"What about you?"

Essa didn't answer that.

They ascended through Deadbeat, negotiating the tangle of stairs and switchbacks. Every other person here seemed to be carrying a wooden box, stacked high with pieces of stiff paper.

A final flight of metal stairs and they were almost at the top of the town. This part of the Well was made of steel plates with rivets weeping tracks of rust. The Door set into it was crooked, leaning at an angle—a rectangle with rounded edges, braced wide open. There was an equally rusty metal wheel set into its centre.

A brass platform hung from the side of the Door, under an arrangement of pulleys. Now the pulleys whirred into life and more of those boxes ascended from the town on a rope in jerky steps, nearly spilling their paper cargo. A harried-looking Cog hurried out of the Door, took a box under each arm, and disappeared again.

Ben looked around. Deadbeat spread itself out beneath them, crisscrossed by those huge steel cables. Looking left along the curving wall he could see a blue glow beyond the edge of the town. He craned his neck to look, mindful to stay well back from the edge. The glow was coming from what looked like a forest, horizontal trees sticking out into the Well. No, not trees—they were mushrooms, huge ones—

A shove from Hektor that nearly knocked him off the stairs, and then they were through the Door.

The corridor of rusted iron was tilted too. Ben had to lean to the side as he walked so he didn't tip over. "What is this?" he asked.

Essa shrugged. "Ship, probably."

"You can get onto ships from the Well? Not just, you know, buildings?" he asked. This was interesting.

"You can get anywhere," said Essa. "Anywhere there's a Door at least, assuming you can find the Door."

If it was a ship, it must have been aground because they weren't moving; the floor just stayed at that same angle. Boxes lined the already narrow corridor, overflowing with more of those papers, and Ben saw they were riddled with holes. Punch cards.

They passed a doorway and Ben blinked at the nightmarish whirl and clash of brass gears and struts inside. The machine filled the room beyond—they must have had to dismantle it to get it in—and Cogs surrounded it, feverishly feeding those punch cards into it and, once the machine had spat them out again, stacking them into boxes and hauling them out of the chamber. Ben had to flatten himself against the wall to let one go by.

Essa nodded. "They're planning something big. It's that Door, has to be—Ben?"

Ben stood in the doorway at the end of the corridor, orange light bathing his face, and said, "Wow." Lud trundled between his feet and stopped too, red eyes flaring as it stared.

"Wow," Ben said again.

This was evidently the ship's bridge. One wall was dominated by a huge curving window. The other side of the window was streaked with salt, and beyond it was an ocean under clouds tinted a toxic orange. Strange wind- and water-carved stone spires pierced the water, thousands of them, all the way to the horizon.

Another of those machines occupied the centre of the room, only parts of this machine were people.

A ring of brass looped around the machine. At intervals, skeletal metal harnesses sprouted from the ring, and strapped into each harness was a person. They were all ages, genders, sizes, and hanging over each of them on articulated arms were split-flap displays, like in an old-fashioned airport, the flaps never stopping but flipping forwards and backwards endlessly, a blur of motion that made a headache bloom in Ben's skull just from glancing at it. He blinked and looked away.

"Order."

Everyone in the circle said it, almost in unison. Almost—there was the tiniest pause between one voice and the next, so the word took a second to run around the room.

"The Committee, I presume," muttered Essa.

The Committee ignored her. "Captain?" they said, the word beginning somewhere at the back of the circle and ending in front of them.

Poinkaré stepped forward, cleared his throat. "Per special directive: 'Essa', Librarian; 'Lud', apostate, under sentence of corporeal forfeit, no fixed abode; one Naive worldsider, relationship to others unknown." Behind him Houellebek had a pair of nail-clipperish looking things and a blank card, which he was rapidly punching holes out of; he finished as Poinkaré stopped talking and pushed it into a slot on the side of the machine.

The Committee's eyes rolled as a new eddy rippled through the chaotic rush of information on the clicking boards. Ben wasn't paying attention. It was the first time anyone had said Essa's name around him since he'd had his shot, and when the word had twisted through his head, what he'd heard was 'orphan'. He looked at her, but she was picking at the dried blood on her neck and didn't look like she was in the mood for any personal questions.

The Committee still weren't saying anything. Water sprayed against the big curved window, streaking and dissolving the salt. Ben looked through it at the sea, dotted with spume dyed orange by the light from the clouds. Immense waves crested and broke from one side of the window to the other, thrashing against those strange stone spires. At some point a haze of mist and spray had swallowed the horizon. As he watched, something broke the surface of the water all the way out there, something like a serpent or a tentacle. It thrashed and collapsed into the water again in a chaos of raging foam that slowly closed over it.

Ben took a step backwards, nearly tripping over Lud, who nipped his ankle with a claw. He didn't feel it.

He must have misjudged the distance.

It couldn't have been that big.

He turned as the Committee cleared its throats in a circular ripple of phlegm. "Take them to the cells," they said. "Our Priority is our new Door. We cannot have Librarians in Deadbeat until it is secure. We cannot have interference from the Treaty. Once we have secured the Door, we will deal with them."

"Wait," said Ben, "if I can—"

The Committee weren't even paying attention anymore. Ben felt Hektor's single hand on his shoulder and let himself be led out of the chamber.

Ben wasn't thrilled when Poinkaré and Houellebek stayed inside the Committee chamber, leaving them at the mercy of the one-armed Hektor.

Hektor didn't look too thrilled about it either, but he didn't try any police brutality as they left the ship. He led them along a narrow bridge to a tower Ben hadn't seen before, a cylinder of windowless wood. At the top, just below the roof, metal girders stuck out from it like the spokes of a stripped umbrella. Steel guy-wires anchored the tower to a few open Doors.

Beside the tower's heavy wooden doors was a counter with a bored-looking soldier. He spoke to Hektor in the clicking Cogs language—which Ben supposed hadn't been included with his shot—and Hektor faced them and beckoned with two fingers—*give it here.* "Bags," he grunted in Creole.

He hardly bothered with Ben's messenger bag. He looked inside, saw the laptop, sniffed, then pushed it back against Ben's chest hard enough to almost knock him over. Essa wasn't so lucky: Hektor took a look in her bag at all the climbing gear and his eyes gleamed.

"Hey," protested Essa.

Hektor snorted and threw the bag on the counter, where the bored soldier made it disappear. "Confiscated," he said in that thick Cogs accent.

"There's black iron in that bag. I notice you didn't declare it. I want a receipt—"

"Confiscated."

Essa's eyes flashed dangerously. She seemed herself again, more or less, and Ben could only imagine how she felt—she'd kept that bag safe at Chifley for a year, waiting for her Door to open, and one day in the Well and she'd lost it. She didn't say anything about the bag, though. Instead she pulled the hip flask from her back pocket. "How about this, big man? Going to confiscate this?"

Hektor eyed the flask apprehensively.

"Going to take on a Library grievance?" Essa let the silence linger, then stuffed the flask back in her pocket. Hektor let it go. After seeing what Essa's dust, "Whisper," had done to the skulker in the gym, Ben wondered why.

The centre of the tower was an empty circular shaft, like the Well itself in miniature. Instead of Doors, though, there were round galleries, one on top of another, and in each gallery a line of emaciated figures trudged in circles. Each of them pushed a wooden spoke, like sailors around a capstan. A tremendous grinding and creaking echoed through the tower.

The floor was a metal grille, and through it he could see immense gears turning slowly.

"Winders," said Lud at Ben's feet. "Winding the town."

Ben's shoulders tightened up just looking at them. "Are we going to be doing that?"

A clatter from the crab that could have been a laugh. "We're criminals. They're apostates. Winding's too good for them, if you ask me."

"Didn't that Poinkaré say you were—"

"*I* am an Apostate Minor. I have rights. *They* are Apostates Major. And *you* are an insulting little shit—"

"Shut it," rumbled Hektor behind them, and Lud shut it.

In the very centre of the tower, a freestanding spiral staircase wound up and up towards the roof. There was no railing. Ben kept his eyes on his feet as he climbed.

At the top of the staircase was a circular wooden platform surrounded by a ring of iron cages that dangled from short lengths of chain. Each cage's floor was padded with a lumpy mattress covered with indeterminate stains. Their doors stood open and Hektor half-pushed, half-threw them all into the same one. It was only after he'd slammed the door and padlocked it that Ben got a chance to look around.

His first surprise was the girl, the one from the House of Green Lights. Winter. She was sitting on the cell's single bench and staring morosely at the floor. She didn't look up as Hektor pushed them into the cage, just kept rubbing the back of her head, for all the world like Poinkaré hadn't put a bullet in it an hour ago.

The second surprise came when Hektor kicked a lever that extended from beside the door and the whole cage started moving. It rattled out towards the tower wall, and then beyond it. The jolting drove Ben to his knees. He thought of those spokes radiating out from the top of the tower—the cage must be hanging from one of those—

Then he was falling.

Ben's guts shot up into his throat and his feet almost left the floor, but after only a moment of freefall the cage stopped again, slamming him into the padded floor. It wasn't *that* padded, and pain shot through the elbow and hip he'd landed on.

He groaned and picked himself up. Essa was doing the same, and Lud was on its back, having some trouble flipping itself over on the uneven mattress. Ben let the little snitch flop around for a while.

The girl with grey hair hadn't moved at all. She sat on the bench with her head down, like nothing at all had happened.

The cage was swinging in long vertiginous arcs, the chain above them creaking and groaning. There was twenty feet of empty space between them and the windowless tower wall.

The cage was already slowing. He realized the mattress under him was damp and thought for a moment he'd wet himself when they'd fallen, but a discreet check of his jeans showed otherwise. He was relieved for a moment, then realized that meant the damp patch might be anything. He got unsteadily to his feet and staggered over to the bench, plonking down on it next to the silent girl.

"Well," said Essa, "this is just fantastic."

The mattress muffled Lud's reply.

"How are you feeling?" asked Ben.

"Full-voiced and full-lunged, thanks."

"Sorry?"

"You're a Choirgirl." Lud had succeeded in toppling over onto its legs. "I knew it."

"Raised in a tithe-house. Never made it to the Choir."

"Afraid of the surgery?"

"Can't carry a tune in a bucket." Essa staggered on the shifting floor as she too sat down on the bench, on the other side of Winter from Ben.

"What's a tithe-house? And your name is 'orphan'?" asked Ben. The way the word twisted on its way from his head to his lips still set his teeth on edge.

"It's not 'orphan'." Essa switched to English. "That's the problem with language in a bottle. You hear 'orphan' because you don't know the idea behind the word, and your brain just picks the closest thing it knows. It means a child without a blood tie stronger than the fourth degree, no Door to their motherworld, no Claims. You're supposed to change it if someone does Claim you, but I'm not ashamed of who I am, so I didn't."

"I don't know what any of that means," said Ben.

"Exactly. Anyway, that's just my name in Creole. In Cogs, it's *Essa*"—a hiss like steam escaping a boiler—"and in Vats it's *Essa*"—the vowels oily, the s a bluebottle buzz—"and in Library it's *Essa*." This third was entrancing, a breathy whisper like fine sand slipping down the face of a dune.

"I like the Library one best," said Ben without thinking, then wished he hadn't.

"This is all fascinating," said Lud in Creole, "whatever it is, but—" It clacked and scurried away from Essa's barely aimed kick.

"We're here because of you, you little...thing," said Ben.

The crab hoisted itself up on its rear legs, its front pincers clicking.

"Yeah?" demanded Ben. "What are you going to do with those?"

"Leave it, Ben," said Essa wearily. "It doesn't matter."

"We're in *prison*."

"Only until they've bagged their new Door," she said, rubbing the bridge of her nose with a gilded forefinger and thumb. "Then you get deported, and they send me to the Library."

"And how long's that?"

"A few days, tops."

"I don't *have* a few days," said Ben. "I need to go *home*. Or what am I going to tell them? 'Don't send me to prison, I was in prison?'"

"What do you mean, prison?"

There it was.

"I broke into a couple of servers, leaked a few things to the news. Stupid hacktivist thing." He was going to go into detail, then realized it didn't matter. "Then I bragged about it to the wrong people. If I don't make my court date, they're going to…make an example of me, I guess. Try me as an adult."

The arrest and everything after had coloured every one of his thoughts for weeks, and to express it now in so few words felt odd. "What about you?" he said. "What happened back there on the Vine?"

"Library locked me down. The Bindings"—Essa spread her fingers, showing off the circuitry in her hand—"they work both ways. I can use them to talk to the sand, command it if you like, but it can turn around and do it to me, too. The Library uses it to catch renegades. And to punish them."

"Catch you for what? Punish you for what?"

Nothing from Essa for the longest time. Then, quietly: "Murder."

"You…" Ben didn't know how to finish.

The silence lengthened inexorably before Essa, mercifully, broke it. "She died. I didn't kill her, but I…if I wasn't there, she wouldn't have died. So." Abruptly she stood up and walked to the other side of the cage.

Ben looked out his own side. With no windows, there was no way for the guards in the tower to keep an eye on them—but when he looked down, Ben understood why. They were dangling right over Deadbeat, and if they tried to get out of their cage, anyone who looked up from the innumerable boardwalks and alleys and bridges would see them do it. And the way the Cogs were all in sync, Ben bet they'd waste no time in alerting a soldier. There were plenty of soldiers—Ben tracked a pair of those tall shakos along a boardwalk and into a Door. From up here, that creepy regularity the Cogs had was clearer and more unnerving than ever. It was like there was a pattern to the flow of goods and pedestrians that he could *almost* make out.

"Huh."

Essa was looking at the Well, at the scaffolding under that big stone Door. Cogs were swarming up and down, adding strut after strut to bring it up to the Doorstep.

Still looking through the bars, she unscrewed the cap of her flask. That familiar ribbon of red dust streamed out. With a few strenuous-looking permutations of her fingers—he could hear her knuckles crackling—she spread it out into a ring that hovered in the air just outside the bars.

Ben glanced at Winter, the girl who'd slept off a bullet to the back of the head the way some people slept off a hangover. She hadn't said anything yet, and neither had they, and the longer nobody said anything the harder it was to start.

He turned his attention back to Essa and Whisper. "How come they let you keep it?"

"Because *she*, not '*it*,' has rights. And technically she's a prisoner too, so why shouldn't she be here? They know we won't try anything. The Treaty is very specific about using an Ism on a representative of a Power. I'd be in deeper trouble than I am already. If such a thing were possible."

A few more gestures and whispered commands, and Ben blinked as he saw the air inside the circle of dust ripple. He nearly fell backwards off the bench as the Door seemed to leap towards them. He recovered and realized it hadn't moved at all: Whisper had somehow bent the light passing through her, made herself a lens.

Which was impressive, but she didn't seem to do anything else. Essa just stood there, lost in thought, looking at the Door. Lud seemed to have powered down, its mainspring barely ticking over.

Once again Ben found his gaze drifting through the bars, down into Deadbeat. Now that he'd had some time to look over their surroundings, he saw that they weren't quite in view of *all* of Deadbeat. The town had expanded, and new buildings and roofs blocked off a lot of the streets. There were blind spots.

As he leaned over for a different angle on things, he bumped against the silent girl's shoulder. "Sorry," he said. It was the first thing anyone had said to her since they'd been put in the cage. He thought she'd ignore it, but then came a minuscule shrug of her shoulders.

He was going to say something else when Essa's voice cut through the silence.

"Now *that's* interesting," she was saying. Characters were rippling through the dust around the magnified image of the Door, changing as fast as he could focus on them.

"What is?"

"That big Door…" Essa shook her head. More of those gestures flowed through her hands and wrists, like he'd seen in videos of meditation or yoga. Those were more flowing, though. Artistic. Essa's were businesslike, professional, and with each gesture the view altered slightly, and the characters flowing around the ring of sand changed.

"It's not…" Essa shook her head. "Not that it matters anyway. Not until I can get somewhere to crunch the numbers."

This was interesting. "Which numbers need crunching?" said Ben, flipping open his messenger bag and taking out his laptop. He didn't really think he'd be able to help, but this might pass the time at least. "And can't it do it itself? It's a computer, isn't it?"

"*She*, not 'it,' *she*, is a *person*, Ben."

Lud clicked. "How can a cloud of dust be—"

"Because she chose to be. As is her right. Anyway, Ben, she's smart like a person, not like a machine. She doesn't do grunt work. But if you think it'll help…"

With a shrug and a flick of her wrist, Essa sent a shiver through the floating lens and the circle of dust shrank into a red ribbon that poured itself through the air towards Ben's laptop. "Wait a second—" he said, but it was already blowing into the vents, streaming through the case.

The screen glitched, recovered, glitched again. Ben winced. Then the image cleared as the dust swirled out of the laptop. It probed each port in turn, then settled on the Cat 5, tiny red lightning rhythmically striking the contacts.

"Well?" said Essa, looking over his shoulder.

"Well, I doubt that it…*she's* using any kind of protocol the computer'd understand," said Ben, "but if I can see the raw info coming in the port…can you give me a second?"

"One thing, Ben."

He looked at Essa.

"My friend who died. More than a friend, really. A research partner. Which for Librarians is more like a lover."

"And they think you murdered her? Why?" asked Ben quietly.

"In the Library we use…we call them Chants. Like songs, but also…prayers, if you like. Or spells. They can get stuck in your head, like any song, but when they get in there they can do some serious damage. You saw what happened to me on the Vine."

"Right."

"I would have exposed my friend to the Chants I composed. The same Chants I'll need to use on the data you give me, to figure out what's happening with that Door. I don't think it'd do you any harm—you're not Bound or wired—but I didn't think it'd do her any either. So…"

Ben paused, but only for a moment. "Let's do it."

He could have told himself he was being brave, but he knew that wasn't it. He wanted to tackle this for the rush…and here it came again, the world going away, narrowing down, becoming nothing more than the problem he was looking at right now.

He glanced at the battery indicator—sixty-eight percent it said, but that could mean anything with the battery as old as it was—and got to work. He wasn't much of a hardware guy, and this was a lot deeper into the OS than he usually went, but eventually he was looking at a window with a display of ones and zeros flickering past, in time with the electrical pulses that Whisper was sending through his port.

It was coming in surges, each one followed by a lull. Surge, lull. He played with the dimensions of the window, although he didn't know if he would recognize what Whisper was trying to tell him if he saw it.

Then he saw it.

A pulsing pattern of concentric circles, flicking through one formation after another like iterations of a fractal, before it looped around to the original pattern again. Sixty-one percent, said the battery indicator.

He turned the screen around, showed Essa. She raised her eyebrows, grinned at him, and he grinned back. Then she crouched beside him, all business. "How many patterns are there?"

Ben was already counting. "Seven…wait…nine."

"So what you're looking at are vectors in nine-dimensional space. But we need to translate them, twist them around a little bit, so Whisper can understand them."

"A matrix transformation, sure," said Ben. "Which one?"

It was slow going. When it came to notation, they didn't have a lot of common ground. Not being able to google anything made things even slower, but they got there eventually. Ben hit Enter, then winced as the fan kicked in while the CPU churned through the calculations. Fifty-two percent. Forty-six.

It was at forty-three and Ben was beginning to worry when it came back, another circular pattern pulsing on the screen.

"Ha!" Essa crowed and punched Ben in the shoulder, hard. Ben couldn't help grinning. Whisper let go of the laptop, hovered in front of the screen for a moment, then arranged herself in the same pulsing pattern. She leaped into the air in front of Essa, who shook out her fingers like a pianist limbering up before a concert.

"Are we done?" Ben asked. She nodded, barely listening, and he slapped the laptop shut. The case was hot to the touch.

The pattern Whisper was displaying was two-dimensional but Essa pulled it apart into a sphere, and then again into a kind of meta-sphere that made Ben's eyes itch. He wondered, a little late, if he should close them, but Whisper was already whirling back into her flask and Essa was staring at the Door. For a moment Ben thought she'd frozen again, like on the Vine, but then she whispered, "Lady's teeth." She lashed out with a foot, catching Lud on the carapace and making it ring hollowly.

"Ow!" it said, its voice slurred at first but regaining its pitch as its mainspring ticked to life. "What—"

"We need to get out of here," said Essa. "Right now." She shook the bars, setting the cage swinging again. "Hey!" she yelled at the ceiling. "*Hey!*"

"Essa—" said Ben.

"Stop—" said Lud.

"Why," said a quiet voice, "do we need to get out?"

They all turned to look at Winter, still sitting on the bench, who raised her head and looked up at them.

"Our Librarian friend would seem to have gone mad," said Lud to Winter.

"You know each other?" said Essa.

"We move in the same circles. Or overlapping circles, anyway."

"Crooks, you mean," said Essa.

"I mean people who have been forced by circumstances to seek a living outside conventional—"

"Crooks," said Winter softly. "Why do we need to get out?"

Essa took a deep breath, blew it out. "That Door. The one that's going to ripen any time now."

"You said it'd take a week," said Ben.

"I was wrong." She paused, struggling with what came after that, then said it all in a rush: "The Exile's behind it."

The pause that followed was broken by a harsh clattering. Lud's laughter. "Lunatics. I'm locked in here with lunatics."

Winter wasn't laughing. Her eyes narrowed as she looked at Essa. "How do you know?"

"Long story short: that Door up there didn't grow on its own. Someone planted it."

"Impossible—"

"Quiet," said Winter in her rusty voice, and the crab obeyed.

"Planted it," Essa repeated. "I know two people who can do that. I'm one of them."

"Bollocks," said Lud.

"You can grow Doors?" asked Winter.

Essa nodded. "Me and the Exile. And I didn't grow that one. So…" She was looking up at the cage's ceiling again. "Where are the guards? They must be planning to feed us. If they winch it down in a bucket, we can put a message in it…"

"If you want to escape," said Ben, "I might have a couple of ideas about that."

Now everyone was looking at him instead.

Chapter Twelve

As soon as the walls begin to sag, Essa and the two Librarians with her pick up their pace from a jog to a full sprint. Even so, they barely reach the intersection before chunks of the ceiling start falling behind them, exploding into loose sand on the floor.

There's another group of three waiting for them. Rachana is among them. She's barefoot, like Essa, her skin cloudy with nicks from running along sand for the last four days.

"They're really going at it," says one of the Librarians who arrived with Essa.

"We need more breaks," says Essa. "We've stopped it this side of the dorms, but if we don't lay down more breaks, it'll punch right through the refectory."

"I've got it," say Rachana. "Nura, with me." She and Essa grin. Then, like they weren't expecting to, they lean in for a quick kiss, and she and Nura are gone.

"You together again, then?" asks the other Librarian with Essa. His fingers are moving unceasingly, calming the ceiling and walls in the intersection. The skin of his cheekbone is abraded away, blood dripping from his chin. "I thought you were with that guy from the Halls."

"I didn't ask you to keep track, Guim," says Essa, "and we're not 'together,' I hate that word."

"Oh, Rachana must love that."

Essa changes the subject. "It got you," she says, touching her own cheekbone.

One of Guim's hands still moves while the other reaches into his robe and produces a bandage that he slaps on his face. The bandage is Vats work, a living flap of skin with dozens of tiny claws that dig into his cheek to hold it in place. Instantly the flow of blood slows to a tiny trickle.

"Right," he says, "so—"

They're interrupted by a rumbling from deep in the Library. The intersection shifts and tilts ever so slightly, red grit raining from the ceiling. The tension among the group rises as the tilt becomes more pronounced, and when it stops, no one relaxes.

"Really stirred up this time," says a Librarian between gulps of water from the gourd at his belt.

"Who is it, anyway?"

"Sails and the Heptacomb. We're not taking sides, just putting out the fires."

"What are they fighting about?" asks the remaining Librarian from Rachana's group.

"The usual thing," says Guim.

"Meaning what?"

"Exactly," everyone says in a tired chorus.

"All right," says Guim, "break's over. Back to work."

He takes the lead. They find a staircase leading out of the dorms, so narrow they have to ascend it single-file, but stable.

"What are you even doing here, Essa?" Guim asks as they trudge up the stairs. "You've got your own…" He gestures at the flask hanging from Essa's belt by its leather thong.

"Whisper's sitting this one out," says Essa. "It's not her fight."

"It's not yours either, is my point. That's why you picked a new Ism, isn't it? So you never had to choose a side, never had to stand and fight."

"She picked me. And I did it so I could choose which side I was on. Not be forced to choose one. I'm here to help, wherever I can."

Guim grunts and hoists himself out of the stairwell into a service corridor, where a burst of superaccelerated sand blasts out of the wall and strips all the flesh off his arm. He stares at the skeletal remnants for a moment, then the ceiling caves in on top of him, and he's just gone.

Chapter Thirteen

T here. And there."

They were all standing at one end of the cage, and their combined weight was tilting the floor alarmingly—a lot more than Ben thought it should be tilting, in fact.

Ben pointed. "There too. Gaps in the traffic, where there's hardly anyone on the streets. They're regular, I've been watching. They cycle every twenty minutes or so. See where those patrols are crossing on that bridge? That's where they always cross."

Essa rolled her eyes. "Cogs."

"Bigot," said Lud.

"But now they're all gone. See? That building's in the way, they can't see us. The point is—well, it's kind of academic, because we're stuck here, but if someone can get out, and climb back up to the room we were in, and do it in about five minutes..."

"If they can get out," said Lud.

"Yeah."

"And if they climb up and…what? Go back down the stairs in the tower full of soldiers?"

"I guess." Ben's face was hot. "Anyway, they'd have to take you with them. Go to the stables, get your spider, come back for the others."

"Wonderful. I'm winding down again. Let me know if anyone has any *non*-academic ideas—"

"Who's going?" said Winter, looking down at the street.

Ben looked at her. "But we don't—"

"Say we did. Who's going?"

Now Ben and Essa looked at each other. "You're the better climber," he said.

Essa grimaced. "Not right now. I feel like I've pulled every muscle in my body." She looked at Winter, who shook her head.

"I'll go," said Ben instantly.

"Seriously?" asked Lud.

"But we still can't get out of—"

Winter reached out and took hold of a bar of the cage in each of her hands and plucked them out of the frame, the metal shearing off at floor and ceiling with a screech. She tossed the bars down on the floor of the cage, and sucked at her finger where the metal had nicked it. Her blood was thick and black with a rainbow sheen.

"Wait," said Essa, her voice suddenly tight. "Is she..." No one answered. Essa looked at Winter with wide and shining eyes. "Oh Lady," she said. "Oh Red Lady, you have got to be kidding. I never thought I'd meet a..."

Winter said nothing.

Ben would have liked to know what was going on, but he didn't think they had time. He looked down. With the bars gone, creating a space he could easily fit through, it seemed a lot further to the boardwalk than it had a moment before. Below them, the traffic was in one of those lulls, but he didn't know how long it was going to last.

A squawk from Lud. Winter had picked it up in one hand and dumped it in Ben's arms. Ben yelped as Lud's pincers dug into his shirt.

Then Winter took off, charging for the far end of the cage.

"Wait—" said Essa.

Winter hit the bars with a clang. The cage creaked, tilted, and began to swing.

That tilt nearly tipped Ben and Lud out of the cage. He grabbed the bars and hung on as they reached the end of their swing—and Winter whipped past him and smashed into the bars on their side.

They were swinging violently now. Ben heard a scream of tortured metal from somewhere above them. He wondered about the chain they hung from, how strong it was, then wished he hadn't.

Another clanging impact from Winter, and they were really moving. The end of their swing took them close to one of Deadbeat's newer buildings, and Ben began to get an idea of what Winter was doing. Evidently so did Lud, because it gave a metallic moan and shuddered.

Back they swung, towards the tower, just grazing its wooden side.

"Now," said Winter, and Ben swallowed and braced himself in the gap in the cage. And when it was at the other end of its swing, the new building's gabled roof below them across what seemed like endless empty space, he tensed and jumped.

He landed on the roof, started to slide off it, grabbed a narrow chimney stack with one hand. His other held Lud to his chest, but the crab had its own ideas, clambering around him onto his back like a knapsack, hooking its little brass legs over Ben's shoulders.

Ben ducked behind the chimney just as a shout came from far above him. Evidently someone in the tower had seen the cage swinging. Ben didn't think they'd be able to see him, but he wasn't sure. He risked a look around the chimney: the cage was already slowing to a stop. Unless the guards could see through its solid ceiling, they wouldn't know Ben was missing.

"Well?" said Lud after a moment.

"I'm going," said Ben, and after a moment convincing his legs to move, he went.

He slid awkwardly down the roof until he was dangling half off it, and finally his feet found a rusty pipe he could balance on. He put more weight on it and it held, although it gave a dangerous-sounding creak. The roof was level with a boardwalk belonging to a higher layer of Deadbeat, and the pipe continued under it, with enough clearance that Ben could crouch and sidle along under the planks.

Holding onto the underside of the boardwalk, he inched his way along, keeping low. There was a ramp or something ahead, a downward slope, but he thought he could manage it. Just an overhang problem. Just like bouldering in the gym.

He glanced down. Below the ramp was part of the machinery that spread through the town, a nest of spinning gears. If he fell into that, he'd be grease.

So not *just* like the gym, then.

Green light shone through the gaps between the boardwalk's planks. He'd seen that glow before. He had an idea of where he was— if he made it past the overhang, it was a straight shot to the Door where Lud had stashed its spider.

He could do this.

He edged along, the pipe creaking under him. Lud whirred in his ear, and from the corner of his eye, Ben saw a red glare as one of the crab's eyes extended itself on an articulated telescope, swivelling to look over his shoulder.

It was easy, really. Even when he dropped his gaze to check his footing and looked into the void and the twinkle of Doorlight speckled across the Well below him, he didn't feel a thing. He sped up, letting go with both hands to grab the next strut or pipe or rope. He felt Lud tense, the little legs gripping his sides and shoulders harder.

The pipe here ran along the very edge of the boardwalk. He could see the Well. He could see the great stone Door that had Essa so freaked out.

It was open.

Far away, someone screamed. Now that he wasn't concentrating on climbing, he realized they'd been screaming for a while.

He froze. It wasn't just one voice, it was all over Deadbeat. Screams, shouts, cries, robbed of urgency by distance and sounding thin and flat. Then a *crash* from somewhere a lot nearer, and another scream, cut off suddenly like someone had thrown a switch.

Something on the boardwalk above him hissed.

Slowly, very slowly, he drew back underneath. He eased his head into a shaft of light coming down through a gap between the planks and looked up.

Something was standing on the boardwalk almost directly on top of him. Something he couldn't see. Except…he could see *parts* of it, dark blue ribbons that floated there like they'd been drawn on the air, so thin they disappeared when he looked at them edge-on.

The thing moved slightly, the lines bunching and sliding over each other, and Ben got it. They were tattoos. This thing was invisible, but the ink in its skin wasn't.

Down through the tangle of pipes and cables under the boardwalk, he could see a wooden staircase, far below. Someone was running down it, a Cog, half-dressed and panting wildly, his arms flailing as he sprinted, taking three steps at a time—and then he stopped dead and bounced backwards, like a gif Ben had seen of someone running into a glass door. The Cog sprawled, and then just as quickly rose again— only it wasn't him doing it, something was pulling him up until his feet dangled a foot off the ground. Ben saw his hair flatten against his temples as the half-invisible thing gripped his head—and then with a tiny clear *crack* his skull caved in. He dropped again, and this time he stayed down.

Ben wanted to look away but couldn't. The thing that had killed the man was a blur in the air with thick purple bars coiling up its long limbs, making him think of those orange-peel people in Escher prints. Before he could see anything else, the invisible thing flowed across the boardwalk, almost too quick to see, straight up a wall and over a roof out of sight.

Ben looked up at the stone Door again. The air around it seemed to boil, translucent figures slipping out and climbing down the Well, spreading through Deadbeat.

He had to move.

The little crab gasped a little—it sounded like tiny gears grinding—when Ben started down the overhang, making as little noise as possible. He thought they were below the House's ground level now, which meant they were climbing down the wall of its basement. The pipe he was on zigzagged down with him, providing both foot- and handholds. The worst part was not being able to see what was ahead, just the wall he was facing as he descended into who knew what. His eyes came level with a crack in the wall and he pulled himself closer to look—he was definitely under the House now, looking into a dark room full of weird hanging shapes like translucent cocoons. Something stirred inside one of them, and the outline of a face pressed itself up against the slick membrane of its skin. He thought of what Essa had said about the Empty Ones—*grown, not born*—and swallowed.

He only realized he was at the bottom of the wall when his foot prodded around for purchase and found nothing but air. He let his legs dangle and just held onto the pipe in front of him. As it took more of his weight, the brackets that held it on the wall began to creak, and Lud moaned again.

Inside the room of cocoons, something hissed.

Ben froze, perfectly still. In the distance someone screamed, once. He could hear gunfire now, scattered flat *cracks*.

He scanned the room through another gap in the wall. Something was stalking through the cocoons, setting them swinging. Ben felt horribly exposed—he was sure it could see him through the wall, just like he could see it—but he didn't dare move.

The cocoons slowed and stopped. His arms were burning. Nothing was moving now. After what seemed like an age but was probably less than a minute, Ben took a deep slow breath and started down the wall again, legs dangling, until finally he was below it and could see the way ahead, along the underside of another boardwalk.

He'd been afraid that there'd be nothing for him to hold onto down here, but there were metal struts underneath the boardwalk holding the planks together—he could hand-over-hand his way along them. Just like the monkey bars at primary school. And even better, he could see the Well here, and the stable door, dead ahead and a little below him. Almost there.

He'd covered maybe half the distance when he put his weight on a strut and it creaked, and right away he heard the crash behind him.

He twisted to look. Something had smashed through the wall of the cocoon room, and chunks of wood were arcing down and away. Ben's eyes involuntarily tracked the debris as it fell into the Well, and suddenly every one of his muscles was locked up with fear. His hands tightened on the struts he was holding, unable to let go.

Over his shoulder he saw something approaching, crawling out of the room and along the underside of the boardwalk. Stripes of dark red ink crossed its invisible flesh. Ben watched it come, frozen.

Lud was poking him in the side, hard. He barely felt it. Then one of the crab's brass pincers darted out and snipped off a sliver of his ear.

"*Shit!*" he yelled as he turned and grabbed for the next strut. For a sickening moment he thought his sweat-slick hand would slide off it, but then he was swinging to the next, and the next, convulsing his whole body each time to propel himself forward. The thing behind him was hissing, louder and louder, and now he heard an answering hiss from the boardwalk above. The surface of the Well was only a few feet away, but he felt the tattooed thing's hot breath on the back of his neck and he knew he wasn't going to make it.

He let go.

He was swinging forward as he did it and his momentum carried him through the air, towards the surface of the Well. Lud shrieked. Ben reached out, felt the stone wall strip the skin off his fingertips, and then he was falling past the stable Door. As he fell through the gap between the Door and the wooden platform surrounding it, he managed to get his arms in front of him and they slammed down on the Doorstep, stopping his fall. He felt something deep in his shoulder pop.

He slid backwards but managed to grab the Doorstep with the hand that wasn't numb. Black fireworks burst behind his eyes. Lud's pincers dug into his skin as the crab crawled up his back, over his shoulder, and through the Door. He watched it through a haze of pain as it scuttled away across the plain.

Oh, you little—

He couldn't pull himself up with only one good arm. As he dangled there, something slammed down onto the platform behind him, and he felt its leathery palms grip his head. *This is it*, he thought, and wondered what it would feel like when his brains imploded.

From above him, a clattering voice said: "*Right.*"

He looked up at the brass spider towering over him. One of its legs shot out over his head and Ben heard the *thud* as it speared the tattooed thing. The hands on his head tightened, then relaxed. Lud retracted the leg—the platform shook as the invisible thing fell dead— and hooked it around Ben's waist.

"All aboard that's coming," Lud said, perched on the spider's head.

The brass basket unfolded on the spider's back and the leg dropped him inside. Ben screamed as the impact jarred his shoulder and he dropped to his knees as the spider came to life, the mainspring in its belly ticking faster and faster. He could hear a strange clacking noise and he thought something had gone wrong until he realized what it was.

Lud was laughing.

It kept laughing as the spider rampaged down the boardwalk, legs sweeping and stabbing, clearing a path for itself. The spider's carapace dipped as something climbed on, the air rippling as it came towards Ben. Without thinking he stood and aimed a clumsy kick at it. He couldn't put any of his weight behind it but it stopped the tattoo for a moment, and a moment was all Lud needed. The spider bucked violently, knocking Ben backwards and jarring his shoulder again. The thing slid off, invisible claws scrabbling on the carapace, and Lud noisily trampled it to death.

Without warning the spider hoisted itself up onto a roof, slamming Ben into the side of the basket again, his vision blurring from the pain. Something leaped from an upper level of the town, coming straight down at him; he cringed but the spider extended a leg almost lazily, and the thing neatly impaled itself. Invisible blood rained on the roof and the thing's tattoos jumped and danced as its muscles twitched in death. Lud casually flicked it off, and Ben lost track of it in the air until he saw the wall of the next building over shatter as the thing fell through it. Then they were past the crest of the roof, and looking over the prison tower and the cage swinging from it.

The heavy chain connecting it to the winch looked blurry, and it wasn't just from the pain. More tattoos were climbing down it, towards the cage.

The trickle of invisible things out of the stone Door had become a flood, and Deadbeat was pandemonium. Bursts of gunfire echoed through the town. A fire had started somewhere, and fingers of black smoke were weaving through the streets.

Winter had seen them before they'd seen her, and she was already setting the cage to swinging. As she crashed into the bars, something reached a red-and-blue-striped arm for her, and she grabbed it almost casually and twisted it off like a drumstick. Whisper was out of her flask, spinning in a helix around Essa's forearm like weird jewellery.

As the cage swung towards them, Lud's spider reared up, nearly sending Ben tumbling off the back, and hooked its two front legs into the bars, holding it steady. Its rear legs dug two tracks in the roof, sending splintered tiles flying as the weight of the cage tried to drag them off.

"Hurry *up!*" screeched Lud.

Essa tossed Ben's bag into the basket. She hopped out of the cage, managed to steady herself and clamber one-handed over the spider— she had her other hand extended, a coil of red dust spinning around her forearm, and now she spoke backwards and part of it shot out too fast to see. He heard something behind him splatter. Winter leaped out of the cage and grabbed a handhold on the spider's thorax. Her fists were dripping with colourless blood. She was bleeding herself, a black trickle from her hairline.

The spider disengaged its legs from the bars and the cage went sweeping back towards the tower. No one in the tower seemed to have reacted to any of this. Ben guessed that they had bigger problems on their hands.

"*Are you—*" Ben yelled over the clicking of the spider's mainspring, and then he had to lean hard to the side as Lud began to lope back along the roof. Without thinking he steadied himself with the hand of his bad arm, and the bones of his shoulder grated together with a vibration he felt in his teeth. It must have shown on his face, because

Winter hoisted herself up level with him, looked him up and down, and before he'd even processed what was happening she'd put one hand on his collarbone and the other on his bicep and *wrenched*, and he felt his shoulder pop back into place. It hurt too much even to scream; he managed a whimper that turned into a gag as he fought not to throw up.

Lud hadn't left the roof, and when Ben could see again through the pain he realized why. The boardwalk they'd just left was swarming with tattoos, ink overlapping ink in a lurid abstract splatter.

No one said anything. The only sound was Winter cracking her neck, one side then the other, with a sound like a latch clicking into place.

"How," said Essa, "are we getting through that?"

Lud said nothing. The spider swayed as it looked one way, then the next, and then it said: "Down."

Almost instantly Essa dropped. Ben remained standing, dazed, until she screamed "*Ben!*" and grabbed him by his bad arm. His shoulder stayed in this time, but he yelped and went down too, and just as his head dropped below the lip of the railing, more brass rods snapped into place above him, turning the basket into a cage.

Then everything lurched, and they were weightless.

It jumped, it jumped, thought Ben, *that's it, we'll fall forever—*

But then the cage swung around and over, dumping them on the ceiling, which was now the floor, and it was moving again, sliding and jerking and throwing them against the walls each time. From overhead came a rhythmic, metallic slithering.

Ben couldn't see a thing, just a whirl of light from the town beneath them as the spider shuddered and shook. Then he figured it out, and his stomach lurched and he very nearly threw up for real.

Lud had leaped onto one of the massive cables that formed the boundary of Deadbeat. The spider was upside down with its legs wrapped around the cable, sliding itself along. If a leg slipped, if it lost its balance…and what if those invisible things were coming for them? And where was Winter?

Both those questions were answered when he heard a hiss from above, followed by a *crunch*, and something bounced off Lud's carapace hard enough to rattle Ben's teeth. The thing hissed in agony, the sound fading as it fell away. Now he could hear the footsteps ringing off the cable above them. Winter was running along the top of the cable, keeping pace with Lud underneath, the rhythm of her footsteps interrupted by more blows and hollow screams.

Lud had reached the Well, and the basket lurched and righted itself. Ben landed on his back with Essa on top of him. His ribs creaked. The basket was juddering, shaking him and Essa like dice in a cup. And then it unfolded itself again, opening up, and Essa rolled off him, groaning. Ben took a deep breath, clambered to his feet, leaned out over the railing and threw up.

"Watch it," said Lud, "that just got polished," as the coil of vomit vanished into darkness and Lud climbed up the Well, away from Deadbeat.

Whisper was still flickering around Essa's wrist, and now she unscrewed her flask and it disappeared inside. Ben saw she was bleeding again, from an eye this time. Winter had been hanging off the side of the spider, and now she vaulted onto its thorax, sitting there cross-legged and shaking the colourless blood off her hands.

The spider was leaving Deadbeat behind. Ben could see smoke rising from one roof, and he thought there were fewer lights on than usual, but otherwise it looked just the same as when he'd first seen it. He imagined travellers coming in, not knowing what had happened until invisible hands closed around their throats. He shivered.

"We have to warn people," he said.

"Excuse me," said Lud, "what we have to do is get the hell out of here. The Cogs'll have telescopes on Deadbeat, *they always take care of their own.*" Bitterness in the clashing voice. "They'll know."

"It's not going to make any difference," said Essa. She hadn't bothered to clean up the blood and it streaked one cheek below her red eye, like tear tracks.

DownWell, they could see the huge stone Door through which the tattoos had poured. Something else was coming out of it now. It was little more than a shadow at first, dimming the lights of Deadbeat, and Ben thought it was more smoke, but it looked different somehow. Paler. The colour of bone.

It spread through the town in discrete streams, sent tendrils slithering along the Well. One of them was coming towards Lud, and it seemed like it was moving slow until he realized how far away it was, and how fast it was closing in.

"Lud," said Essa carefully, "is this the fastest you can go?"

The spider sped up. Its legs scrabbled at the Well, out of sync, jolting them hard each time. The tendril coming towards them was blocking out the lights of Deadbeat with its own pale glow that leached the colour out of everything.

Ben and Essa had to crouch inside the basket so they wouldn't be thrown out as the spider's eight limbs slammed into the Well, pulling them upwards. Lud's mainspring ticked faster and faster, but the white dust was still gaining on them. Essa just watched, not making any move to back away from the bone-coloured cloud. Now it was almost level with the spider, curving towards them, ever closer. They weren't going to make it—

And then they had. The dust thinned as it rose, until it was nothing but wisps that fell back towards Deadbeat.

"We made it," Ben gasped, "we outran it—"

"No," said Essa, "we just weren't worth bothering with."

"What was that thing?" he asked.

"The Exile," said Essa.

"Bollocks," Lud grated. Winter said nothing.

"So…" said Ben.

Essa turned on him. "If it can wait until I've stopped bleeding from my eyeballs? Yes? Good. Get some sleep." She sat down, pulled up her hoodie, and folded her arms like she was slamming a door.

He didn't push it. He was too exhausted. He sat down beside her—there wasn't anywhere else to sit—and tried to sleep himself, but it wasn't going to happen. His thoughts were running away from him, chasing each other around, his brain revving up like it was in first gear and he had the accelerator down. Eventually he wore himself down far enough that he did sleep, if you could call it sleep—an uneasy circular dream, where he ran from invisible things through a tangle of rope and wood and endless night.

The brass spider marched along the endless curved wall, heading upWell, away from Deadbeat. The barbed black spikes at the end of its spindly legs left a double row of holes in the wall behind them.

It was hard to wake up; he had to struggle out of uneasy dreams like tangled bedclothes. It was the endless night of the Well, he thought. He'd never had jet lag—never even left Chifley—but he thought this was what it must feel like.

His brain kept slipping gears, he couldn't concentrate on anything. Essa was curled up beside him, asleep. He felt a surge of jealousy— that was *his* sleep she was having, she was stealing it from him.

Great. He was losing his mind.

Winter wasn't sleeping. Did she ever? She crouched on the spider's thorax, shifting with it as it moved, keeping her balance effortlessly. Over the clicking of the mainspring he could hear her talking to Lud, although he couldn't make out the words. Lud replied and she nodded, reached into her jacket and pulled out a pair of leather bands that she slipped over her hands. They had rows of black metal hooks on them, sticking out from her palms. She tightened the bands, making sure of them, then gripped the basket's rail and vaulted over the side.

Ben's stomach turned over. It had looked for all the world like she was throwing herself into the void, but when he looked out and down he saw her. She was climbing alongside Lud, using the spikes to keep her grip on the Well. That was how she'd pulled off that horizontal trick the first time he had seen her.

She barely seemed to touch the Well as she leaped along, crabwise, easily keeping up with Lud's long legs as they climbed side by side.

Just for something to do he turned around, grimacing—he ached all over and his shoulder throbbed painfully—and looked at the Well as it scrolled past. It was made of coarse-grained wood, but as Lud lumbered past it changed.

He'd seen the Well change before, climbing up into Deadbeat, but that had been under the influence of the skulker spores and the memory had deliquesced like a dream does. The wood grain twisted until it was a curling regular pattern, while the wood itself lost its colour and softened, becoming wallpaper. It was peeling in one spot and he reached out as the spider passed and tore off a swatch. Behind it was more wallpaper with the same pattern. He wondered how far down it went.

He rubbed the swatch between fingers and thumb. It was thick and expensive-looking, printed with sinuous tentacular curls that almost looked like writing. It *was* writing for all he knew. They passed the Door in the centre of the wallpaper (peeling white paint and louvered slats) and then the wallpaper hardened, the pattern losing regularity and becoming varicoloured swirls in marble. Whatever the material, Lud's legs drove in effortlessly and anchored him to the endless wall.

Another Door, rich wood with gleaming bronze hinges, the panels inlaid with mosaics. As they passed Ben caught a flash of brilliant light between Door and frame, and he thought he heard, very faint, the laughter and chatter of a crowd.

He shook his head in wonderment and looked out on the Well. Lichen fields glowed like nebulae among Doors like stars. Mushroom forests waved in up- and downdrafts, shining blue and green and purple. Beside Lud, a swarm of beetles trundled along the wall, their carapaces picked out in bioluminescent dots. Lizards with glowing fronds sprouting from their spines like the manes of seahorses darted around them, picking off the insects at the edge of the herd.

As the scene dwindled behind the clockwork spider, Ben heard a low hiss from the darkness ahead, at first at the edge of his hearing but growing steadily louder as Lud marched on. The air had grown damp and he could see tiny beads of water forming on the railing of the basket he and Essa sat in. The Well here was a field of sodden plaster sprouting clusters of small frilled mushrooms, and Lud's claws squelched as they punched into it. Ben smelled salt. The noise built into a roar. The Well changed to rusted iron. And then he saw the waterfall.

It shot out from a tall narrow Door, a jet of foam shining white in Lud's headlights. It blasted out horizontally at first and then in a great arc out into the void, losing cohesion and turning into rain. The spider crossed the Wall above it, and Ben trailed his hand in the air and brought it back sparkling with droplets of water. He tasted it. Salt.

"Sunken ship, probably," said Essa next to him. She had to lean close and talk loud to make herself heard over the waterfall and the spider's clattering. "There's a world out there where the sea level's dropping, very slowly."

Ben reached out and touched the water-slick wall. "What's it made of?"

"The Well? What it looks like. To an inch or so down, anyway. After that, it looks the same, but nothing can even give it a scratch. Well, one thing." She pointed at Lud's leg, the black spikes that tipped each one. They drove rhythmically into the Wall, puncturing the steel like it was a pincushion.

"'Black iron,' you called it. What is it?"

Essa looked past him at Winter, still keeping pace with Lud. Then she looked away. She unscrewed her flask and Whisper leaped out, circling in the air. She shied away as Essa raised a hand.

"Come on, girl," coaxed Essa. "You know we need to." She passed her gold-inlaid fingers through the red dust, then winced as a shower of sparks erupted around them. She closed her hand gently and withdrew it. "There. All done."

She turned to Ben, opened her hand. Tiny beads of crystal glittered in the folds of her palm. "The Well is bad for Isms. The fight glassed her, burned part of her out. Once she's in the Library she can build herself up again. And we'll get there, baby," she said to the cloud. "We will."

Whisper darted around her hand, through her fingers. It was oddly intimate, and Ben looked away. He glanced back at the waterfall. Something silver flashed through the Door in the middle of the jet and fell, squirming. The darkness swallowed it.

"So what was the white stuff back there?" asked Ben. "Another Ism, like Whisper?"

"Part of one. It used to be, anyway. That's what happens when you take the chains off an Ism, hurt it and hurt it until it's a beast, a mindless thing that just dismantles and destroys. The Boiling Dust."

"So it's from the Library? The thing that attacked us?"

"It was. More or less." Essa looked like she was going to say something else, but then she just sat back down, making Lud rock a little. A flicker of leftover acrophobia made Ben tighten his grip on the rail.

A hollow *bang* from somewhere beneath them shook the basket, rattling them around inside. "Shit!" yelled Lud from its harness ahead of them. Something was grinding in the spider's brass body. Ben heard screeching metal and the basket tipped alarmingly to the side as Lud fought to keep the spider's legs going.

"*Shit!*" it screamed in a voice like rending metal, and the spider changed course, heading for the nearest Door, a nondescript metal rectangle in another concrete wall. Something hung from the doorframe, bright blue and yellow.

They only just made it.

Chapter Fourteen

The Well around the carved Door is empty. The remains of a Cogs siege line still guard it, nominally, their analytical engines waiting for any sign the Door is opening, but the automated emplacements haven't moved in seasons, their outlines blurred by moss and mushrooms. It's easy to sneak in. But no one does.

The Door is barely even there any more. The seasons have smoothed it away, as they have the immense scars on the Well around it. One can still make out, barely, the bas relief of a face that fills the Door, heavy-lidded with sensual lips and long dangling earlobes. Essa sits on a collapsible ledge beside the Door, anchored to the Well by a single black iron piton. Whisper darts around the Door, sparks clicking between her and the stone surface. Essa sketches in a notebook. Without turning, she says, "Congratulations."

"Thank you. Where did you get the iron?" asks Gregor. He's atop a small platform with a multitude of suckered pseudopods that stretch and contract as they ooze across the wall.

"I worked for it. Did a Stacks job for the Green Mirror."

"You and your Ism are getting quite a reputation for 'Stacks jobs.'"

Essa just sketches.

"I've been approached by several Isms regarding your exploits. They seem to believe you may have strayed once or twice into their own domains on your expeditions. They hinted rather strongly that you were due a reprimand. At least."

"So that'll be your first official act now you have a front-row seat at the Mandala, then? Issuing me a reprimand?"

Gregor doesn't answer. He's watching Whisper scout over the Door.

"Then what are you here for, Gregor? Just playing tourist?"

"Rachana said you'd be here. She's worried about you. No faction, no rooms—where are you sleeping, anyway?"

It's Essa's turn not to answer.

"Or *are* you sleeping? Between all the grey-market odd jobs you're buying Mandala time with, and the Mandala time itself—you're running yourself ragged. Literally."

The hem of Essa's tattered robe is hanging over the ledge. Essa tucks it under her leg. She hasn't looked at him once.

Gregor turns to take in the scars that splinter the Well around the Door. "It did this in its last moments. Before we pushed it through the Door. Do you think it was angry?" he murmurs. "Or afraid? At the last?"

"Whatever it was feeling, we don't have words for it. 'Anger,' 'fear'…you're not just anthropomorphizing, you're trivializing." She looks up at the Door. "You know more than me. You're in the Spires now, you can look at the sealed Stacks. How did they choose this world?"

"It was the only empty one they could find at short notice."

"No world is empty. Something had to build a Door."

"Dead, then."

"How's Ra?"

"She's well," says Gregor, moving smoothly to the new topic. "Her Proof is coming along. With the Group's resources—"

"If you came out here for a recruitment pitch," says Essa, talking right over the top of him, "you can turn your tentacles around and creep right back to the Spires."

"You could do research all day, every day, Essa. No need to resort to thievery—"

"Is that an accusation—"

"You would have time to *eat* and *sleep*—"

"Because if that's a formal accusation, let's take it to the—"

"Do you think it's not obvious what you're doing here, Essa? We glassed the Exile's entire Library. This is the one place there's any trace of it left. If you're taking readings, and bringing them back to the Mandala, I won't need a formal accusation. They'll be happy to run you out of the Library on the mere rumour."

"Then do it. Go ahead. Give Ra my best."

His platform is already crawling away. Essa sits there for a moment, head lowered, then hurls the sketchbook after him into the Well while Whisper dances in jagged, anxious arcs around her.

CHAPTER FIFTEEN

Oh you snot-nosed, logger-headed—"

Lud's tail thumped against the abdomen of its spider in time with its curses. Ben, hanging upside down with a rope tethering his waist to its thorax, tried to tune the crab out as he wrestled with a bolt.

"—grout-brained, long-eared, short-haired—"

The bolt finally gave and Ben spun it loose. It almost got away from him but he snagged it before it fell into the void. That made the rope creak, which made him clench his teeth; the rope had come from a compartment inside the spider, and it was old and starting to fray. Tucking the bolt into the upside-down pocket of his jeans, he carefully levered up the brass inspection hatch set into the oversized pocketwatch of the spider's belly.

"—filthy scabby damnable villainous—"

The spider's insides were a nightmare of clockwork—cogs large and small, cams of all kinds, and hundreds, thousands of gears, some the size of his head and some barely bigger than his thumbnail. Other things, too, that Ben didn't know the name of, and some things he wasn't sure *had* a name in his world. He wasn't even sure what was damaged and what was in working order. There was damage, though, definitely: the brass was pitted and corroded right through in places, more like lace than metal. He supposed the smoke, the Boiling Dust, had done that, and shivered as he thought about what it would have done to him.

Meanwhile the little crab had been cursing non-stop, a cavalcade of profanity that kept cutting out into random noise when it strayed from Creole into his native tongue.

"—shitten, stinking, snot-nosed—"

"You said that already," said Ben.

"Piss off. Ready?"

"I think so," he replied, looking at the spider's clockwork guts.

He heard the crab drop into its harness with a *click* and the spider shivered to life, one section of gears spinning up. Another section followed it, then another—and then a shower of sparks burst over him with a screeching noise like an icepick in the sinuses.

He jerked back. "It's still doing it!"

The gears spun down with a sound like something dying. Ben winced as the spider rocked, making him swing at the end of his rope. That was Winter, crawling around on Lud's other side. Something was up with her. For a start, she weighed a lot more than someone her size should. A *lot* more. Ben remembered her setting their cage swinging back in Deadbeat.

She came into view, not wearing a rope, holding an assembly of gears she'd lifted from her side of the spider with the hand she wasn't hanging on with. She said something to Lud in his own language, pronouncing those metallic clicks and clangs effortlessly. Whatever she said, it evidently wasn't good news, because it sent Lud off into another tirade of curses that fortunately Ben couldn't understand.

"That isn't helping," he said as he clambered back up the rope and put a foot through the Door.

"It's helping *me*," said Lud.

"I mean it's not helping anyone else."

"Piss on 'anyone else'," said Lud. "Piss on the lot of you." The tiny crab reared up, digging into the spider's thorax with its sharp little legs as it waved a pincer at Ben. "I am *a hundred seasons old*, and after a century you know the difference between trivial things and the things that matter. And do you know what that is? What matters? Go on, guess."

"Family?" said Ben. He shouldn't have, it just made him think of his own family. They probably thought he'd skipped bail, run off somewhere rather than face prison. His bag was just inside the doorway, and he was absurdly grateful that Essa had retrieved it from Deadbeat, although there wasn't anything in there he could really use. He'd checked his laptop's clock before Lud had called him out to help with the spider: his court date was in two days.

Lud snorted. "Piss on family. Family die. Everyone dies."

"I don't know, then," said Ben, wishing he'd never opened his mouth. "Being a good person?"

"Ha," said Lud, mirthlessly. "Live long enough and go far enough, you see the 'good' you grew up with turn to 'bad' and then back again. And vice versa. And you realize it doesn't mean a thing."

"Okay," said Ben, "you tell me. What really matters?"

"What matters is *stuff*." One claw tapped the surface of the spider. "Stuff, and the money to get it."

"Stuff doesn't last either, though," said Ben, pointing at the useless spider.

"But there's always more just the same, or better, if you've the money for it. It never ends. And to watch it go, let it trickle through your fingers…there's nothing like it."

"So why're you so—"

"Because I *don't* have the money for it. And I have debts."

Ben had had about enough of this. "Lud," he said. Lud ignored him, muttering more curses as it probed at the spider's controls with a claw. The knob on the end of the pocketwatch-shaped abdomen shot out, spring-loaded, on a long metal rod. A cluster of brass spines unfolded in stages, thin fabric snapping taut, until a giant pinwheel had assembled itself at the end of the rod, and began to turn in an updraft, winding the spider's mainspring for him.

"*Lud!*" He said it more sharply than he'd meant to, but it worked. The muttered profanity cut off and the crab's eyes swiveled to face him.

"Just tell me whether you can fix it," he said. "And how far it'll get us if you do. Can you do that?"

The red lamps of Lud's eyes flared and for a moment Ben thought he'd be on the receiving end of another tirade, but the crab only said, "Give me time. I'll see what I can do."

"Thank you," Ben replied, doing his best to sound sincerely grateful, and left Lud to it.

The Door they'd come through was set into smooth purplish rock that formed one wall of a narrow canyon, only about fifty yards wide. A stream trickled through the middle of it, spindly bushes growing along the banks. They were on the canyon floor, the sky a pale thread between the towering walls.

Ben clambered into the canyon. He looked back at the Door, wondering where it had led when it was just a door. No way of telling now, not without tunnelling into the rock beside it.

Looking into the Well was easier here—he could convince himself that the whole Well was behind the canyon's rocky walls, so that sense of space not fitting together right didn't make him sick. Winter was crouching next to Lud on the spider's thorax, looking at the knot of gears she'd dug out of its belly. They were talking softly, prodding at the thing with pincer and hand.

He had no idea what to think about Winter. She was a stone-cold badass, she'd established that during their escape, but she fit almost none of Ben's ideas about what a stone-cold badass would be like. She took no *joy* in it; if he could do what she could, he'd allow himself at least the occasional smile. Ryan had been the scariest guy at Chifley and *he'd* certainly seemed like he was enjoying himself. Winter, of course, could have taken Ryan apart (a sudden flash of Ryan spread over the gym floor, the skulker feasting) but she just seemed…not sad, not exactly, but…blank. Cold.

Except with Lud. They were business partners, he supposed, but they seemed closer than that, even though Winter was about nothing but self-discipline and Lud seemed totally depraved.

Now, shockingly, Winter burst out laughing, her head thrown back, presumably at something Lud had said. Her laugh was creaky, like a rusty hinge, but surprisingly warm. Ben felt a smile spread over his own face as he listened: it was that kind of laugh. She grinned down at the crab as it waved a pincer.

The stream widened into an almost-still pool a hundred yards away. It wasn't deep, and he could see eel-like things flopping around in it, raising ripples. Essa was watching them with her back against the canyon wall. Ben sat beside her. "They're working on it," he said.

Essa shrugged.

"Look," said Ben, "is anyone going to talk about what happened in Deadbeat?"

"I think everyone's finding it a bit difficult to fit inside their head."

"Right. Sure. I sure am, because I don't even know how to start! Don't just blow me off, all right? I just risked my *life*, okay, to get Lud's spider, and I saved yours. I saved everyone's, I nearly *died*—"

He stopped talking, but it was too late. *Congratulations*, he told himself. *You've taken the only heroic thing you've ever done and turned it into something petty and small. Nice going.*

The sun of this world chose that moment to cross the sky above the canyon. Instantly, everything was plunged into dazzling bluish light. "Lady!" Essa exclaimed, and pulled her hoodie over her head. Ben didn't have one so he could only screw his eyes shut against the pounding glare that seemed to soak right through his eyelids.

Then, as abruptly as it had emerged, the tiny sun was over the other lip of the canyon and they were plunged into darkness.

Ben blinked, trying to get his vision back. His skin itched and he held his arm up to his face. He appeared to have a light case of sunburn.

Essa chuckled.

"Very funny," said Ben.

"Not you. Just…there's always something new. That's what I love about the Well. That's what I'm going to miss."

"Miss?"

Essa sighed. "All right. Question time. So what do you want to know?"

Ben opened his mouth to ask a question, and then realized he didn't have the faintest idea which one to start with.

Essa nodded. "Yes, it's a bit like that, isn't it? All right, we'll start from the beginning. Bear with me…"

Most worlds that had Doors (said Essa) didn't even know it. They had no organized presence in the Well, just the usual trickle of explorers and looters and chancers that wandered through a Door pretty much by accident. By the same token, most towns and cities in the Well (like Deadbeat) were just that, in the Well, only reaching into a few—mostly lifeless—worlds to anchor a cable or scavenge for raw materials.

In some worlds, though, knowledge of the Well was widespread, and they'd made an effort to colonize.

"Most of them are small-time, of course," she said, "but there's three—" and she stopped and her gaze flicked over to the Door behind which Lud and Winter were working. "There's three big ones," Essa continued, "we call them the Powers. There's the Vats—you remember the House of Green Lights." What Ben remembered was the room under the House, the swinging cocoons, and he shuddered a little and nodded. "They do biology, drugs, genetics. The Cogs make machines, like Lud's spider. And then there's the Library, and they deal in information."

"The Committee, back in Deadbeat. They talked about a Treaty," said Ben.

Essa nodded. "The Treaty between the Powers. That's what you were invoking, without knowing it of course, when you pulled your diplomatic immunity stunt in the House—nice going, by the way, that could well have worked."

Ben shrugged. "It didn't."

"Nice going anyway. The Treaty is pretty new, relatively speaking—we don't have any records of *anyone* being in the Well until a few hundred years ago—but it's mostly worked, kept everyone from knocking heads all the time. Which is not to say you don't get the occasional squabble—things got nasty between the Vats and the Cogs for a while. But that's all small-time. We aren't the Powers, we just work for them. The Powers are the Intellects."

"Intellects?" said Ben. "Like AIs or something? Artificial—"

"I know what it means, thank you. Wellside, 'Intellect' just means anything big and old and smart. There's a ton of minor ones—L'Esprit d'Escalier, the Νομοθέτης, the Shifting Sky. Some of them go into business as consultants or oracles or whatever, but they're still kind of small-time.

"The *real* Intellects—the Library Isms, like Whisper here,"—she held up the silver flask—"the Cogs Analyticals, the Vats brain-kraken—*they're* the Powers. And they don't go to war. If they did, we probably wouldn't even know why, we'd just get caught in the middle and squished. But for now, the Powers keep the peace, stop things getting screwed up."

"Screwed up how?" asked Ben.

"Well, just for an example, if the wrong Door gets opened and a horde of invisible monsters pours out. The Cogs are probably marshalling an army right now—the Vats too, so they can get in on the reconstruction after they've put the invasion down. Except they're not going to put it down."

"Because of the Exile."

"Because of the Exile," Essa agreed. "Who came from the Library, like me…"

Chapter Sixteen

Some Librarians chatter through their Defence, explaining every step, pointing out each salient in their Proof.

Essa never says a word, just the occasional grunt of effort as she twists her fingers around each other. Beside her, Whisper diagrams the Proof, circles shifting inside circles, Library notation for Wellside math. Under Whisper, the Mandala turns, each axiom and conclusion like raindrops falling, spreading tiny ripples as it absorbs them.

Some Librarians structure their presentation, building to a dramatic revelation that the sand beside them echoes triumphantly. Fireworks. Essa just brings her hands together while Whisper shrinks to a sphere beside her, then she stands back and folds her arms, hunched like she's bracing for a blow.

The panel in front of her haven't moved once the entire time, just their eyes, flickering between Whisper and the Mandala.

A short silence. Essa doesn't drop her guard. Gregor is in the gallery, she sees, and doesn't allow herself to react.

"Where did you get your data?" asks the panel chair, looking at the sand lectern in front of his seat, the symbols tracing themselves on it.

Essa relaxes, not because the blow has missed, but because it has landed and she's still on her feet. Gregor is a blur in her peripheral vision, but she can tell he hasn't moved.

"My own research. Also certain Stacks, it's all in the—"

"Your bibliography," says another Librarian, of the same species as the Governess back in Three Suns, her bright red corneas staring down at Essa, *and how appropriate*, she thinks, "is in the notation of several Isms, all obscure and some defunct. While we can verify that the data are present and accurate, determining *where* they are, that is to say, their relationship with other data, their provenance, will be almost prohibitively difficult."

"None of this is against the rules."

"The letter of the rules, as opposed—"

Essa uncrosses her arms, stands taller. "The data are accurate, and accurately cited. That's the reason the bibliography exists, to confirm that. That's the reason *you* exist."

"We are not here," says the lady with red eyes hotly, "only to determine the accuracy of your data, but *ethical*—"

The Chair raises a hand. "Have you had any contact with the Exile?" he asks.

The flatness of the question shocks even Essa, a little. "No, I have not." Gregor gets up and leaves.

The Chair stands. "That this panel shall seal the thesis data and arguments?"

A chorus of soft "Aye"s.

"*What?*"

"The thesis is sealed and will be isolated from the Stacks," he says. "The author shall receive a passing grade and is dismissed."

Essa doesn't move.

"There's no way you're sealing this," she says. "Because this is worth money. Isn't it? Even if it had come from the Exile itself, you'd still use it."

"The author—" The Chair is losing his patience. His red-haired neighbour is seething.

"So you're just going to *take it away from me*, that's what you're doing—" Two Librarians are coming to escort Essa out, but she waves them off. She draws breath to say something else, then turns abruptly and leaves.

Gregor finds her in the Cathedral. She's alone on a packed sand pew, forehead resting on the back of the pew ahead of her. The Cathedral is both church and churchyard—the towering windows are made from dead Isms, glassed in the fight against the Exile—and they dapple Essa's hair and robes with varicoloured light. Her shoulders are shaking, but as soon as she hears his footsteps she freezes in place.

Her flask rattles as he sits in front of her and to the side. The cap unscrews itself and Whisper leaps out. She darts at his head, hissing, but he doesn't turn or flinch.

"Going to rub it in?" Her voice is clotted with tears. "Thought you had more class than that."

"I was going to tell you you were right in there. Absolutely right. They're terrified of what you've done. Where it might have come from."

"If I thought there'd be any danger—"

"It doesn't matter. They're taking it away from you."

"Well, thank you for saying that out *here* rather than in *there* where it might have done some good—"

"It wouldn't have. There's too much money at stake. You were right about that, too."

"What are you *here for*, Gregor?" His name turns into a sob and she clenches her teeth, hard.

He turns, leans over the back of the pew, his pale eyes boring into hers. "I have an answer."

Chapter Seventeen

No one knew who had built the Library (said Essa) or if it had been "built" at all. The Library was part of Red Sand City, which lay in an endless desert behind a Door a thousand miles downWell.

Explorers from the Well had found the City deserted, hundreds of miles of halls and pinnacles all made of sand that formed and reformed endlessly according to some unguessable plan. Quite a few explorers had been lost when they'd picked the wrong room to make camp in and been buried alive while they slept, their lungs filling with sand grain by grain.

They'd learned to read the hieroglyphs that etched themselves endlessly in the sand, and to write them. They'd opened a dialogue with the City. And the City had directed them to the mile-high mountain in its very centre, atop which was the Library.

The Library was the mind of the City, and its hunger for information was vast and insatiable. It hadn't known about the Well, and had jumped at the opportunity to have others gather information for it from countless worlds. Those who did had become the first Librarians.

Librarians didn't own, or even run the Library—they were the hired help, collating, curating, taking care of the Library in the few ways it couldn't take care of itself. It was the sand that owned the place.

Except it wasn't that simple, because within the sand-mind of the Library were innumerable factions, coming into being, growing, merging, splitting, fading—

"The Canted Plane," said Ben, remembering what 鐘 had said. "The Heptacomb."

Essa nodded. "The Static Void, the Slow Walker, the Thousand Sails. And a hundred thousand others. Isms. They're not even entities, really, more like…movements, or philosophies. Cataloguing systems, taxonomies, ways of looking at the Library's data. The biggest are *huge*, and ancient, older than anything."

At some point Winter had emerged from the Door, and now she crouched by the pool. Her arm blurred, and then it was dripping wet and she had something slimy clutched in it. It squirmed and struck at her wrist with its blunt head until she cracked it like a whip, snapping its spine. She threw it onto the shore of the pool and went back to staring.

That was dinner, he supposed.

"Librarians can sign up with an Ism—you pretty much have to, if you want to be able to search the Stacks," Essa continued. "The biggest ones have hundreds of Librarians. The place where Isms interact, talk to each other, we call that the Mandala."

The word seemed to fit clumsily in Ben's head, and he had the idea this was another concept his new language wasn't getting across, an almost-but-not-quite-good-enough approximation.

"There are different ways you can sign up with an Ism. But we all take the Wire." She raised a hand, circuitry glimmering in the gloom of the canyon. "Some more than others. Some are Wired head to toe, their Isms can control them completely."

"The tattoos."

"Exactly. Wherever the Exile is, it's bound those invisible monsters to it. Lucky for us it couldn't make the bindings invisible, too, or we'd still be in Deadbeat right now, and also dead."

"So which Ism are you signed up with?"

"You have to ask?" Essa smiled sadly and touched Whisper's flask. "When I stepped up to the Mandala to make my choice, she'd only just come into being. Brand new, but smart and curious as hell. And she wanted to see the worlds, like I did. Pretty much killed any hope I had of a career, but who needs one of those?"

"And the Exile?" Ben asked. "It's another Ism?"

She sighed. "Right. Well. The thing about Isms is, they don't always get along. Half of the time we don't even know why, we don't have a clue why one's locked another out of some ancient chunk of data. Most of the time it's small stuff, doesn't affect the Librarians one way or the other. But sometimes…

"Sometimes they go to war."

Wars between Isms were vicious, and could lock whole Stacks away for days as the combatants tried to erase each other from the Library's memory. The battles spilled over into the architecture of the Library itself; the towers and halls belonging to each antagonist would droop and collapse, rooms chopping themselves up into labyrinths like misshapen honeycombs where the unwary would get lost and starve. The ends of the wars were as inscrutable as their beginnings; sometimes they would not be over until the total destruction of one party—or both—and other times they just…stopped, with nothing apparently resolved.

Librarians could join in the wars, and often did, if their own

Ism was at stake; they laid traps in the Library, tampered with its architecture to wipe out enemy strongholds. But the sand was alien, you never knew quite what you were fighting for, and so Librarians tended to stay out of any conflict unless it was obvious survival was at stake.

As had been the case with the Exile.

Night had fallen in the canyon, but the sky between the walls was almost as bright as it had been in the day. Because the sky was…

Ben's primary school science club (one of his dad's ideas, that one) had gone on an excursion to a dark-sky park once, a place cut off from cities and streets and light pollution, where you could see the night sky the way humans had seen it for millions of years. They'd only had a glimpse of the naked sky, the Milky Way arching over their heads like an inverted river, before the clouds had rolled in. The club had spent the rest of the night waiting fruitlessly for them to roll back out again, getting eaten by mosquitoes the whole time. But that half-hour of stars had been impressive.

Not next to this, though. The sky here was crammed, packed, *bursting* with scintillating stars, sparkling white and blue and angry red. He craned his head back further, and nearly fell into the campfire Winter was building.

"Sorry," he said.

"No problem," said Winter. She took a sharp stone from her pocket.

"We can light it," said Essa, Whisper streaming out of her flask, sparks flickering inside her.

Winter didn't look up. She just ran the stone along her finger—her bare finger—and a fountain of sparks showered into the campfire. The wide-eyed look Essa gave the grey-haired girl was hard to decipher, but there was wonder in it, and sadness too.

The fire gradually rose and dimmed the stars, somewhat to Ben's regret. It was warm, though.

"Where are we at right now, Lud?" said Ben.

"More time."

"Seriously?"

"About as long as we've taken already, to find out exactly what got bollocksed up. Then maybe a Dial to fix it."

"A what?"

"A Dial. Ninety thousand measures." The crab's tail beat time on the spider's shell again. "That's a measure. And that. And that. Ninety thousand of those. All right?"

Ben did the math in his head and came up with a day. Ish. That was it. No way he was making it home in time. And when he did—if he did—what was he going to say? If he made something up, they'd call him a liar—rightly—and throw the book at him. If he told the truth, he'd maybe avoid prison but he'd end up somewhere that also had bars on the windows, and for a whole lot longer.

"You were going to talk about the Exile," he said to Essa, just to stop thinking about it.

Essa glanced at Winter again, and it wasn't with sadness this time. Ben thought it was apprehension. Or fear.

"It can wait," she said.

Winter looked directly at Essa, for maybe the first time. "I don't have a problem with it. I wasn't even born."

"It's still the Library's fault."

"The Library kicked you out. It's fine. Unless you want to keep dancing around it, congratulate yourself for feeling guilty about it. I might have a problem with that."

Essa swallowed, then nodded. "Fair point."

"You might as well tell him," said Lud lazily. It had flipped itself over so the fire could warm its clockwork guts. "No one ever really bought the Library explanation anyway. Everyone thinks you've been holding out on us."

Essa nodded again. "We have."

"The Exile," said Essa, "was one of the old Isms. Old and vast and strange. It didn't even have any followers, it was way too…abstract. We called it the Stranger. Then the Enemy, when we were fighting it, and the Exile after."

She shook her head. "I'm crap at stories. Help me out, Whisper." The red dust swirled above the fire. As Essa talked, it formed patterns in the flickering orange light, not pictures exactly, more abstract, but complementing what Essa was saying.

"It wanted—well, we don't really know what it wanted. It belonged to another Library, in another sand city. There are a few of them—Red Sand is the one we know best, of course, that's where the Door is, and we've figured a little bit of it out—but the others are still just…alien.

"They all share information, so they all learned about the Well, and about us, and what *we* were learning about *them*. Well, something we learned must have ticked the Stranger off, because its whole Library, the whole mile-high pillar of sand, started moving. Heading for Red Sand City. Heading for the Door.

"The Librarians had no idea what to do. Take on an Ism, sure. Take on a whole Library? It came right up to the Door. The other Powers were screaming, wanted to cut the Library off, but Red Sand City isn't some no-name world. The Powers' whole economies were built around exploiting the Well by then, and without the Library and all its information, they'd crash hard. So they hesitated before they shut our Door on us.

"Which would have been a waste of time anyway. The Librarians were three deep around the Door in Red Sand City, ready to hold the Stranger off, and the Stranger just made its own."

"Its own Door?" Lud said, and gave a tinny whistle.

"It opened up Wellside right next to the Library Door, and then the Stranger—the Enemy by that point—started sending itself through. You saw the Boiling Dust in Deadbeat?" Ben nodded, and Lud twitched its tail in assent. "Like that, only more of it. A lot more. Tendrils, pseudopods, miles long. And they started lashing the Well."

"Sorry," said Ben, "when you say—"

"Just striking the Well, over and over. Where they landed, Doors bloomed. Bloomed fast, too, like a whole Season in five minutes. So many they started to overlap, merge with each other. A few Librarians have published on that, on what that would have done to the worlds behind those Doors. Something drastic, probably. We never heard from them again, of course, so no way to confirm it.

"When we discovered the Well, we used to think it was untouchable—the structure of it, I mean. Eternal. As far as most people are concerned, it still is. But when the Stranger came... it opened up cracks. Deep ones."

"I never heard this," said Lud.

"No, because everyone in the Well who saw them either died, or went mad and *then* died. At any rate, the Library managed to stop the Stranger—"

"That part I know," said Lud.

"That part the Library won't shut up about," agreed Essa.

"What happened?" asked Ben.

"A team of Librarians managed to get into the Stranger's Stacks, plant a couple of conundra—malware, I suppose you'd call it—and cut it off at the root. None of them made it out again. There are two-hundred-foot statues of them all through Red Sand City. Then all the other Librarians managed to push the Stranger out into the Well and through a waiting Door, which they slammed. Problem solved.

"Until now. The Lady knows what's going to happen now."

"Why isn't it attacking the Well again?" said Ben. "Making its own Door, like it did before?"

"I don't know. They hurt it quite a bit last time, and Isms can take a long time to heal. But it's back, and it presumably has something in mind."

No one said anything. The fire crackled, wood turning to ember turning to ash.

"What did they see?" asked Lud curiously. "The ones who saw these cracks in the Well. What was inside them?"

"We rather think that was what drove them mad. All the Library could get out of them—all they could get out of the ones who lived long enough—was that they saw something big, moving."

"How big?"

"Big. They were very emphatic on that point. *Big*. And moving.

"And seeing it killed them."

Chapter Eighteen

Essa pauses at the threshold of Gregor's rooms.

Gregor is already striding in. "It's just a room, Essa."

"It's the Spires. I promised myself once I'd never set foot here, so give me a moment."

"You're not going to catch institutionalism or whatever you're worried about. Come here, I want to show you something."

Essa shakes her head, then steps into the rooms.

The first thing she notices is the sound of water, a rare thing in the Library. It runs down one wall in slow rippling waves. Plants sprout from the wall, leaves beaded with moisture.

Essa flicks a leaf with a finger. "If you're trying to make me believe you're serious about this and not just another Spires showoff, you're not doing too good a job."

"My one indulgence," says Gregor. "I'm from the Thorn, I missed the green. You're from Three Suns?"

"That's where I ended up anyway. Choir orphanage."

"Hence your name." Gregor nods. "I've never heard the Choir; it must be something special."

"I wouldn't know, I'm tone deaf. They couldn't get rid of me fast enough. Show me what you wanted to show me so I can go back to work."

Gregor leads her to an alcove curtained with rich Thorn silk. He draws it aside and Essa whistles long and low.

The packed sand wall at the back of the alcove churns, never-ending concentric circles pulsing and revolving. It's the Mandala. A mirror of the Mandala, technically—they're all through the Stacks, for Librarians to consult, but those are tiny, with only the largest rings visible. Gregor's reproduces the real Mandala in vivid detail. Essa examines it with her nose a finger's-width from the circling sand, then flinches back as with a gesture Gregor sends the Mandala's focus flying over the Stacks, the circles shifting chaotically before they settle on a new pattern.

Essa's eyes narrow as she takes it in. "What am I looking at?"

"What I came to the Spires for," says Gregor. "You said the Exile had been burned out of the Stacks; well, that's not entirely true. If you know the Isms well enough, you see the interstices, the fault lines between them where old material lies forgotten…"

Essa already has Whisper out and they're examining the patterns together.

"You're at a dead end with your Proof, and after that debacle of a Defence, no one's going to give you the resources to complete it. I can give you those resources. And no, this isn't another invitation to the Group. You'd be off the books entirely. No strings attached."

"And Ra?"

"Rachana's Proof is…not working out. We thought she was close to something, but nothing's come of it."

"You're kicking her out?" asks Essa instantly. "To make room for me?"

"I'm kicking her out regardless. You saying yes or no to this won't make any difference."

"So why?" asks Essa.

"You asked me once what the point of the Spires was. The point of having power. *This* is the point. The ability to be flexible, to bend the rules. What you're doing is important, Essa."

Essa hesitates, then lifts her arm. She looks at Gregor, who nods.

She reaches out, the sand falling away before her fingers, and soon her arm is in the mirror up to her elbow. Suddenly she snatches it out. "Red Lady," she says under her breath, examining her trembling fingers, sparks cracking between them.

"Well?" asks Gregor.

Essa plunges her arm back in, and Gregor pushes his own in beside her. Whisper swirls around Essa's arm, then around both of them, turning ecstatic figure-eights. Essa begins to laugh, and Gregor chuckles with her.

Sex is almost an afterthought.

Chapter Nineteen

Ms. Buckley wrote something on the board but Ben wasn't paying attention, he was looking out the classroom window. The window faced west, towards the town; if he stood up he could have seen his house.

The daylight was dimming, and changing colour. Now it was a dirty yellow. Now the colour of rust. Now blood. Something was coming up over the horizon, a towering wall of smoke, miles high and shot through with lightning, and even as he watched, it raced towards the school, blotting out the world.

"Ms.—" he said, turning, and the smoke blasted through the open window. He could barely see Ms. Buckley as she turned to him with her face cracking and crumbling like dry clay. *Everyone* was crumbling, coming apart, his classmates were falling to bits in front of him. He saw Victor Jia trying to stand; his leg burst apart as he put his weight on it and he fell. His head hit the corner of the desk and caved in. It was hollow inside. People were struggling towards him, holding out crumbling hands, pleading with eyes that turned to dust in their sockets as the storm grew and darkness fell—

Voices woke him. He stirred a little, then his sleep-addled brain managed to latch on to a few words.

"…no idea. But he can handle himself. And he's smart, you saw what he did with that machine of his."

It was Essa, and she was talking about him. He lay still and listened.

"What are you going to do?" Winter's rusty voice.

"Run," said Essa, without missing a beat. "That's what. Run and never stop." Pause. "But there's…there's something I need to know first. And Ben needs to go home. So we have to go back. Somehow."

Winter said nothing.

"I have no idea what we're going to do, though. We need to find whoever's organizing the fight back there. Except they're downWell from us, we'd have to sneak past Deadbeat, which *no thanks*, not with those invisible things running around. Even assuming Lud gets his spider working."

A pause. Then, carefully, Essa said: "What are *you* going to do?"

Winter said nothing. Essa spoke again, hesitantly, like someone feeling their way through a dark room. "I mean, are you taking off? You know, going your own way?"

Then Winter's voice, hollow and flat like it was echoing off metal: "You'd like me to?"

"*No*," said Essa. "Red Lady, am I going to be walking on eggshells this whole time?"

"Are you?"

"Fine," Essa snapped, "forget it."

Silence.

"But for what it's worth, I'm sorry."

"Why?" Winter's voice was soft. "Were you in on it?"

"Come on," said Essa, "look at me. I was screaming and pooping myself in a Three Suns nursery when the Rust hit."

"Would you have gone along?"

"Probably." Essa sighed. "Just then, *everyone* was pooping themselves and screaming, to hear the old ones tell it. I don't do that sort of thing, if you want to know, I never once voted to slam the Door on a world that needed help. But the Exile…yes. Probably. It was just *so* fast, it ate your world from the—"

"Not my world," said Winter. "I never knew it."

Essa stumbled but kept going, sticking to whatever script she'd worked out in her head: "—from the inside out and…I mean, no one knew *anything*. What if it got into the Well? So yes, I would have gone along, I would have shut the Door on you. I'm sorry about that. I'm sorry."

Nothing, again, for the longest time. Ben thought Essa had gone back to sleep. Not Winter though, Winter never slept.

"Where did you…" said Essa, out of nowhere.

Nothing. Ben pictured Winter waiting, that cold and patient look in her eyes.

"…learn?" Essa finished. "To be one? To become one?"

Pause.

Essa's voice betrayed her increasing frustration. "Look, you know what I mean. An—" then something he couldn't make out, *Eyes on* something.

Pause.

"Okay," said Essa, "fine, have it your way, I just—"

"Worldside somewhere. Nowhere special. *Where* is one of those things that just doesn't matter, when you're talking about the Art. In *here* is where you learn."

Ben held his breath, and he could imagine Essa doing the same. Along with her speech over the fire, this had to be the most Winter had said since he'd first seen her. Certainly the most she'd said about herself.

"She found me, or said she did. I don't remember. I just remember training." Toneless, no spin on it at all.

"But was she—you know—an original?" Essa almost whispered the last word.

Ben didn't see what Winter did, but he thought she must have nodded, because he heard Essa's breath catch in her throat and when she spoke there were tears in her voice. "What happened to her?"

"She died," said Winter. "Like the others."

Another pause, on Essa's end this time. "I'm so sorry," she said finally, and Ben could tell she meant it, it wasn't just something to say when you didn't know what to say. Whatever had happened to Winter, Essa counted herself responsible in some way. She sounded like she was about to cry.

"Are you…do you want to help us?" she asked after a moment, tentatively.

"Help the Library." Winter's voice was toneless.

"I know," said Essa, "but one thing you might want to consider is where the Rust came from. What brought it down on the Eisenwelt."

Ben heard the word clearly. It wasn't the one she'd used before, but it was close.

"The Librarians were responsible for shutting your Door on you, I'm not arguing that at all, but the one who *made* the Rust is sitting in Deadbeat right now. So if you ever considered taking a shot at it…"

Winter said nothing.

"And one more thing," said Essa. "If the Exile makes it back to the Library, it'll do the same thing to other worlds that it did to yours. And it probably won't stop."

He thought Essa was going to say something else but then he heard her clothes scraping along the concrete floor as she lay down and got comfortable. Winter didn't say anything at all, and presently Essa's breathing deepened into sleep.

Eisenwelt, mouthed Ben. He had no idea what it meant.

Ben, covered in grease, emerged from the Door just as the sun began its short arc over the canyon. He winced and jerked his head back, grabbing the Doorframe so he didn't topple backwards into the Well. Behind him Lud's spider ticked over in a complicated pattern of clicks and thumps.

He stayed there, blinking away the swarming spots in his eyes, and was just about to swing himself back worldside when something made him cock his head and listen.

That clicking hadn't been coming from the spider's carcass, but from somewhere above. He leaned back further, wincing at the pain in his neck, and squinted at the glimmer of light that had just appeared upWell.

Lud must have heard it too, because the spider's searchlight fired up with a whine and swung up to shine past Ben.

There was an army coming at them.

As the light swept over them, Ben saw clockwork bugs the size of houses, with ten, twelve, twenty legs. Things on treads, bristling with cannons of every size of barrel and bore. Troop carriers with scores of Cogs soldiers strapped into them like vertical rollercoasters. And other things too, not Cogs, enormous and indescribable things that slithered and oozed and flopped down the Well. All of it lit by Lud's searchlight, with Ben's own shadow looming huge over the horde.

A red flare out there in the Well, a glowing sphere hanging in the darkness. It was a balloon, a huge one, slowly descending.

A hand closed over Ben's mouth.

He struggled fiercely. Not fiercely enough. More hands grabbed his arms and wrenched them around behind him. Something drew tight over his wrists. It was over before he'd fully realized it'd begun.

The hands shoved him through the Door into the canyon. He landed on his chest in a cloud of dust, the impact driving the breath out of him, and they rolled him over and grabbed the front of his shirt, yanked him up, shoved him against the wall. Ahead of him he heard

Essa draw breath to yell, then a *thump* as she landed in the dust beside him. He sat there and blinked dust out of his eyes until he could see what was happening.

Essa's hands were behind her back, presumably tied up like his were. There was something over her mouth, a gag of some kind. She was staring at the ground—glaring at it, not scared at all, just monumentally pissed off.

A sinewy figure stood over her. It looked something like the Empties he'd seen in the House of Green Lights in Deadbeat—the same blue-grey skin, the same grotesquely long arms—but there was none of that plantlike growth on it. Its hair was a cluster of blue spines, like a hedgehog's quills, cut close to its scalp, and it wore a wraparound visor bolted to its temples. Its needle-toothed grin split its face practically in half. Instead of those white shiny scrubs, it was wearing a matte black thing with a high collar, like a wetsuit, that seemed to drink up all the light around.

Lud sailed through the Door and landed in a cloud of dust, skidding along on his carapace before a foot landed on him. The foot had a thumb. It belonged to another sinewy thing, this one with multifaceted eyes and mandibles instead of a jaw. Lud's legs writhed uselessly.

They were scouts, maybe, for the advancing army, who'd looped around and snuck up on them from downWell. They hadn't snuck up on Winter, though. Three more of them, all in those suits like holes cut out of the world, stood in a loose arc around her. Winter's stance was relaxed, her hands open. Ben had just enough time to take all this in before one of the things went for her. Or at least that was what he assumed had happened—all he saw was a blur, then a split-second freeze frame of it bent double with Winter's fist buried in its solar plexus, then another blur and a thump that shivered through the ground, and the black-suited thing was on the floor, fetal and wheezing. Winter stood loose-limbed and patient, with no sign that she'd ever moved at all. None of the others seemed all that eager to follow the first one's lead.

Essa took a deep breath. She said something incomprehensible through the gag, which slithered tighter on her face—it was *alive*—and she grunted with pain.

Ben looked at it. What he'd taken for pale cloth was a long fat body, segmented like a centipede's, clinging to Essa's face and squirming between her teeth. Essa tried to say something else, and its legs dug into her face as it tightened further.

The one with the visor glanced at its fellows. It covered the distance between itself and Essa in one long stride and knelt beside her. With a finger-length blade that appeared in its hand like a conjuring trick, it severed the cord that bound Whisper's flask to Essa's belt and tossed it to the one holding Lud down. That taken care of, it reached behind Essa's head and did something that made the gag let go of her face. She took a whooping breath as the grinning thing stroked the gag like a pet. It scuttled over his arm and down his torso, burrowing into a pocket at his waist.

"Okay," said Essa through her teeth, "that does it. You thugs untie me *right now.*"

One of the things laughed, a high-pitched titter that set Ben's teeth on edge. He tried to pull his wrists apart and then froze as he felt the thing binding them squirm a little.

"I am invoking right of passage to an Annex-listed mediator," Essa was saying. Spots of blood stood out around her lips where the gag had dug its claws in. "Right now. I claim this right under the Treaty, as a Librarian of Red Sand City—"

"Except," said a voice from the Door, "I'm afraid that's not quite true."

Someone stood there, someone tall dressed in a robe of coarse black cloth, the same robe as 鐘 in his shack in the grasslands and

Essa's sketches back in Chifley. A Librarian. Their hood was up, their face in shadow. Something gleamed under there.

The darkness under the hood turned this way and that, taking them all in—a long look at Essa, shorter ones for Lud and Winter, barely a glance for Ben—and two glittering hands emerged from the robe's sleeves and pushed the hood back.

He had the same kind of circuitry as Essa, but more. A lot more. It shone in the gloom of the canyon, the lines and swirls covering every inch of his shaved scalp, extending over his face and neck, marching over both sides of his hands. He glanced at Ben and Ben's first thought was that his eyes were all red, like Winter's were black. Then he saw they did have pupils and irises, they were just bloodshot as hell.

"Oh," said Essa with disgust, "you have got to be *kidding* me."

"Hello, Essa," said the Librarian.

"What do you want, Gregor?"

"I apologize for all of this, Essa, but—"

"It was you, wasn't it? You declared us non grata. Why? Just because I walked out on—"

Gregor held up a glittering hand. "We needed you, Essa, and quickly. The Cogs were supposed to hold you in Deadbeat until I could come for you. In any event, things moved a bit too fast for that."

"The Exile's in Deadbeat, Gregor."

"We know."

That stopped Essa. "You what?"

"We know it's the Exile. We need you to stop it." Gregor crouched in front of her, red eyes intent. "The Exile has been opening Doors up- and downWell for almost half a season."

Her eyes narrowed. "You didn't tell me."

"I wanted to. No one outside the Spires could know. We've managed to find the Doors before they ripened, seal them, but the Cogs didn't want anything getting in the way of exploiting their new world. So they didn't declare the Door, and things went a little further than they should have."

"A little further, yes. The Door's open. The Exile is in Deadbeat right now. It's got a Bound army and the Boiling Dust."

"Well, the good news is that we believe we can still head things off," said Gregor, "and that's where you come in. I assume the reason you've resurfaced is that you…did it?"

Essa looked away.

"This is important, Essa. Not for me—"

Essa snorted.

"Not only for me. You finished your Proof, didn't you? You grew a Door, that's how you made it back Wellside. We can still stop the Exile, but we need that Proof."

Essa looked at the ground. Ben knew that look on her face; it was one he was familiar with, he'd seen it in the mirror in the days after his arrest. She was hunting for an alternative, any alternative, to what she had to do now, and not finding any.

Finally she muttered, "Red Lady in a box."

"That's the spirit," said Gregor with a chummy smile.

"I won't give you the Proof."

The smile remained, but the warmth was gone.

Essa looked up at him. "I won't give it to you. But I'll come with you."

"Good enough." He stood, and turned to Winter. "Now. You. *Eisenkünstler.*"

He said it coldly. Ben wondered if he knew Winter could twist his head off any time she wanted. Her expression didn't change.

"Do you know how many of you there are left?" Gregor cocked his head, waiting for a reaction. "I can tell you if you like. It's fewer than you think, I suspect." He stepped forward, right up in her face with lunatic self-confidence. Ben expected Winter to pull him apart, but she just stood there.

"The Library thanks you for protecting our colleague, but now, unfortunately, we take our leave—"

"Hold on a minute," said Essa, cautiously. "If you know what she is, you know she can fight. I've been talking to her, can we at least—"

Gregor held up that hand again. "We can't have her, Essa, you know that. Operationally it's unnecessary, and politically it's just impossible."

"Winter—" said Essa anxiously.

"Go," Gregor said to Winter. "Or stay here. Either way, you're not coming with us."

"*Winter*—"

Winter stepped forward, and Ben winced—but she stepped past Gregor, turned and stood with the Door at her back, surveying the canyon. Her eyes met Essa's for a second, and Ben saw a flash of emotion in them—weary contempt, the eyes of someone who'd always known she'd be let down and was utterly unsurprised to find that that was, in fact, the case.

She shrugged, stepped backwards through the Door and was gone.

Gregor sniffed. "Theatrical."

"You didn't need to do that," said Essa, but that was all she said. She looked up at Gregor. "So what now?"

"Now," said Gregor, "we're joining the army."

Chapter Twenty

Essa wakes and at first she's not sure why. She reaches for sleep again, but it trickles through her fingers and drains away.

Voices in the antechamber. That's what woke her. Gregor is out there, his tone calm as ever.

She stirs, and feels the sheets sliding across her skin, and remembers she's naked. She doesn't see her robe, or Gregor's. Usually they're puddled on the floor between the bed and the Mandala mirror's alcove on the wall. They've spent the last week crossing that short stretch of floor, doing nothing but work, screw, eat, and sleep, although they don't always have time for the last two.

Gregor isn't finished talking, but his interlocutor talks right over him, voice taut and bright. Rachana.

Essa lifts her eyes to Gregor's waterfall-wall beside the bed. Something tiny and yellow trundles across a patch of water-bejeweled moss beside her head. Probably one of only a few dozen insects in the whole City. The walls tend to mistake anything smaller than a cat for refuse, and absorb it.

She's listening harder, although she doesn't want to. "I have it, Gregor," Ra is saying. "It took a while but I have it."

"The Proof?" asks Gregor evenly.

"Well, not the Proof, you know I don't have the Proof yet."

Rachana is talking a mile a minute, her voice tightening up until it creaks. Essa knows that voice. She's on something, probably has been for days. "But I can see there from here. I have a Chant. I just need to run it through the Mandala. I just need Mandala time. This is it. I'm sure."

"Rachana, this is the same thing you've told me a half-dozen times. The Group's resources, my resources, are not infinite. I told you this already. I asked you not to come here."

"I never said I was sure before. I never said I was sure. I'm sure now. Come on, Gregor," Ra says with a high-pitched giggle. "Just queue it up for me and—" Her voice cuts off like someone threw a switch on it.

Very clearly, Essa remembers how her robe felt sliding over her skin when Gregor took it off. They'd had to take a break while a Servitor cleaned his rooms, and they'd had a huge fight in the Spire Gardens over how to elaborate the Chant they were working on (nose to nose, yelling in each other's faces) and they'd continued the fight all the way back to his rooms, and once inside they hadn't even made it to the bed. Her robe they left on the floor of Gregor's antechamber. Where Rachana is now.

With the care of someone stepping away from some precariously balanced thing, Essa disengages. She stays exactly where she is, staring blankly at the surface of the pillow an inch from her face. Gregor's sheets are from the Thorn, from huge worms that never stop eating and spinning, each sheet one long continuous thread. This information has exactly the same weight as the knowledge Rachana is out there with Gregor. She stops listening, hears only the tone of their voices, Gregor's cool, Rachana's increasingly hysterical. The door to Gregor's rooms is a panel of sand, and doesn't slam—it hisses open and shut, a soft sound that's just the same regardless of what exit you're making.

As soon as it's closed behind Rachana, Essa crosses the floor between the bed and the mirror in two long strides, not bothering to dress, and plunges both her hands inside. At some point Gregor joins her. They don't speak.

Chapter Twenty-One

The attack was scheduled for 2674 hours by the Great Dial. Four Cogs crawlers, *chasseurs-à-l'araignée*, awaited the signal, deployed in a line half a mile upWell of Deadbeat. Their grizzled sergeant observed the sweep of the fourth hand on her chronometer, then looked down at the silent town.

Nothing moved there. The buildings that had burned during the invasion had been quickly doused, the invaders making use of the town's hydrant system, pumping water from a river in another world. Now the stink of charred timbers rose upWell, and black water rained down.

The crawlers shifted, mainsprings fully wound and creaking with tension. Their riders, sitting horizontally and strapped tight into their saddles, held the reins with white knuckles.

It was time.

The sergeant's mouth was a cluster of metal keys surrounded by twisted scar tissue, and they clattered out her words as she barked the order to advance.

Their mainsprings drove the Cogs' crawlers forward, rushing downWell towards Deadbeat. They spread out as they approached the town, randomly sidestepping left and right against the possibility of missiles fired from below. None were, and they were well into the outskirts before the counterattack began.

As they passed through the narrow gap between two buildings, a single tattoo, half its body solid blue and the other no colour at all, burst from a ragged hole in a wall and landed on one cavalryman's mount. An invisible claw opened his throat, and as he sagged in his saddle, the other *chasseurs* wheeled to face him. Their rotary clockwork cannon chattered, blasting the tattoo into shreds of inky flesh and peppering the luckless Cog's mount with holes.

The guns fell silent, and the three remaining cavalrymen paused for a moment, listening. They heard nothing over the ticking of their mainsprings but the dripping of water and the occasional creak of wood as a building settled. Droplets cascaded on their faces and the lenses they had for eyes, and they didn't see the heaving mass of invisible bodies brachiating up through the town at them until it was almost too late.

The cannon cut them down, brass casings and colourless blood raining into the darkness. The cavalry advanced in step, two in front and one covering their rear. Their metal spiders descended through the town, their guns mowing down tattoos by the dozen, hurling them backwards like brightly coloured paper caught by the wind.

A trapdoor in a cellar disgorged a stream of ambushers who leaped down on the rearmost *chasseur*. His cannon blasted through them, playing from side to side. He realized too late that he hadn't left himself enough time to sidestep the falling corpses, and began to scream as they hammered into his spider, knocking a leg free, then two, then pulling it off the wall entirely. He kept screaming as he fell.

Two Cogs were left, the sergeant and one other, cutting down tattoos to their left and right. A swarm of them burst from a Door where they'd been hiding: the cannon raked them with fire that raised a cloud of splinters. When it cleared, there was nothing left of them but splashes of blood.

And then, like a switch was thrown, the attack ended. They heard the last of the casings rattle through the buildings below them, and then nothing. The spiders made their way through the silent town.

A breath of wind, like a rueful sigh. The lights around them seemed to dim.

The sergeant chattered to the other cavalryman in the Cogs' high-speed combat code. The other was silent. The sergeant tried again, and her comrade finally turned. His face was crumbling to dust.

"*Aide-moi,*" he said. The sergeant backed away in horror, raising a hand to ward him off—and then she saw her hand was full of holes like ragged lace, and as the sergeant watched, the holes grew larger.

A thousand yards above, standing on the platform of the Cogs' command tent, *Chef de Bataillon* Henriette-Marie Poinkaré, of the 31e *chasseur-à-l'araignée* regiment of *L'Armée du Puits*, surveyed the aftermath of the assault with a contraption of brass and mirrors, a horizontal periscope. The remains of the sergeant and private still clung to the wall, fragile and grey as the ash on the end of a cigar.

She collapsed the periscope and stood back from the platform's edge. She felt sick. "Any sign of the *Dédaigneuse*?"

Houellebek consulted the insides of his lenses. "Nothing. The College may have chosen to keep her in reserve," he said diplomatically.

"Protect their own lily-white arses, you mean."

Houellebek shrugged. "We still have the *Généreux*."

Poinkaré looked out at the balloon and its complement of Librarians, keeping pace with the army as they descended towards Deadbeat. "Let's hope it's enough, then."

"So what now?"

She hawked and spat. "Now I draft letters to those *chasseurs'* spouses.

Somehow I don't think *Général* Karrère will volunteer to do it." She glanced inside the brightly lit command tent.

The attack order had hardly been unexpected, but was no less bitter for that. Evidently *le Général* had seen the four little brass spiders on his campaign map that represented Poinkaré's scout unit—all that had been left of it, after the disastrous retreat from Deadbeat—and, since integrating them into the siege line would have necessitated rewriting his already-neatly-typed plan, had decided to wager them on a surprise attack. A "test of the defences." Which had probably seemed like a brilliantly bold and audacious move, not to mention a retaking of the initiative.

But then, words like "bold" and "audacious" tended to change their meaning the closer you got to the line of battle. And *le Général* wasn't the one who'd had to slap those *chasseurs* on the back and wish them well before sending them to their deaths.

But they'd known the score as well as anyone. With an infinite number of Doors out there and new threats pouring out of them all the time, sooner or later one would have your name on it.

Unless you were a general, of course.

A blur of motion coming through the advancing war machines, here then gone, there then gone again.

"The creeps," said Houellebek.

"Remind me what they were doing, again?" said Poinkaré, not looking.

"The Librarian took them out. He said he was getting reinforcements."

"Reinforcements that fit on two lizards?" Poinkaré squinted at the approaching mounts. She saw the Librarian, the creeps…and two others. There was something familiar about them.

The things that had snuck up on them were called *creeps*, or anyway that was what Essa had called them. Unless it was just an insult. She was certainly in a pretty foul mood.

Their mounts were lizards, two giant geckos with bulging black eyes and black scales that drank light, like the creeps' own suits did. As a creep had manhandled Ben out of the Door and into a harness, the gecko had twisted its head around to face him and yawned, its tongue a vivid blue rope of muscle against the wet pink of its mouth. Ben flinched, and the creep had tittered as it strapped him in beside Ella and tested the buckles, leaving Ben's feet dangling into the Well.

With Lud stuffed into a bag that hung off one lizard's saddle, they'd set off. The army had advanced downWell past their Door, so they were in the middle of the clanking, slithering mass. The lizards changed course constantly to avoid being run over, moving in a winding path that tilted Ben rapidly this way and that—now on his right side, now his left, even upside-down for stomach-churning minutes as the lizards raced over the wall on the sticky pads of their toes.

"Creeps?" he asked as Gregor, on the lizard ahead, had a muttered conversation with the grinning one.

"From the Vats," Ella replied.

"I thought the Vats just did medicine and stuff," he'd said, rubbing his wrists. He'd caught a glimpse of the thing that had bound his hands when a creep had removed it—another of those tapeworm/centipede things, like Essa's gag. His skin itched where its legs had dug in.

"Biology, is what the Vats do. Anything that creeps or crawls or oozes. It's the same when we go to war, everyone has a specialty. Cogs are the firepower, Library has the Dust, and the Vats"—one hand waved at the creeps—"are intelligence, infiltration, all that stuff."

"Ninja," said Ben, unable to prevent a grin.

She rolled her eyes.

They were headed for a huge spider with broad legs like a tarantula's and a wide, flat abdomen that extended a dozen yards out from the Well. The lizards circled it and ascended to the level of its belly, which Ben saw had a tent perched on it. Ben and Ella's gecko leaped nimbly onto the spider and a creep threw a release on his harness. Ben slithered unceremoniously off his gecko and the creep grabbed him by the back of the shirt and hauled him into the tent.

A red glow bathed the inside of the tent, coming from an odd-looking lamp on the wall. A matchstick-and-string diorama replicating Deadbeat and its surrounding stretch of Well took up most of the space, balancing on gimbals that kept it level despite the spider's shaking. A Cogs soldier with lenses for eyes was placing small brass figurines around the diorama, stopping occasionally to stare into space. The figures were spread around the town in an Ω-shaped siege line. The sleeve of the soldier's uniform ended at the elbow, and a bandage crusted with dried blood emerged from the ragged end and bound his arm all the way to the wrist.

Dangling over the diorama, suspended from the canvas ceiling, was an assemblage of gleaming arms and pincers and shining crystal eyes. They swivelled to take in the new occupants of the tent: Gregor, Essa, and now another haggard-looking Cogs officer who entered behind them.

He didn't see the bag the creep had stuffed Lud into.

"You," said the Cogs officer. She had a metal nose, and a torn silver epaulette on her shoulder.

"Oh," he said. "Hi. Sorry about escaping."

"Glad someone did," said the officer. She looked terrible, sallow with black circles under her eyes, and she held one arm stiffly across her body.

"Is this her?"

The voice came from behind Ben and made the skin on the back of his neck prickle.

"This is her," said Gregor, indicating Essa. Essa didn't react, just studied the diorama.

Carefully, Ben turned around. The thing on the wall wasn't a lamp. The glow came from a translucent ovoid embedded in a foamy lump that rippled as he looked at it and edged an inch higher. It looked like a slime mould from his biology textbook.

"Right, introductions," said Gregor. "This"—indicating the brass machine hanging from the ceiling—"is *Général-Stratège* Karrère of *L'Armée du Puits*." A few of the crystal eyes tracked them from head to toe but the General didn't say anything. "And this"—indicating the glowing egg on the wall—"is our Vats liaison, whose name is unpronounceable with the standard set of vocal cords, I'm afraid, here to coordinate with General Karrère on—"

"Rachana," said Essa.

Gregor's face went absolutely still. "Now is not the time—"

Even Ben could have told him that was the wrong word to use.

"Time? *Time?* I was trapped worldside for a *year* and now you don't have *time?* What happened to her, Gregor—"

"Essa, that's what I need to talk to you about."

"What happened to Ra, Gregor?" said Essa louder, and drew breath to repeat the question.

"It wasn't you," said Gregor to head her off. He glanced at the Cogs, who were clustered around the diorama. "And can we lower our voices, please?"

"The Vine seemed pretty sure it was me."

"I can reverse that judgment, when we return. I'm sorry about it, deeply sorry, but I needed a pretext to hold you without spreading panic about the Exile."

"It wasn't me? Can you even be sure about that?" said Essa with an edge to her voice.

"It wasn't you. It was Rachana's own Proof that did it. You know what she was researching?"

Essa nodded. "Talking through keyholes. Communicating through a closed Door, even an unripe one."

"She was…erratic, you know that. Wasn't cautious with her Chants. That was all it was."

Essa looked at him distrustfully, but didn't say anything more.

"Now if we can please—?" And the tent shuddered to a halt. Gregor looked to the doorway. "Ah. Looks like we'll be getting more room shortly, anyway."

They were in someone's bedroom. A kid's, from the look of it, or maybe just someone who liked stuffed toys. Assuming they *were* stuffed toys.

"This is weird," whispered Ben, looking around.

Houellebek shrugged. "L'Armée has taken me to stranger places," he said loudly, and Ben winced.

"What if they come back?"

Houellebek had that spaced-out look again. It occurred to Ben that he looked like someone gaming with a VR headset, and that was probably exactly what he was doing—he had some kind of AR setup in those lenses of his. "They will not," he murmured. "You saw the flag?"

There had been a blue-and-yellow flag hanging from a black iron spike above the Door, like there had been above the Door to the canyon. "What does that mean anyway?" Ben asked.

"It means L'Armée has surveyed this world. 'Safe every day until 0321,' says the flag. It is now 2763, by the True Dial of the Pewter

Abbey, of course, so we are alone. At any rate"—he nodded at Gregor and Essa, his shako bobbing—"I think your friends will be ready soon. They had better be, the attack is imminent."

He trailed off, still looking inside his lenses. With practiced ease he popped something out of the left lens's barrel, like a vinyl LP the size of a thumbnail, and slotted another one in.

Ben dug at the contents of the tin in his hand with his spoon. Houellebek had rustled up some Cogs army food, and Ben had been so hungry he'd gone through three tins of the spongy pinkish meat already.

Gregor and Essa were on the other side of the room, cross-legged on the floor back to back. Gregor had found a Librarian's robe for Essa. It made her look different, older. They hadn't managed a change of clothes for Ben, but someone had given him a Cogs infantryman's jacket, which cut the chill a little.

Whisper danced in front of Essa's eyes, and Gregor's own Ism danced in front of his. Gregor didn't have a flask like Essa, he'd just exhaled the stuff like it lived inside his lungs. Essa had rolled her eyes. "Flashy. What is it?"

"A fragment of the Thousand Sails. I'll be your Second, when you erase the Door."

Erase, not close. Creating and destroying Doors was what this was all about. A lot of Essa and Gregor's conversation had been in Library math, but Ben had gotten this much: no one had thought it was possible, but the Exile had created its own Door years ago, when it had opened up those rents in the Well. Essa had been researching the same thing, how to create a Door, at the Library. She hadn't cracked it before she'd left (why she left was something she and Gregor talked around without meeting head-on). But when she'd been stuck in Chifley, she'd finally managed to work it out.

As for Gregor: Ben had been to his share of courses and camps for "gifted" kids, and Gregor reminded him of more than a few people he had met there. The ones that thought that because they were smart, everyone else was stupid, and good for nothing but pushing around, manipulating to get what they wanted. He could see that there was pretty clearly some history between Gregor and Essa. He wasn't sure how he felt about that, or how it might be colouring his opinion of the tall Librarian. But just because he was probably jealous, that didn't mean Gregor *wasn't* an arrogant shit.

Anyway, his plan was…here was where Ben's grip really started slipping off the half-math half-Creole they were speaking, but Gregor apparently thought the same technique Essa had used to create her Door could be used to cancel out the Exile's, set up some kind of interference pattern that would prevent it from making another.

The Cogs and Vats were going to launch an attack on Deadbeat, and in the confusion, Essa, Gregor and the creeps were going straight for that huge stone Door, to trap the Exile behind it for good.

And Ben was going home.

He checked his laptop before he shut it down (thirty-two percent, said the battery counter). He'd had to show Houellebek its timer, so the soldier could calculate how long it would take to get Ben back to his Door. He'd make it, as it turned out. Just.

Whisper and Gregor's dust (it wasn't a whole Ism like Whisper was, but a fragment of one) had merged in a cloud above their heads, and now, before Ben could close the laptop, a tendril of that cloud extended lightning-fast towards Ben, and flicked curiously through the laptop. The screen flared white for a moment. "Hey!" said Ben, snatching it away, but the tendril had already withdrawn.

And now Houellebek was leaning out the Door, looking up. Gesturing for Ben to come over. His ride was here.

The army had a balloon, the one Ben had seen before the creeps had snuck up on them. It hovered in the Well a few hundred yards away. Its wooden gondola looked like a sailing ship, and there were Librarians on board to support the invasion. The one that lowered itself outside his Door wasn't nearly as big, its gondola barely a dinghy.

It stopped a few yards from the Well, the Cogs soldier inside expertly manipulating the hissing gas cylinder that provided the flame, bringing it level with the Door. She threw something at them, a lead weight at the end of a line. Houellebek neatly caught it and drew a wood-and-rope bridge from the dinghy across to the Door.

"Now, if you please," he said. "You will want to be well clear when the attack begins."

"What about Lud?" asked Ben.

"The Apostate? It will be joining the attack, in return for which the Cogs will grant it special dispensation for its heretical and achronological beliefs. Although perhaps I am misspeaking, by implying it had a choice."

Lud had been drafted. Ben didn't think it'd be dealing with it that well. "You're going to win, right?" he asked. "They're going to be all right?"

"Yes." He reflected. "And possibly. Respectively."

"I know you can't be sure, I know that, but—"

"This is *L'Armée du Puits,*" said Houellebek, like that was an explanation. Ben stared at him and he shrugged. "We win always. We may have to grind flat every inch of Well we take, but we win. Victory, in L'Armée doctrine, meaning at least one Cog is standing when all the other side have fallen."

That was not reassuring. "Well, can I say—" said Ben, but Houellebek was already ushering him onto the swinging bridge to the balloon. He had time for one backwards glance at Essa, still sharing a trance with with Gregor, and then he needed both hands and his eyes on the bridge.

"How long?" he asked the soldier as she rolled up the bridge he'd used and stowed it under the gondola's deck. She raised her hands and said something in the clacking Cogs language—*no Creole*. Ben hoped she knew which Door they were heading to.

The balloon swayed and drifted along the Well. They were taking a looping path around Deadbeat that stayed well clear of the town.

The Cogs siege line spread itself out around them. Below, the fortifications were going up, horizontal walls that doubled as walkways, anchored to the Well with black iron spikes and cables strung through Doors. Above them, tiny clockwork trilobites were scuttling along the wall dragging paintbrushes behind them, drawing out the lines that future emplacements would follow. The army itself was like a restless snake bowed around Deadbeat, twitching and shivering as all those crawlers and troop carriers and cannon rearranged themselves, one neatly slipping into the gap another had left behind.

That was what Ben was going back to. Back to playing Tetris with his family and his life, trying to keep things together. Only he wasn't a Cog, and it wasn't going to work.

He didn't even know if making his court date was going to make a difference. He'd disappeared for a few days—that probably wasn't going to look all that good to the judge.

Something made him get his laptop out as the Cogs soldier reached up to adjust the gas burner. They were drifting past a huge Cogs war machine on ten thick legs, bristling with gleaming cannon.

Twenty-eight percent. There was a new icon sitting in the middle of his desktop. The name was a garble of ones and zeroes run through Unicode—Chinese, Sanskrit, Cyrillic, all mashed together. Probably that red cloud had left it there when it whipped out at his laptop.

When he'd seen Essa for the last time.

He was sick of this. He should just pitch the laptop out of the gondola, aim for Deadbeat maybe, see if he could hit a tattoo.

Instead he clicked on the new file.

A second and a half later, he snapped the laptop shut, stuffed it into his bag, buckled the bag, then stood up and leaped out of the gondola.

CHAPTER TWENTY-TWO

Gregor's hands twist, and a streamer of dust from the tiny cloud circling his wrist streaks down the narrow lane of sand towards his opponent, whose own cloud lashes out to stop it. The shock drives the opponent to his knees, and the chime from the judge's pavilion indicates a hit. It's Gregor's third, and the duel is over.

Scattered applause from the scattered crowd in the Spire Gardens. Dueling is a vestige. The Spires keep up their tournament for tradition's sake, but its days are numbered.

Gregor is naked to the waist and gleaming with sweat, and as he returns to his bench he accepts a towel from his second and presses it to his face. His second is some guy from the Spires that Essa doesn't know.

Essa sits at the end of the bench, watching the patterns play through Whisper as she darts around her head, offering an occasional comment via a precise gesture of her hands. She hasn't looked up at the duel once.

A Librarian passes the bench. "Well *done*, Gregor. Breath of Dust, what a duel," he says cheerily.

Gregor acknowledges him with a wave. Essa rolls her eyes. "'Breath of *Dust*'," she mimics as he passes from earshot.

"Pyotr is a little old-fashioned."

"He's *our age*. Pretentious, is what he is."

"Perhaps a little over-conscious of the traditions we uphold. You have to accept some of that, in the Spires." He slings the towel onto the bench, shrugs on his robe.

"Do I."

"It's just ceremony. Like the duel itself. It doesn't have to define you—"

Essa isn't looking at him. "I'm not going, Gregor."

He clenches his jaw. "It's just a banquet, Essa. You're not going to *compromise* yourself. You've been in the Spires a month, do you feel compromised?"

"Would I, if I was? I'm going back to the rooms." She never calls them *his* rooms. "Back to work. I—oh no."

A commotion beyond the dueling lane. Someone is coming into the Gardens, fighting the flow of the crowd as they leave. Someone stumbles, disturbing the flow, and they can hear a slurred voice overapologizing.

Essa gets up, then sits down again. The Gardens only have the one entrance and there's nowhere to go.

"You should have an end to it, Essa," murmurs Gregor. She shoots him a glance brilliant with hate. Then Rachana is there. She's carrying a large cloth bag, weighing her down on one side.

"Where are you going, Ess? Sorry, did I not give you a chance to run? Again?"

There's a tremor in Rachana's translucent hands, and the pulse of life inside her seems subtly out of sync. *Pills again?* Essa wonders. Librarians are used to the panoply of neurological weirdnesses that comes from Communing too closely with Isms, but there's something *off* about this that Essa hasn't seen before.

Gregor's second is talking with a few older Librarians, their Isms dancing between them, replaying Gregor's duel as they offer commentary.

Now he sees Rachana, who shouldn't even be in the Spires, let alone at Gregor's bench. He starts for her, but Gregor waves him off.

"What are you doing, Ra?" asks Essa.

"I'm working. That's what I'm doing." She's talking to Gregor now. "I'm cracking it, you know."

"I'm happy for you, Rachana—"

"I'm cracking it, and I don't need you. It didn't start going wrong until I took your help anyway. Don't need your *Group*. Your *rooms*. Your *bed*." She's back to looking at Essa.

Essa looks away, but the only thing to see is the knot of onlookers drawn by Rachana's raised voice. Their eyes are bright, greedily taking in the drama. Essa wonders who they are. Who she is.

"Ra, you can call me whatever you want, don't—just don't be a child. Meet me in the High Gardens?" That's a mistake, she knows it as soon as she says it; the High Gardens were the setting for any number of their trysts. "Send me a message, we can—"

Rachana bursts into harsh peals of laughter. "Send a *message*. Set up a *meeting*. You are so full of shit, Ess. Have fun with Gregor, until he gets tired of you. Oh, here." She tries to fling the sack at Essa but her hand is shaking too badly and it flops to the ground. "Your clothes. That you never picked up. You—"

She pauses for a second. Her violet eyes lose focus. She shakes her head abruptly and turns away, stumbles for the exit.

Gregor turns to Essa but her hand is already up in his face. "*Don't.*" She watches Rachana go, and when enough time has passed that she knows she won't meet her outside, she leaves too, stopping only to snap something at a nearby Servitor, who hustles to pick up the cloth bag and dispose of it.

Chapter Twenty-Three

The gondola swung wildly as the Cogs soldier grabbed for him with a strangled shout, but Ben was already lunging through the void. He hit the curved brass surface of the war machine and started sliding off, but his foot came down on one of its many gun barrels and he was able to grab the top rung of a ladder that ran down the thing's flank.

At the bottom of the ladder was the thing's head. A hatch was unscrewing itself, someone wanting to ask him what the hell he was doing, probably. He leaped from the machine before he had to answer, because he wasn't at all sure himself.

He didn't entirely remember what had happened when he opened that mystery file. A pattern, like the one he'd seen when Whisper had interfaced with the laptop, but different, more like the symbol Essa had shown him after he'd had his shot, the one that had made Creole flower in his brain. An urge. A certainty.

He had to see Essa. He had to tell her something.

He didn't know what.

His memory kept flickering in and out, which was just as well, because if he'd been present for half of the stuff he was doing, he'd have frozen with fear. The army was so tightly packed it wasn't even much of a jump from one machine to another, but missing his footing even once would have sent him falling down into Deadbeat. Fortunately this was a Cogs part of the siege line; he didn't want to be crawling all over anything from the Vats.

Then he was climbing down past that bedroom Door, where the creeps were strapping Gregor into one of the lizards' harnesses.

Ben hung back. Looking at Gregor, he felt a surge of anxiety, paranoia almost. An effect of whatever bomb had gone off in his brain just now.

The lizard, with Gregor and creeps on board, scuttled away from the Door, and now the other lizard crawled over, two creeps hanging off it, and Essa stepped out of the door and down into her harness.

"Essa!" he yelled as he leaned out and grabbed the Door.

"*Ben?*"

The creeps with her had bulbous compound eyes, like an insect's. One of them, sporting serrated mandibles instead of a lower jaw, drew a sinuously curved blade, but Essa waved it off. She was furious. "Red-Eyed Lady, Ben, what the hell do you think you're doing?"

"I have to—" He stopped. He didn't *know* what he had to do. He just remembered the pattern—

The pattern. He fumbled at his messenger bag.

"Get him out of here," Essa was saying to the creep, "don't hurt him but—"

Then Ben had his laptop open and Essa was looking into that pulsing pattern.

Essa stared at it wide-eyed. Then she hissed, "*Gregor.*" She turned to the insect-eyed creeps. "Are you Vats? Are you here serving the Vats? Or did Gregor buy you off, are you his pets instead?"

The creep grinned.

"If you're Gregor's, you might as well cut our heads off right now, because we're most likely going to try to stop him. We might need your help. You might have to cut up those friends of yours."

The one with a jaw fingered his matte black blade for a moment, then shrugged, said something in its oleaginous voice.

"Good," said Essa. "Ben? I think the Well is in terrible, terrible danger, and I have no idea how I'm going to save it but I'm going to try. I'll need all the help I can get, so will you come with me? It'll almost certainly mean both our deaths. Also, I'm going to kill that shit Gregor."

"You should have led with that," said Ben. "I'm in."

Essa nodded. Despite the jokes, she looked as sick as he felt. She turned to the creep. "Buckle my friend in. He comes too."

They'd left the siege line behind, arcing out towards a pale blue glow somewhere beyond Deadbeat. He could see the lights of the town in the distance—they twinkled peacefully in the dark, but Ben remembered the last time he'd seen them, amid the screams and the hissing of invisible killers.

He could hear intermittent hollow explosions, shots from the siege line. Softening Deadbeat up, maybe, before the attack. They trailed off and silence fell as the glow became brighter, resolved itself into the mushroom forest he'd seen on their way to the Committee chamber. It looked like they were going to climb through it, although he didn't see how it helped them sneak up on the town, since they'd still need to go through the siege line.

The mushrooms' spreading caps blocked out the Well. Ben felt everyone relax a little. The stalks creaked in the breeze, and tiny things skittered through the luminous licheny undergrowth.

Dark humped shapes stood among the fungi, irregularities protruding from the Well, their jagged edges smoothed by a nubbly carpet of glowing toadstools. They were foundations, the stubs of immense beams and girders made from the same stuff as Essa's piton and Lud's claws, "black iron" she'd called it. He reached out and brushed a clump of mushrooms from the broken end of a strut; underneath, it was smooth and seemingly new, unpainted but without a hint of rust.

"What is it?" he whispered under the noise of the vertical forest. He looked at Essa and was astonished to see tears on her face, shining tracks reflecting the weird blue light.

"The Fourth Power," she said hollowly, looking up at the ruins. "The Eisenwelt. What's left of it."

Ben was about to ask what that meant when something caught his eye above them. A huge fleshy body swayed through the luminous trunks, keeping pace with them on spindly legs. Ben's eyes fixed on the blind half-formed head swinging from side to side on its serpentine neck before he lost sight of it among the stalks. A thin bleat that made his throat close in remembered terror sounded through the forest, but it had come from below them, opposite the one he'd seen. How many skulkers were sharing the forest with them?

"Essa," he whispered. "I think—"

"I know," she murmured, her breath soft on his ear, making the hairs at the back of his neck prickle. She jerked her head at the creeps. "I think they're counting on it."

"Essa, what are we doing?"

"Whisper saw something, when she was Communing with Gregor's Ism. He's not going to erase the Door."

"What about saving the Well?"

Essa shook her head. "I don't know what he's thinking. Don't much care. Whisper saw…wait." Her fists clenched. "Get your head down."

Ben ducked. They could see Gregor's lizard up ahead, and he turned, a silhouette against the pale glow of the mushroom stalks, to check Essa was with him. Essa gave him a thumbs-up.

Lights, shining between the mushrooms—at first just the occasional glimmer, then longer glimpses, gaslight dimming the ethereal blue. One of the creeps on Gregor's lizard reached silently into a pouch at its waist and withdrew a square of glossy plastic that it slit open with its blade. Instantly, the air was full of a rich rotting scent that made Ben gag and clap a hand over his mouth.

Another bleat, louder and closer, a note of urgency in it. All around them, the sound of things stirring to life.

Now Essa got a whiff of whatever it was in the bag and began to cough, loudly, but by then the creep had drawn his arm back and was whipping the bag around, pitching it like a baseball. Essa followed it with her eyes, and even while she was spluttering she managed to say "Oh no, you *wouldn't!*" and—

A Cog sprawled on one of Deadbeat's boardwalks in a sticky puddle of blood. A cloud of tiny flies hovered over the corpse, landing on the body a few at a time to feed.

The body shook. The insects fled. The corpse, suddenly animated, rose into the air, arms dangling like a marionette's, feet dragging through the blood. It made its way to the edge of the boardwalk, limbs flopping, then its feet left the floor and it swung through the air once, twice, and pitched into the darkness as the invisible things carrying it hurled it into the Well.

Poinkaré watched it through her field glasses as it fell, losing the illusion of animation and becoming just a corpse. The netting below Deadbeat had been shredded during the tattoos' invasion, and the body tumbled through the ragged remains and fell towards the siege line. The line had its own netting up, black iron pickets driven into the wall with wire mesh strung between them, and now the dead Cog landed on it, bounced, lay still. A couple of infantrymen hauled it down, casting worried glances upwards, and carried it away, towards the Vats HQ. For dissection, presumably, although who knew what they would learn from it that they hadn't from the last dozen.

Poinkaré lowered the glasses and rubbed her eyes. She stood on a narrow walkway resting on black iron pegs hammered into the wall, that snaked and switchbacked through the Cogs positions. Below and to her right was the Vats tent, a bulge of living skin clinging to the wall, veined and pulsing slowly. The Dial knew what they did in there; certainly no useful information had come out of it, nothing that had reached Poinkaré anyway.

The attack was due shortly. The Librarian, Gregor, was to give the signal, although they had been vague on what the signal would be. It didn't matter to Poinkaré; after her *chasseurs* had been butchered, she was an officer without troops. She was that least useful element of any campaign: the *observer*.

The *Généreux* was drifting closer to the town, its balloon the dull red of a dying star. As it reached eye level, Poinkaré could see the gondola's deck and the black-robed figures lining the rails. Flames roared from the burner, lighting the whole scene up—they were Librarians, all shapes and sizes, humans and machines and tall skeletal things and man-sized slugs, each with a silver censer on a long chain. A breeze picked up, carried their voices; they were chanting, a steady deep drone. They were here to neutralize whatever the thing in Deadbeat—the Exile, they said, although Poinkaré could hardly believe it—had used on her troops. She hoped they knew what they were doing.

Beyond the siege line, Poinkaré saw the mushroom stalks bending and swaying, heard a low rumble that rose to a roar, thin shrieking over the top of it. Uprooted fungi began to rain into the Well.

Then the first skulker broke from the forest.

"*Tabarnak vert,*" swore Poinkaré, forgetting her adopted religion for a moment, and started yelling for the bugler.

Ben held on to his harness until the tendons in his hands creaked. The lizard rushed out of the forest and into the open at a pace that made the world a blur. The stampede was on in earnest, skulkers ahead and behind, above and below them, their bleats turning into thin theremin wails as they caught the scent of whatever the creep had thrown. The lizards couldn't keep up, they were falling back into the herd. Some of the skulkers were *huge*, three times as big as the one in the gym. Four. Essa, hanging on beside him, was staring intently ahead of them, at Gregor's lizard.

Ben yelled at her, "*Was that bait?*" Not much point in keeping quiet now.

"*Kind of!*" Essa screamed back.

"*What?*"

She shook her head. "*They don't want to eat it! They want to have sex with it!*" Seeing his face, she added, "*You asked!*"

The creeps were grinning wider, faces splitting open to show mouthfuls of shark teeth, blades like bizarre surgical instruments in their long-fingered hands. Over the thunder of the stampede, Ben could hear the crackle of gunfire. Then a bugle, the tune cutting in and out like whoever was playing it was running like hell at the same time. The Cogs siege line loomed up ahead of them, soldiers turning surprised faces in their direction; evidently they hadn't been told what Gregor had been planning. Some raised muskets, a few even managed to get a shot off, and then they were flinging themselves into the nearest Door as the skulkers stampeded over them, the lizards close behind.

Flags were waving all along the siege line. Muzzle flashes like short-lived constellations spangled the darkness of the Well, and puffs of dusts bloomed in Deadbeat where the shots landed. A couple of skulkers exploded as shells hit them, filling the air with black spores. Ben felt the texture of the air change as he breathed them in. He hoped his shot was still working.

Now the front line of skulkers reached the town, splintering wood and tearing metal as they crashed into the buildings on the outskirts. Screams and hisses rose up into the Well as debris cascaded down.

Gregor's lizard piled into the wreckage after the skulkers, and their own lizard followed. The jagged end of a plank swept past Ben so close he felt the breeze on his face as they angled down, descending the wall. The creeps sprang from their backs and fanned out, leaping and loping through the town, blades whickering through the air and slicing through invisible bodies. The lizards scampered on; Ben hoped they knew where they were going. Essa had Whisper out, spiralling around her wrist, and now she barked a couple of syllables and a tattoo came apart in an explosion of colourless blood. Ahead of them, Gregor's own red dust split into dozens of tendrils that sliced through anything they touched.

They crossed a boardwalk and plunged into a cloud of pale smoke. Ben's skin was instantly slick with cold sweat, but the Boiling Dust was retreating before them, thinning—streamers of red dust were coming from somewhere out in the Well, and where they met the Dust, it crackled with lightning and rained out of the air as soot. His eyes tracked the streamers back to their source and he caught a glimpse of that huge balloon floating just beyond the town.

He looked back around just in time to see Gregor's lizard speeding through a gap between two buildings. Their own had just followed, creeps regrouping around it, when the building's windows and doorways boiled with floating ink. An ambush.

A swarm of tattoos descended on them. One of them slammed the mandibled creep sideways into a wall, and invisible jaws tore its throat out. Black blood fountained and coated the tattoo's face—for an instant Ben saw it, almost human but twisted and reptilian with huge bulbous eyes. The other insect-eyed creep stabbed and sliced, knife arm a blur, and then, impossibly, they were through.

"Follow him!" Essa yelled to the creep, who nodded. The great stone Door loomed ahead of them, and then it was behind them and receding fast as they climbed the Well, on the heels of Gregor's lizard, until they were facing the canted Door of the Committee chamber.

Two of the creeps were flanking the Door, holding off a swarm of tattoos. A blur of invisible bodies encroached on the creeps like mist as they hacked and sliced. Gregor was already off the lizard and leaping through the Door, his black robe flapping, creeps falling in behind. Ben didn't realise they'd stopped until he felt Essa yanking on the buckles of his harness. She was pulling at him, yelling *"Come on!"*, and he climbed awkwardly over the lizard after her. And then they were inside.

Chapter Twenty-Four

The wake in the High Gardens is a formality, and the Servitors with trays of drinks, paid for by Gregor, outnumber the participants. Essa stands at the parapet, looking at a cloud drifting by.

She hears Gregor approaching but doesn't turn around.

"Is this where she did it?"

"Essa," says Gregor.

"They just said she jumped. Actually, they said she fell, but they weren't there."

"Essa—"

"No one was there."

"Essa, do you think I'd have her wake here if it was?"

"I have no idea why you do what you do. What do you want, Gregor?"

"I haven't seen you since it happened. Where have you been sleeping?"

"Around. I've been sleeping around." She cranes her neck to follow the cloud as it drifts behind a tower.

Gregor takes a moment. "Are you coming back to the Spires?"

Essa says nothing.

"Our presentation before the Mandala is next week, and the Proof's not done. I've spent quite a bit of social capital to arrange this. Postponing it now would not look—"

"I'm leaving."

Gregor bites down on his first response, then carefully chooses another. "I need you, Essa. You're the only one who can take us the rest of the way. I'm sorry about Rachana, deeply sorry, but this is bigger than her. This Proof is going to change the Well, and we don't just need the Proof itself, we need to be ready to take advantage of the opportunity—"

Essa whirls, her robe flaring. "Take *advantage*."

Gregor backs up, his hands raised, realizes he's holding a drink in one of them and sets it down on a bench. "That was a poor choice of words."

"I'm done. I am done and disgusted with the whole thing. You, the Spires, the Library. Me."

"We have...additional resources," says Gregor, speaking rapidly. "A new source in the Stacks. If you can take a look—"

"You look," says Essa. "Do whatever you want with it with the work. It's yours. Give me something to sign, I'll sign it right here." She sketches a prompt in the sand of the parapet and gestures, inviting him to fill it in.

"You're running. Would Rachana want you to do this? Run again?" says Gregor.

Essa gasps. For a moment, they just stand there facing each other. Then Essa giggles, the high-pitched sound of something taut and ready to snap.

"How long have you had that in your pocket, Gregor? Saving it for an emergency? Well, at least I know you don't have anything more to say to me. Glass yourself, Gregor. I'm going Wellside. I'm going to show Whisper the worlds like I should have done months ago. Like I should have done with Ra—"

Then she's weeping, great heaving sobs. She doesn't run, though. She walks, weeping, to the door of the Gardens, and Gregor doesn't follow. He takes a deep breath and lets it out gently, centering himself. Then he picks up his glass and hurls it over the parapet, roaring. No one sees him. All the other guests have left.

Chapter Twenty-Five

One of Gregor's creeps led the way, its scalpel stabbing and sweeping through the tattoos that tried to hold the corridor. Gregor strolled along after it, his other creep close behind.

Essa followed him, Ben and the insect-eyed creep bringing up the rear. The creep was the only thing between Ben's shoulder blades and a horde of monsters, and he couldn't help glancing over his shoulder every couple of steps. He kept stumbling as he put his feet down on invisible corpses.

A blurred silhouette, chest and scalp elaborately patterned in red ink, lunged through a door, holding a length of pipe overhead ready to bring down on Gregor's head. Instead it went reeling backwards, the patterns falling apart as its head fell off and rolled along the tilted floor.

"That's enough," Gregor was saying. "That's enough. I think we've made our point, don't you?" Ben didn't think he was saying it to the creep.

"*Gregor!*" Essa bellowed.

Gregor turned. "Essa, thank goodness. You made it."

Essa hissed a command, her fingers twisting, and Whisper leaped out of her flask, forming around Ben and Essa in a fast-turning circle.

Gregor shook his head. "No need for that. Listen, Essa—"

"What happened to Ra, Gregor?"

Gregor stared.

"You have her Proof, in that Ism of yours. Whisper found it. The Proof you said she couldn't crack. The Proof she went mad for. Died for. *You had it all along.*"

Gregor exhaled, and now his own Ism was in the air. It and Whisper feinted at each other, lighting crackling between them.

"So why?" continued Essa, bearing down on him remorselessly. "Why tell her she failed when you knew what it would do to her? Why did you want to talk through keyholes? Who did you want to talk *to*?"

Gregor took a step backwards.

Essa drew a deep breath. "*Who?*" she screamed.

A voice from inside the Committee chamber, a voice that covered Ben in gooseflesh.

"Enough of this. All of you. Come."

They stood there silently in the doorway, Ben and Essa, Gregor and the creeps, looking into the great round Committee chamber.

Outside, the ocean was shrouded in twilight. A last glimmer of reflected sunlight from the clouds cast just enough light to see by.

For a moment Ben thought the Committee, hanging in their cages around the machine, had been replaced. Then he recognised the little girl nearest the door, and the old woman next to her. This *was* the same Committee, just…changed.

Their skin was grey, cracked like dried hardpan, sloughing off in places to reveal white bone. Their hair littered the floor, and their eyes were like glass balls full of grey smoke. A low squalling and screeching filled the chamber. The machine that held them was out of phase, gears grinding, metal warping, slowly shaking itself apart.

One after another, the Committee raised their heads. Despite the creeps fanning out into the room, soaked in colourless gore up to the elbows, blades dripping steadily onto the floor, they didn't seem at all alarmed.

"So," the Committee said, through split and bleeding lips, "the Library is here."

Gregor surveyed the room. "You speak for the Exile?"

"We are the Exile, or a part of it. Or it is a part of us. We are not sure." Their voices were harsh, broken. "You are the one who sent the message?"

"Oh, no," said Essa. "Oh, Gregor."

"'Do whatever you want with the work,' that's what you said, Essa. So I did," said Gregor. "And now you can join me. You can be part of this."

"What did you do?" Essa shook her head. "Gregor, what did you *do*?"

"Save the Well," said Gregor. "That's what I'm going to do." He'd dropped that urbane act of his entirely. Sweat was beading on his circuitry and his voice was tight.

"Which is our host?" said the Committee. They spoke haltingly, like they were unfamiliar with their own vocal cords.

Gregor turned to them. "Very realistic show you put on, out there," he said. "But I think you've made your point. It's about time to beat your retreat."

"Which is our host?"

"What do they mean, 'host'?" said Ben.

"One moment, please," Gregor told the Committee.

"No," said the Committee in their alien voice.

"We need to prepare ourselves. To act as host. Please."

The Committee stirred, moaned, but said nothing.

Gregor stepped close to Essa, and Whisper fanned out in front of her in a razor-edged shield that almost took the tip of his nose off. Gregor's creeps stepped up beside him, knives out, and he waved them back.

He spoke low and fast, nothing like his earlier drawl. "Right: yes, I've been talking to the Exile; yes, I betrayed Rachana to do it; yes, I was the one who slammed the Door on you and left you in that shitty little world." He glanced at Ben. "No offence."

It was Ben's turn to step forward, Essa's to wave him back.

"It was the only way to light a fire under you, get you to finish your Proof. I had to do it. I had to keep it secret. If the Spires knew I was speaking to the Exile—"

"They wouldn't let you climb any higher. Because that's what you're about, isn't it? Climbing the Spires and just...*squatting* there at the top, like a *toad*. That's about as far as your imagination goes, isn't it? Ra and I *cared* about each other."

"And look where that got you."

Essa choked.

"Now just *listen*, Essa, for once in your life." A rivulet of sweat trickled down Gregor's temple. "I've put myself at considerable risk to arrange all this. Not just for my own benefit. For everyone's. Literally everyone's.

"All the people we lost, all the worlds we lost, all the havoc the Exile wreaked on the Well, and no one, not one person, ever asked *why. Why* it had done it. They conjectured, they postulated, but no one just asked. I asked. And you know what it told me? It told me something's *coming*."

Another moan from the circle of decaying Cogs. Gregor glanced at it, then back to Essa, speaking faster and more urgently. "As soon as our friend there loses patience, we're going to have to make a choice. So: something's coming to the Well, and soon. We got a taste of it the first time the Exile got loose. Those things in the cracks, moving. They come from somewhere else. Not the Well, not the worlds. Another place. Whatever they are, they know about the Well and they're coming for us."

"To do what?"

"Essa, *please.*" Another frightened glance over his shoulder at the restless Committee. "Nothing pleasant, all right? And the Exile was trying to fight them off. Perhaps it would even have succeeded, but we broke it and trapped it on a dead world instead. But those things in the cracks are coming for us, they are *appallingly* dangerous, and the Exile knows how to stop them. Or it does now. Your Proof filled in the final gaps. And Essa? It's not going to be like it was before. No chaos of Doors, no cracks in the Well, no danger. A simple operation. But the Exile needs a host. It needs someone it can Bind to carry this out."

"What about the Committee?" asked Ben.

Gregor waved him off. "Please. Just look at them. It needs someone who knows what they're doing. A Librarian." He ran a hand over his gold-inlaid scalp.

"And that'd be you."

"*No.* That's what I'm saying. Look: it's *your* Proof the Exile will be using. You know it better than anyone. And Essa...anyone who plays host to the Exile will wield *terrible* power. I don't...I don't trust myself with it."

Essa was already drawing breath for a retort, but at this last from Gregor, it died in her throat.

"I'm ambitious, you've pointed that out to me enough times. With that kind of power...I can't be sure what I'd do." Gregor looked at Essa beseechingly. "I know you, though. You never trusted power. The fact that I had to lie to you to even get you here is proof of that. You can do this, for the sake of the Well, and relinquish it afterwards before you destroy yourself. You can walk away. It's what you do.

"If this is to be done, it has to be done *now*. You host the Exile Wellside, it does the necessary, the Exile retreats behind the Door which we then erase, just like everyone out there"—he swept out an arm, taking in Deadbeat and the armies beyond it—"assumes the plan was all along. The Exile grows a Door to wherever it likes, a billion miles downWell, and we'll never see it again."

"You announce you've personally defeated the Exile and saved the Well, and you can write your own ticket from there on."

"*We* can, Essa. You can do it with me."

Essa stared at him. Then she started to laugh.

"Enough," slurred the Committee. "Bring the host to us. Now."

Gregor's brow furrowed. "What are you *doing?*"

"Almost had me. I admit it. Almost. But you? *Share* anything? Get glassed."

Gregor snarled, that pleading look gone in an instant. He grabbed Essa's arm, pushed her towards the Committee. The Committee raised their heads, dropped their jaws, and churning white dust fountained out of their mouths.

Everything happened very quickly after that.

Whisper was the first to act, flying into Gregor's face, a miniature thunderstorm playing around his head as she did battle with his Ism. Gregor grunted and let go of Essa as his hands flew to his face, just as Ben stepped up and shoved him from behind and he went tumbling into the Committee's machine.

The white dust surrounded him, coated his circuitry, swirled in his face. Whisper fled, just before Gregor's Ism flared and rained on the floor in a shower of glass. "Wait," Gregor was saying, "*wait*," but the cloud around him kept thickening. One of the Committee burst, crumbling to a dull grey powder. In the white cloud, black lightning arced, like cracks in the fabric of the world.

Essa and Ben backed up, step by step, as unobtrusively as possible. Whisper was circling in front of Essa and she passed a hand through her, watched her eddy. "Oh no. Oh, Whisper."

"Is she all right?" asked Ben, keeping his voice low.

"No. That Ism of his tore the guts right out of her." Essa bit her lip. "We have to fix this, Whisper, if we're going to get out of here."

Whisper contracted, shivered.

"Oh my baby, I *know*, I know, but we need you. I'm so sorry, but you have to be strong. Be strong for me now."

She held her hand inside the cloud of dust, sparks crackling around it. She bit her lip harder, and blood trickled down her chin. A surge of electricity ran through the cloud, Essa gasped in pain, and part of Whisper fell out of the air, grains of glass rattling on the floor to mingle with the remains of Gregor's Ism.

Essa took a shuddering breath, then stood straighter, Whisper following the contours of her hand like a red gauntlet. "*Right*," she snarled, then paused.

Gregor hadn't moved. He looked like Essa had on the Vine, every muscle locked up, the tendons in his neck standing out. The white dust reached for him and with effort he managed to thrust his hands out, warding it off, but it was inexorable. "Wait," he kept saying, his tone almost casual, "just wait a moment—"

The dust lunged for him.

Ben waited for him to fall apart, but whatever this was, it wasn't what the Exile had unleashed on Deadbeat. It blasted into Gregor's nose, his mouth, his ears. Gregor drew a hitching breath and *screamed*.

Ben had thought the creeps with Gregor would have tried to stop them, but evidently the Vats assassins had decided that things were too messed up to stick around for. They were heading for the door of the Committee chamber when a streamer of smoke lashed out of the white cloud and took two of their heads clean off.

One made it out, and he swiftly outpaced Ben and Essa as they ran down the corridor outside. He was almost Wellside when tattoos came boiling out of a side door and fell on him. The creep had a knife out, hacking away, and even managed a few steps' progress before they bore him down, filling the corridor with a splatter of overlapping ink. Invisible fists pummelled the writhing creep's skull and torso. They went *thud* at first, then they went *splat*.

"Stop."

Ben and Ella had already stopped, there was no way out, and now they turned to see who'd spoken. It was Gregor, or it had been. He held himself differently, like he wasn't in charge of his muscles anymore.

The tattoos were edging towards Ben and Essa. "No," said Gregor's voice, and they backed off.

He smiled so wide his lips cracked and bled. "Not yet," he said. "I want them to see this. I want *her* to see it."

"See what?" Essa said.

From all around Deadbeat, the artillery volleyed and volleyed again, smashing holes in roofs and walls, chewing at the town's edges like a plague of oversized mice. The flank Poinkaré was on had taken a little time to join in—they'd needed to regroup after the skulker stampede had sent them scurrying into any Door that would open. She *very* much wanted to know whose idea that had been. Presumably the line had not been informed to preserve the element of surprise, and that part had worked just fine, she had to admit. That part had worked *very* well.

They were reforming now, though, and their own guns' voices joined the crashing chorus. The tattoos had tried a couple of sallies against the line, and the line had thrown them back decisively, chewed to pieces by the Cogs' cannon and poisoned, liquefied, and incinerated by the Vats' hellish living artillery.

Poinkaré had only half an eye for all that. She was looking for the stuff that had eaten her *chasseurs* the way locusts devoured a field. Then she saw it, questing out at the line, and a fist of ice seized her guts—but at that moment she heard the singing.

A jet of flame lit up the *Généreux*'s balloon as it rose up over the town. A sonorous chant rose from the black-robed figures on its deck, as they swung their censers. The metal globes spilled red clouds of dust, illuminated by tiny flashes of lightning. It mingled in the air off the *Généreux*'s port side, then braided itself into thick streams that all at once were streaking out into the Well, down towards Deadbeat.

Poinkaré raised her telescope, focused it with trembling fingers. The Librarians' dust was invading the town, and the pale stuff gave way before it. The tendril she'd been looking at didn't even make it halfway to the siege line before it broke up and rained downWell. Shakily, she released a breath she hadn't known she'd been holding.

It was working.

They were winning.

She couldn't even see any tattoos now, but the guns kept hammering at the town. She and Houellebek had found each other after he'd dispatched the Librarian's boyfriend, or pet, or whatever he was, back home. Now she grabbed his arm.

"That's chainshot. They're firing chain."

They could heard the whistling as the chains flew through the air, the deep twanging as they severed the town's rigging. It was putting more weight on the massive steel stays, and at least one of them was looking a little frayed.

"Who the hell is doing that?" she muttered. Houellebek looked at nothing as he scanned the order of battle he'd loaded into his lenses, but the answer didn't really matter; Poinkaré had no authority to order them to stop. She hoped someone did, and would use it. Deadbeat had expanded fast in anticipation of exploiting their new world, and she doubted the foundations had been adequately surveyed before all the new construction. Lose one cable, and who knew what would happen.

Now came one of those odd lulls that swept a battlefield, everyone reloading at the same time. Without warning, coils of crimson spiralled out from the town into the Well. Heads all along the line turned to follow it: the Librarians' dust, returning to the *Généreux*. The timbre of their chanting changed, voices raised in exaltation as they held the censers up to receive it.

Houellebek's lenses clicked as he looked up. Poinkaré brought up her telescope. The Dust looked different somehow. Darker.

She said "What—" and then "—no. *No.*"

It wasn't their dust. It was darker, the colour of a fresh bruise, and the flashes inside it were the colour of blood. The Librarians' chant began to falter.

It looked like it was heading for the gondola and the censers, but at the last moment it reared up over the balloon, forming a roiling, curving mass reaching out either side to flank it, like a cresting wave or the hood of a cobra.

"*No!*" Poinkaré roared.

The wave broke. The Dust rolled over the balloon and where it passed, the cloth skin bubbled like blistering flesh. Long rents appeared in the balloon's surface, their edges fluttering as hot air rushed out and upWell, rippling the Doorlight above. Hatches slammed open and sailors rushed up onto the deck, climbing up the rigging with foot-long needles in their teeth, carrying spools of thread. The balloon suddenly lurched and a few lost their grip, wailing as they fell. The Librarians staggered against each other, the chant falling apart into a babble of panicked voices.

The red flame roared, holding the balloon steady for a moment, then sputtered and went out. The ship lurched again and a Librarian fell, its voice adding to the chorus of screams.

Houellebek was rooted to the spot, pale and staring. Poinkaré made herself grab his arm, move her feet, start dragging him along the walkway. "We have to go, *Adjudant*. We have to go *now*."

The dark cloud slid down the skin of the balloon and onto the ship. The sailors and Librarians were all screaming now; Poinkaré saw what the cloud did to them and had to look away. The rents in the balloon had become great ragged holes, the air rushing out in a gale—and then, just like that, balloon and ship were breaking up and falling. She looked down again, saw black rags fluttering amidst the rain of splinters and shreds of silk. The dark cloud remained, illuminated by the lightning inside it. It drew tighter, into a rough sphere, bands of different shades rotating on the surface like a gas giant in miniature. It extruded fingers of smoke that probed blindly, seeking.

Seeking the siege line.

"*Run!*" she screamed at her dazed aide, and together they sprinted for the nearest open Door.

PART TWO

Chapter Twenty-Six

The worst day of Lud's life had been the pronouncement of Corporeal Forfeit upon him (not *it*, not then) for his part in the Schism Minor. The second-worst had been the day before that, the final defeat of the Schism, when he'd watched the last true clock tower topple into the Viridian Falls.

Today was running a solid third.

It came to on its back, on top of a pile of rubbish. Two beggars were fighting over it, their single legs hopping while their single hands fought a tug-of-war.

A puff of gunpowder and Lud's spike of a tail exploded from its body, impaling one of the beggars through the wrist. They both dropped Lud and scampered off as the crab bounced down the side of the refuse pile.

As it slid down, it probed its memory the way one would probe a painful boil. The Cogs had put it on the siege line above Deadbeat, manning a gun emplacement, and everything had gone swimmingly until the dust had boiled out of the town and destroyed the balloon. Then it had swept across the line, sowing destruction. The emplacement's ammunition had cooked off, and that was where Lud's memory ended. Evidently the blast had thrown it clear, into Deadbeat, and the refuse had broken its fall.

Lud clattered to the bottom in an avalanche of rubbish, and would have winced at the noise if it'd had a face. Sporadic gunfire was still coming from outside the town, accompanied by the occasional thundering crash, scream, or screech of a dying skulker, but the stampede, and the battle itself, was evidently winding down.

Lud limped into the shadows, and stayed there while it recovered from the rattling its poor grey matter had received.

Occasionally loping footsteps would cross the narrow mouth of the alley, accompanied by a tattooed blur. None of them took any notice of the alley or Lud.

Finally it screwed up enough courage to limp to the end of the alley. One eyestalk cautiously protruded into the boardwalk beyond, then whipped backwards as another pair of tattoos rushed past. Once they'd gone, the little crab scuttled quickly across the open space and into the shadows on the other side.

Painstakingly, Lud worked its way through Deadbeat. The Cogs siege line around the town appeared deserted, ragged holes in it where the Exile's smoke had swept by. Once, it turned a corner and saw a fallen skulker blocking the corridor, the mouth in its belly gnashing weakly, tattoos surrounding it and beating it to death as the spider shrank back into the shadows.

Finally the Door to the stables came into view. It was open, which was a piece of luck—when Lud was out of harness, opening doors was a fairly involved process. It was night in the stables' world and two huge moons hung in its sky, bright enough for the rocks on the plain to cast crisp double shadows.

Lud steeled itself, then broke from cover and made a dash across the open towards the Door, just as two tattoos appeared in front of it. They stopped dead, hissed. Lud tried to rush between their legs before they could react, but one of them was quick enough and put an invisible clawed foot down on its shell, stopping it in its tracks. The foot increased its pressure.

Lud dug its claws into the wood of the boardwalk and tried to free itself, but the tattoo was holding it fast. Its braincase began to flex. Finally it just gritted its teeth, or would have if it'd had any, and waited for the end.

It didn't come. The foot scraped along its shell…and then lifted. Lud risked a look upward, and saw it dangling a foot above, its owner held off the ground by a shadow with a hand around its throat. The tattoo just had time for a strangled gasp before the shadow's other fist caved its skull in.

The other tattoo was already lashing out with a patterned fist, which it smashed into the back of the shadow's neck; the shadow didn't move at all, and Lud heard the crunch as the tattoo's fingers broke. A kick sent it sailing through the air, and it slammed into the Well face-first beside the stable Door, where it scrabbled madly for a handhold before losing its grip. It fell out of sight with a hissing wail.

The shadow loomed over the crab, which looked up at it.

"What kept you?" Lud asked.

CHAPTER TWENTY-SEVEN

It felt weird to be pushed around by something you couldn't see.

Two of the tattoos flanked Ben, their rough-skinned hands on his shoulders. All Ben could see of them were the thorny spirals of black ink that wrapped their limbs and torsos. They set a punishing pace, and he found himself half-skipping to keep up; if he stumbled, he was sure they would have no problem dragging him. He glanced at Essa, a little behind him and getting the same treatment. She was glaring at Gregor's back, and at the silver flask his hands toyed with. Confiscating Whisper had been the first thing he'd done. They'd left Ben his bag for some reason, probably because they viewed him as not a threat at all. Correctly.

Deadbeat was practically empty. Ben thought of how it had been before the tattoos had come through the Door, that neat double row of Cogs marching along in time with those immense pendulums. Here came another of the deep thrumming *ticks*, but weaker than he remembered, and no others followed it for a long time. The machinery was running down. He wondered what had happened to the winders in the tower, although he had a pretty good idea.

Gregor didn't even look at them. Assuming it *was* still Gregor after whatever had been in the Committee had poured itself into him. He was leading them straight to the massive stone Door; whoever or whatever he was now, Gregor was done with Deadbeat.

More tattoos were guarding the Door. The ink on these was more elaborate than those Ben had seen so far—purple stripes and spirals suspended in space, stylized animals, trees, faces. It was hard to tell what they really looked like, even with so much of them filled in— lean and sinewy, long-fingered like Vats creeps, but with pebbled skin like a toad's. Their chests bowed out, came to breastbones sharp as knife blades; their faces weren't tattooed, only a few diagonal slashes picking out the blunt snouts and earless skulls. One blinked as Ben and Essa were marched through the Door, its tattooed eyelids closing over its bulging invisible eyes.

The light on the other side of the Door was blinding at first, but as Ben's eyes adjusted, he saw it was overcast in this world, the grey clouds so low he felt he could reach up and touch them. Off to his right, the clouds were dyed orange-red with sunrise, or sunset. Yet again it scrambled Ben's sense of time, producing another wave of instant jet lag. His head swam. The heat didn't help—it was sweltering, the air heavy with water, and he could already feel the sweat breaking out all over him.

He was standing on bare wet stone, mottled with spongy lichen. Behind him was the Door they'd come through, and a Door was all it was—no building, just two tall stones standing upright and another resting across them to form a frame like one of those Stonehenge things. Another stone slab formed the Door itself, pivoted around to stand open. Through it was the Well and the orange lights of Deadbeat. Around it, the stone plain stretched for miles, and covering it, as far as he could see, were Doors.

Thousands of Doors, tens of thousands, freestanding on the plain, all made of quartets of stones like the one they'd come through.

Through a few of them he saw the darkness of the Well, but most were closed and some were fallen, broken rubble lying on the ground.

Mountains punctuated the plain, rising from among the fields of Doors in discrete peaks like limestone karsts, hundreds of feet high, with jagged summits softened by greenery.

And all of them, every one, had a face.

The faces were different shapes and sizes to suit the mountains' different proportions, but they were clearly kin; they shared the full lips, the round noses. Their chins and long-lobed ears rested on the plain, heavy eyelids downcast in prayer or sleep. Vegetation covered their rocky scalps, grew over their jutting eyelids like green brows. The cliffs of their cheeks were stained and mossgrown by centuries of water, streaked as if by tears. They receded into the distance, mountains behind mountains, the waterlogged air turning them into silhouettes that blended with the grey clouds.

Someone had carved faces into all those mountains. The work that must have gone into them was unthinkable.

Ben remained enraptured by the view for he didn't know how long before he became aware of the noise in the distance. A grinding rumble, constant and remorseless. He looked around for its source, and his eyes fell on the clouds in the distance, glowing with sunlight. He stared.

"Oh," said Essa faintly, "would you look at that."

It wasn't sunlight. It was fire.

The hellish glow was coming from the end of the plain, and it was coming towards them. It was another of the carved mountains, but its features had melted and sagged into a grotesque parody of a face. As he watched, it came alongside another of the mountains, which burst suddenly, shockingly into flame. A firestorm swept over its head as the foliage burned, blazing yellow and sending black smoke pouring into the sky.

At the base of the moving mountain was a cloud of dust, rippling in the heat baking off it. He squinted, then gasped. Essa saw it at the same time, and her hand found his and squeezed.

The red-hot mountain wasn't moving, it was *being* moved. It was mounted on something, a colossal sled of black stone. The heat coming off it making the air roil. Immense steel cables led from the sled to…

The shimmer he'd seen wasn't just the heat. It was the tattooed things, an uncountable horde of them. They were pulling on the cables, dragging the sled, and even as they did, the mountain was cooking them alive. As they fried they grew visible; humanoid geckos with bulging eyes and lolling tongues, they burned black and fell and others took their place and were cooked in their turn. More tattoos were clearing a path ahead of the mountain, knocking over the freestanding Doors and dragging the fallen stones out of the sled's way.

"What is this, Gregor?" demanded Essa, her voice tight.

Gregor shook his head, grinning unnaturally wide. "Not Gregor," he said. "Well. Not only."

She looked at him speculatively, but Ben could sense the fear behind the curiosity. "I'm speaking to the Exile, then?"

"A fragment. An agent." Gregor gestured grandly at the red-hot mountain in the distance. "*That* is the Exile." His voice was different, it had picked up that alien quality the Committee had, pulling his vocal cords in odd ways. He still sounded like Gregor—evidently something of him remained in there, and maybe it thought it was still in the driver's seat, but Ben doubted it.

"But why take over a—" Essa stopped, looked around at the carved mountains. "Oh no."

"Oh, yes." Gregor grinned wider still and a trickle of blood ran from the cracks in his lips. "Intellects. All of them."

"They checked the place out before they threw the Exile in here. There wasn't anything."

"They were panicking. The Exile was slipping from their grasp even as they held it. They had less than a day to inspect this world—"

"They're slow." Essa turned to Gregor. "The mountains. Right?"

"We all live such tiny lives," he said. "Even the most ancient Isms of the Library, even the Exile itself—next to the mountains they are a cloud of mayflies, there and gone."

Essa was getting it. "When they search for Intellects, they're really looking for thoughts. Patterns that could be thoughts." She looked around at the mountains. "But they're slow. Too slow to finish even a little bit of a thought in the time the Library had. So they locked the Exile in here," she said, clutching her head and staring at nothing, "with a whole world of Intellects it could take over."

Of everyone there, Ben was nearest the Door to Deadbeat. Now, as Gregor was talking, he heard something on the other side, just faintly. Shouts and hisses. Splintering wood. And under it all, a wheezing roar that grew and grew.

Ben moved sideways just a little, getting between Gregor and the Door. Whatever was coming, he doubted it could make the situation any worse for them, and the more of a surprise it was for Gregor—the Exile—the better.

"So why move the mountain?" Essa cast a quick glance at the Door as she said it; she'd heard it too. "Why doesn't your boss just pour itself out and head for the Well?"

Another burst of gunfire from the other side of the Door, and the thing in Gregor's body cocked his head to listen. Ben winced.

Essa, though, kept talking, answering her own question. "Because it's changed. Isn't that it? It's tied itself to the mountain, the sand isn't enough to hold it any more. That's why it needs a host, something to take it Wellside—"

"So why does it need to come to the Door?" asked Ben.

Essa looked at him. So did Gregor.

"Sorry," said Ben, "but why do they need to drag a mountain right up to the Door? Why can't you host it from where it is now? Then walk to the Door yourself?"

"Stop it," said Gregor. His voice was utterly alien now. "Stop *talking*. All you…*insects*. Breeding and swarming and filling the sand with your squeaking. You will not thank me, but you *should* thank me, because I will save you. You have no idea. No idea what's at stake. I have seen it, in the cracks in the walls. *I see it still.*"

Essa was looking at Ben, her eyes narrowed. Had he screwed up somehow by speaking up? But when she spoke, it wasn't to him. "And the line you gave Gregor, how you'll save the whole Well and it won't hurt a bit?"

"There is no Gregor. And I will end the Well. I will seal every Door. For the sake of all the worlds."

Essa exhaled sharply. "Right. Did you hear that, Gregor?"

"*There is no Gregor—*"

"Did you? Are you in there, have you been listening? I don't know how much of a damn you give about the Well, but looking out for *yourself* was always your special talent." She jerked her head at Ben. "So answer his question: why bring the mountain to you?" She spoke rapidly, the words tumbling out. "You knew already, didn't you? That's why you wanted me to…" She waved a hand at what Gregor had become. "Because you won't have the time. Because it'll burn your brain out in about five minutes. Once it's in you, you're going to *fry*."

"*Stop it*." It was an ugly snarl that Ben wouldn't have thought a human voice could have produced.

"So if you want to look out for yourself now, you have to *fight this*—"

Gregor turned away. He spoke to the tattoos. "Enough of this. Kill the boy and gag the girl—" He paused as hissing screams erupted just outside the Door. A coughing roar. And something burst through.

It was a spider, like Lud's old crawler, but this one was immense, its legs thick beams of steel. Jets of steam burst from its workings as it squeezed through the Door, its bulbous abdomen—its boiler, evidently—striking sparks off the frame. Sitting atop it was Lud, and as Ben watched, Winter vaulted off the side of the spider and into a knot of tattoos, knocking them to the ground.

Whatever was inside Gregor shrieked in frustration. The shriek became a harsh bark as Gregor's vocal cords gave. Black dust streamed from his mouth and nose as he strode past Ben towards Lud and Winter.

He'd tied Essa's flask to his belt and Ben, without a thought in his head, lunged forward and grabbed it off him. In the same motion he turned and tossed it to Essa, and for a horrifying second he thought Essa wasn't going to see it. But her hand shot out and caught it, and with a gesture she sent Whisper streaming out and circling her head, her free hand dancing.

Gregor had already sent black dust blowing in a twisting stream from his mouth towards Winter. As he realized what had just happened, Essa sucked in one of those backwards syllables and sent Whisper out to intercept it. The two streams met and split into dozens of threads, braiding and intertwining in the air. Where they touched, lightning crackled.

The spider was slowing down as more of the tattoos piled onto it. Lud was screaming and cursing as it waded through them. Winter had retreated onto the spider's steel carapace, and as the tattoos tried to climb on board, she sent them hurtling back down with crushed skulls and shattered limbs.

Ben backed away from Gregor and Essa, who'd turned their full attention to each other. Dust streaked through the air in dizzying patterns, hundreds of threads branching and merging and annihilating each other as each combatant tried to get through the other's defences, but so far they were deadlocked. That didn't look like it would last for long, though. Essa was barely holding it together—bright blood trickled from her nose and one ear, mingling with the sweat that poured off her face as she twisted her fingers around, hissed desperate commands to Whisper, her eyes flickering over the battleground, trying to take it all in, backing up just a little as Gregor bore down on her remorselessly.

Then a streamer of dust got past her and ripped through the air towards the spider. Towards Winter.

Instantly Lud reared up, putting the spider's head in the dust's path. The dust bored a hole right through the steel, and something inside the spider burst in a shower of sparks. It ground to a halt, Lud toppling off and falling.

"*Lud!*" Essa screamed, her concentration breaking. Gregor took advantage of that to send a dozen more threads of dust at the spider. They whipped through it, slicing through its legs and sending it crashing to the ground.

For a moment Ben thought it had fallen on Winter, but then he saw her a few yards away, fighting with her back to one of those stone Doors as tattoos swarmed her.

Essa was barely fending off Gregor's assault now. Ben looked around, found a stone on the ground and pegged it at the skinny dickhead, but Gregor was surrounded by a bone-stripping hurricane of dust and the stone spun away before it even reached him.

Lud lay where it had fallen. There were cracks in its braincase and fluid leaked through them. Its legs moved weakly and out of sync. A tattooed shimmer picked the crab up—it struggled, nipping with its tiny pincers—and dashed it to the ground. More cracks spread over its brain's crystal dome and the light inside went out. Lud's legs jerked arrhythmically, and an invisible foot came down hard on it, shattering the little crab and splattering grey matter over the stone.

Winter saw it. She screamed, enraged, the sound like rending metal, and shook off the tattoos that were trying to drag her down.

Clear for a moment, she swayed and drove her shoulder into the stone Door she'd been backed up against. It shuddered but didn't give. Winter was *smoking*, wisps of it rolling off her skin. She was still fighting, lashing out with foot and fist, but she was letting more and more hits through. One blow from a tattooed elbow took her in the ribs and she dropped to one knee; then she grabbed the arm that had hit her and snapped it in half. She lunged at the Door once again, shoulder slamming into the stone, and this time it worked.

The Door tilted and fell, the uprights cracking in half a dozen places as they tumbled to the ground. Winter staggered backwards, still smoking, shuddering like a car grinding its gears. The toppling lintel hit another Door, which collapsed into another, filling Ben's head with the thunder of it. The last to fall loomed over Gregor, forcing him to step back—and for one second the whirl of dust around him faltered, slowed.

Essa didn't miss her chance.

She sent Whisper corkscrewing through Gregor's defences to envelop his head, and he reeled. Essa, clearly surprised she'd scored a hit, paused just a moment before pressing her advantage—and Gregor stood up, his hands twisting. An electrical storm in miniature played around his head and half of Whisper dropped out of the air. Glass rained on the stone.

Essa screamed, an agonised keening, as the remnants of Whisper rushed back to her. Ben dived for her as she fell. He didn't catch her but he managed to get his hand under her head before it hit the ground, saving her from a concussion or worse.

Gregor still swayed on his feet, dazed, but he looked like the least of their problems. Ben stared up at the tattoos massing around him and Essa. Behind them he caught a glimpse of Winter, black oily blood running from her face as she went down, tattoos surrounding her, ready to stomp her head in.

"Piss off," he said. He supposed that would have to do for last words.

Something leaped over the rubble of the fallen Doors and landed among the tattoos, smashing a couple of them into the ground with an impact that rattled Ben's teeth.

He blinked at this new thing. It was a head taller than the tattoos, and it appeared to be made of stone.

Two more bounded towards them and charged into the tattoos; and then another, even bigger than the others, colossal. It had Winter's prone body cradled in one arm. He could hear stone grinding and slithering as it moved.

It landed next to him, cracks spreading over the stone around its feet. Gently, it lifted Essa and took her up in its free arm. "Run," it said to Ben in a voice like a rockslide.

So he ran.

Chapter Twenty-Eight

He kept running, following the big one that was carrying Winter and Essa. It was all grey rock, its back craggy and fissured, less like a statue than a boulder that had decided to stand up and walk. He saw plants growing in its crevices, moss and small ferns.

Another two stone things were close behind. They crashed together as they ran; the impact would have turned anything between them to jelly. Ben kept his teeth clenched, waiting for one to stumble and crush him, or for tattooed fingers to close around his neck, or for Gregor's dust to blow through him and powder his flesh. Finally he couldn't stand it any more, and looked back.

One of the statues had stayed behind to hold off the tattoos, clubbing them down with huge swinging blows. Now it went down, invisible bodies swarming over it, worming their fingers into the cracks in its surface, prising it apart. The other tattoos rushed around it, coming after Ben and his guardians. One of the statues behind him peeled off and fell back to engage the tattoos coming after them. That left just him, the huge one carrying Winter and Essa, and one more, right behind him.

His lungs burned. Spit clogged his throat. They were running uphill now, it was only a gentle rise but it felt like murder. He couldn't keep up. A moment of panic as he slowed, thinking the statue behind him would run him down, but the stone warriors slowed too, matching his pace.

Over his own laboured breathing he realized Essa was saying something, her voice shaking with the impact of the huge statue's feet. "Okay," she was saying, "I'm okay, put me down, put me *waaaaagh*—"

They'd disappeared. Essa's shriek was cut off by a loud splash, followed by silence. Ben skidded to a stop, fireworks bursting behind his eyes as he sucked air.

He was looking into a hole in the plain that had been hidden by the rise. It looked fresh, and it was surrounded by debris, like something had erupted out of the earth. Inside was nothing but darkness.

The last statue stood beside him. "You," it ground out in a voice like a millstone turning. "Go."

Ben looked up at it. It didn't have a face, just a couple of shallow depressions where its eyes should have been. "What's—" he said.

Then the statue pushed him in.

Ben landed in freezing knee-deep water. He bit his tongue with the impact, tasted blood, and staggered forward, thrashing through the water and trying not to fall. Just as he recovered his balance, the statue that had pushed him landed behind him with another earth-shaking impact, and he did fall. His bag landed in the water and dread shot through him—his laptop was in there, his only link with the world he'd known—and he grabbed it and held it over his head, ice-cold water running off it and dripping down his neck.

The statue waded past him—its wake almost swamped him again—and grabbed him as it passed, pulling him out of the water and setting him down on wet rock. He looked up and saw the huge one, cradling Winter in one arm like a newborn. Essa stood beside it, looking shaky and leaning on the stone thing's arm, but she was conscious at least. Blood ran from her nose, dripped from her chin. He was about to ask her if she was okay, but the thing in the water spoke.

"Go," it said in its mortar-and-pestle voice, and waved them away. Ben's eyes were adjusting to the dim light coming from the hole overhead. They were in a cave, a natural cavity in the rock, presumably carved out by the underground stream. On the bank near them was a natural pillar, holding the ceiling up. Behind the huge statue was the mouth of a tunnel, darkness beyond. It stooped to enter, beckoning with a three-fingered stone hand.

The statue in the water reached out and pushed Ben in the back. By its standards it was probably a gentle tap, but it drove the breath out of him and made him stumble forward. "Go," it repeated. Essa put a hand on his shoulder to steady him. "Lud?" she asked, hesitantly.

Ben shook his head, still fighting for breath. "Oh no," said Essa, "oh *Lud*." She was slurring like a drunk. They grabbed each other, held each other up as they limped into the tunnel.

A series of splashes made him look back. Tattoos were dropping into the cave, visible from the water they displaced. More of them landed as he watched. He looked at the statue in the water and his eyes widened as he saw what it was doing.

"Essa—" he had time to say, and then the thing drove its fist into the centre of the pillar.

The stone column exploded, chunks of rock flying and choking dust filling the cave, blocking the light. In the dimness Ben saw the stone thing stand erect, looking back at them. It raised a hand, fingers spread. The huge thing in the tunnel with them raised its own hand, returning the gesture.

Then the roof collapsed.

Ben and Essa stumbled backwards as debris spilled into the tunnel. The noise was immense, apocalyptic, and it seemed to go on for hours. Ben took a breath that filled his lungs with powdered stone. Coughing, he squeezed his stinging eyes shut and covered his nose and mouth with his sleeve. He backed up, out of the way of the rocks rolling towards him. They piled up and blocked the mouth of the tunnel, plunging them abruptly into absolute darkness. In the pitch black he could hear the rock still crashing, falling, settling, finally tapering off with a pachinko rattle of tiny stones down through the ruin of the cave.

Silence and darkness, the air full of choking dust. Then light glimmered behind him, his shadow sliding over the rockfall blocking the tunnel. Essa stood with her arm raised, wisps of red dust circling it and shining with a faint red glow. She was staring past him at what had been the cave. Behind her was the huge stone thing, still holding Winter. Like Essa, it was looking at the rockfall, and its hand was still up in the same gesture with which it had saluted its comrade. Then, slowly, it turned and headed away, its head bowed.

"They cannot follow," it said. "Walk now. No need to run."

"Is she going to be okay?" asked Essa.

The statue said nothing.

The tunnel was tight for the big thing, which had to walk with knees bent and head lowered, but it was still wide enough for Ben and Essa to walk side by side. The walking statue blocked pretty much all of it, and all they could see by Whisper's faint light was its back.

It really was stone, he saw, not just some camouflage trick. Stone muscles grated as they bunched and slid under stone skin. Each movement dislodged a cascade of dust and tiny pebbles that rained off its green back. Moss clung to the peaks and valleys of the thing's shoulders like a moving garden. The arm carrying Winter hung lower than the other. How heavy must she be, that she was weighing a thing like that down?

It had two arms, two legs, a head set low on its chest, but that was about as much definition as it had. Everything about it was rudimentary, like it had been hacked out of living rock with no time for finesse. Its stubby fingers were as thick as Ben's wrist, and looked like they'd be good only for bunching into a fist and bludgeoning things with; although, from what Ben had seen, they did that pretty well.

What they could see of the tunnel was bare rock, worn to glassy smoothness. Dust from the collapsed cave swirled in the air, but it was thinning, sucked ahead of them somewhere. Ben glanced at Essa— her eyes were as red as Gregor's had been and they were bleeding in a sluggish trickle down each cheek. Occasionally she tripped over her own feet and reeled against Ben and he had to help her right herself.

Ben had been in a fight once with Matt O'Connor—the usual thing, after school on the football field with spectators chanting in a circle, *fight fight fight*. Just a few awkward punches, really, but it'd been pretty much the only fight he'd ever been in and the aftermath of the adrenaline rush had left him bone-tired and staggering like a drunk. That was what he saw in Essa now.

He wanted to ask if she was okay, but she kept talking.

"Is she all right?" she asked again, her voice tight, like she was forcing the words out. Once she'd said it, though, they came faster and faster, a flood of them under high pressure. "You have to help her. You have to help her, you don't understand what she *is*—"

The grade of the tunnel became steeper, angling upwards. There was a turn up ahead and the stone thing's shoulders scraped the walls, raising sparks as it negotiated its way around. Ben followed it, into warm yellow light.

"Why don't you *say* anything—" Essa was saying, then she ran into Ben, who'd stopped dead. "Damn it, Ben, what are you..." and then she saw what he was seeing and her words became a whisper and trailed off.

They were inside one of the carved mountains. It had to be; there wasn't anywhere else he'd seen on the plain that could be this *big*. But looking at them from outside, he'd had no idea they were hollow.

Dozens of holes in the rocky walls let in differently angled shafts of light. Even so, the space was so vast that all that illumination only added up to a kind of gloomy twilight, with bright circles and ovals here and there that picked out details of the…thing…that took up almost the whole mountain.

Ben couldn't even begin to take it in at first; it was just too complicated. His eyes travelled from one illuminated detail to the next while his brain struggled to piece them together. He didn't know if it was a sculpture or a machine, or both. Its shape was something like a tree, a vast central trunk with stone branches that spread out and soared over them, ramifying throughout the hollow mountain. A dizzying array of stone beams standing at all angles, tipped with polished stone weights, balancing on huge stone discs. It was moving, turning, those beams swinging by each other, perfectly counterbalanced and moving at appalling speed. As huge as it was, it moved in near-silence, the only sound a steady, almost subsonic rumble that he felt more than heard.

Intellects, Essa had called the mountains, and he was pretty sure it was an Intellect he was looking at now.

He was looking at a mountain's mind.

Chapter Twenty-Nine

More statues were coming out of the gloom towards them. Some of them were like Gardenback (as he'd named the one who'd rescued them)—outlines barely human, coarse features elongated like half-finished Easter Island heads, bodies just agglomerations of jagged rocks. The rocks grated against each other when they moved, sparks lighting them up from inside.

Others were more finished-looking, some glittering like quartz, others like smooth marble with swirling veins. They stood even taller than Gardenback, slender and delicate.

Their rudimentary lips didn't move when they spoke; the unearthly sound came from inside them, sharp and clear like the pealing of stone bells. They said something to Gardenback and it replied in the same language, its own voice grating and rumbling. It knelt—its knee came down lightly but Ben still felt the earth tremble at its touch—and extended its arms, offered up the limp Winter with unmistakable tenderness.

Essa was trembling as she watched, face pale. Ben put a hand on her arm. He expected her to shake it off, but if he didn't do *something* he'd end up in the middle of a panic attack, like Essa clearly was.

She didn't shake him off. She grabbed his hand, not saying anything, and they followed the statues like that to the wall of the hollow mountain, where a squat column sheared off at an angle, like a lectern, stood next to a huge marble slab. The slab was twice as long as Ben was tall and the top of it was level with his chest. Winter looked tiny and frail as the living statues laid her down on it.

A deep thrumming overhead made Ben look up. The moving stone that filled the mountain was closer here, the end of one of the huge counterweights narrowing to a point barely ten feet over the slab. Looking up, he could see right up into the machine, a hellishly complicated labyrinth in slow and constant motion, illuminated by crisscrossing shafts of light that bounced off the polished stone and filled it with a thousand sparkling reflections.

Whisper orbited them sluggishly. Ben could tell something was deeply wrong with her after Essa's battle with Gregor. Whatever he had done to her, it had hurt Essa too, even worse than the Vine had, back in Deadbeat—she shook, bloodstained tears streaming from her eyes, but she didn't make a sound. Her hand gripped Ben's so tightly he could feel the bones shifting. He didn't mind. Standing on tiptoe, she managed to touch Winter's limp fingers with those of her free hand. Winter lay still. A thin film of black oily blood coated her face, beading on her skin. She wasn't breathing.

Ben wanted to say something reassuring, something to make Essa feel better.

"We'll remember her," he tried. "We—"

Essa groaned. "Who cares?" she said, sounding a little better but still slurring. "You think she'd care? She could have been the last. The *last* of them, Ben, do you even know what that *means*?"

"No," said Ben quietly. "No, I don't. Because no one's told me." It was easy to be calm. The poison in Essa's voice was nothing to do with him, just her beating herself up.

"Then just be quiet, okay, Ben?" said Essa. She wasn't panicking now; she seemed to have accepted that Winter was gone. "Just don't say anything. Just…just—"

She stopped talking herself as three of the slender statues emerged from the darkness behind the slab, bearing something huge and rectangular and black, like an iron strongbox.

"What's—" said Essa, and then, "oh Lady. Oh Red-Eyed Lady's *teeth*. That's a Book."

It *was* a book, Ben saw, only it was made of metal—its cover, even its pages, were black iron, discoloured with rust. The statues, with infinite care, placed it on the lectern. The spine creaked like a rusty hinge as they opened it, and Ben saw the pages—it looked like they'd originally been half an inch thick—were paper-thin, rusted right through in places. More rust drifted to the floor as they leafed through the book. Ben saw drawings like anatomical diagrams stamped into the metal, and blocks of writing in an indecipherably thorny and ornate typeface. The rust was so far advanced that script and drawings were reduced to almost imperceptible shadows.

"That's a Book," Essa said again. Her knees trembled and she leaned against Winter's slab to keep from falling over. She looked up at the statues. "That's...how did you..."

A new statue was shuffling up to the slab. This one appeared to be made of obsidian and it held an obsidian knife, multifaceted and glittering. Before Ben even processed what it was doing, it had run the knife up Winter's front, fabric parting like water, and pulled it apart to show her pale skin. The knife hadn't even scratched her, and now the statue rested the point between her breasts.

Ben started forward, not knowing what to do but wanting to do something. Essa, to his surprise, extended her arm, brought it across his chest to stop him. "Ben," she said. "I think they know what they're doing."

He looked at her. Her eyes were full of wonder and she spoke almost to herself. "They were rare even before the Rust. The Künstler only ever made one mould for each Book, broke it right after." She shook her head, her eyes shining, that lust for the new and unique temporarily trumping everything else she was feeling. "It's…I can't…I really thought they'd all been lost. I'm looking at a *Book*."

She looked at Winter, on the slab, and now there was something else in her eyes. Ben thought it was hope.

The gleaming black figure bent over Winter again. Ben swallowed, feeling faint, as the knife ran down her pale sternum and over her belly, stopping just above her navel. Her skin didn't offer any more resistance than her shirt had. A trickle of oil ran down her skinny flank.

Now the figures either side of Winter took hold of the edges of the incision and pulled. Spots were beginning to swarm at the edges of Ben's vision, but Essa didn't turn away and neither did he. Winter's skin didn't stretch like skin but bent and creased, like sheet metal, as they opened her up.

Ben had seen Winter bleed and he knew she was different, but he still wasn't prepared for what was inside her.

He had half-expected her to be a machine, and at first glance that was what he saw—iron ribs and spine, black tubes with organic curves like manifold pipes snaking through her, all of it covered by a rainbow sheen of oil. Like someone had built a human with a forge and anvil. But it wasn't just metal. Slick membranes like black plastic pulsed and accordioned. Lungs like leather bellows pressed against her ribs. They dimpled, ever so slightly, and filled again. She was breathing.

And in the centre of it all was Winter's heart, a fist-sized lump of iron flesh that glowed a deep, deep red, and smoked as it beat, her heartbeat a sound like a tiny hammer striking metal, a double blow repeated over and over. Now it stuttered, paused. Essa moaned and Ben watched with his heart in his mouth; the heartbeat picked up again, but irregular, as Winter's workings began to fall out of sync.

Essa bit her lip hard, squeezed Ben's hand harder, but even as she did it a shadow fell over them and they both looked up.

The statues had swung the huge stone weight down to barely ten feet above Winter's head. Part of it was unfolding itself towards them, the tip like a stone lance, wickedly sharp. Gardenback and another big one were guiding it down.

Ben looked back at Winter. "She's not human."

"She's more human than I am," said Essa, pushing the hand that wasn't holding Ben's through her short hair.

"But how—"

"*Eisenkunst,*" said Essa, and the stone machine finished its smooth descent, coming to a stop with the end of the lance a foot away from Winter and pointed straight at her heart. Essa looked up at it, talking as the stone wheels began slowly to spin. "I told you about the Powers, right?"

The Library. The Vats. The Cogs. Ben nodded. The hope shone in Essa's eyes now, and so did the fear, that whatever was happening wasn't going to work. She was talking to hold the fear at bay, and he let her.

"Three of them, right? Well, there used to be four. Or three-and-a-half. Or—anyway, there was another."

"*Eisenwelt,*" said Ben. "Those ruins near Deadbeat. Right?"

Her hand tightened on his. "Yeah. *Eisenwelt* was an iron world, just one big machine."

"Like the Cogs?"

Essa shook her head. "Different philosophies. The Cogs are about order. Eisenwelt was about *power.* Coal and iron. Foundries the size of cities. Smokestacks a mile high."

"What did the factories make?" Ben asked.

"Parts for the factories," said Essa, watching the lance come down.

"But what's the point—"

"What's the point of you? Or me? The factories were the point. They were *alive.*"

Ben tried to imagine it, an organism of iron spreading across a whole planet, devouring coal and oil, exhaling soot. "You've seen it?"

"No." Essa looked at Winter. The grinding of the stone machine above them was faster, more rhythmic, steadily rising in pitch. "No, I haven't." She nodded at Winter. "And neither has she. Because it's all gone. And the Künstler with it."

"They were the ones who built it? The engineers?"

"Engineers, workers, warriors. All the same thing to the Künstler. But no, they didn't build it. We don't know who built it. But they studied it, and all that study, they summed it up in the Book. How to build and how to fight."

Ben looked at the iron book, rusted almost to nothing. The statues pored over it, called out in their ringing voices to their comrades riding the machine. Tiny sparks were cracking across the surface of the stone. Ben could feel his hair prickling.

"We brought them into the Treaty, and they built for us, all up and down the Well. Bridges right across it. Staircases that went up for a hundred miles. Wellscrapers, fifty storeys long."

"What did they get out of it?"

"Left alone, is what they got out of it. No embassies on Eisenwelt, no visas. But they probably would have done it even if there hadn't been anyone else in the Well at all. Building that stuff was a religious thing for them. An act of devotion." Essa was still looking at the black iron tome, shaking her head. "And they never gave away the Book. Not ever."

"Maybe these guys stole it."

"If they'd tried to steal a Book, we'd know about it."

"How?"

"For one thing, they'd all be dead. Measured response was never the Künstler's thing. A lot of people found that out the hard way, when they tried to steal black iron in the Well. Because whatever else they were, the Künstler were the ones you didn't mess with."

It was getting hard to hear her. Sparks crackled all up and down the stone needle. Ben smelled ozone, tasted metal. He badly wanted to step back from the slab, but he didn't want to let go of Essa's hand. Essa didn't even seem to notice the charge in the air, she just kept talking, looking into Winter's face, like if her eyes broke contact for even a moment all would be lost.

"And *because* they were so kickass, people showed up wanting to be like them. Which was an ask, if you know what those first Künstler were like…

"Huge, some of them, the size of city blocks. All iron and fire. We thought they were machines themselves, that their builders had died out and left them to run the factories forever. Turned out that wasn't it at all. They were *human*, or they had been. They'd turned themselves into…whatever they were. You think she was born that way?"

Ben, forgetting for a moment the huge stone machine whirring and sparking above them, looked at the prone Winter. "Wait," he said. "You're talking about—"

"I'm talking about changing your own body, through pure *will*, into *living iron*. That was what they could do. The ones who survived the training, and there weren't many of those. And there aren't any of them, not now."

She kept talking but her voice tightened as the sparks gathered into a blinding blue-white point at the lance's tip. "She has to be okay, Ben. She has to. Because she's irreplaceable. Her home's gone, and she never even got to see it—"

And that was when the bolt of lightning blasted from the tip of the lance and leaped straight into Winter's heart. She convulsed on the slab, her back arching until Ben thought it would snap, and then slammed back down onto the stone and lay still. The whole thing had only taken a moment.

The bolt lingered in Ben's vision, a ghost on his retinas. Acrid smoke curled up from Winter's open chest cavity. She didn't move. Her heart had stopped.

Essa groaned, a sound that rose in pitch like steam under terrible pressure, a sound of pure grief—and then it cut off as Winter convulsed again, her heart glowing orange, a heartbeat like twin sledgehammers. She coughed up oil and opened her eyes.

"They did it!" yelled Essa. "Ben! They *did it*!" She was laughing from pure relief, her eyes sparkling.

The obsidian statue was looking Winter over and she looked up at him too. She raised a hand, tentatively, and he took it in one of his, white in black. His lithophone voice chimed something in a language Ben hadn't heard before, a guttural tongue whose harsh syllables made a strange contrast with the pure tones it spoke in.

Winter paused, and then answered him haltingly in the same language. It sounded more appropriate in her own hollow voice, like heavy machinery had learned to speak. The statue rested its hand on Winter's forehead, crooned something, and she lay back, relaxed, and her eyes closed.

Ben looked at the statue as it directed its comrades clinging to the stone machine. "So who are these guys, exactly?"

"That," said Essa, wiping tears from her eyes, "is an excellent question."

Then she collapsed. Ben managed to catch her this time as she sagged and fell sideways, gone limp all over. "Essa?"

"Just the duel," Essa was mumbling, "just the duel. Takes it out of you." And indeed she didn't seem sick or stunned, just bone tired.

Ben nodded. To the statues, which had turned to look at them, he said, "Look—I don't know if you understand me at all, but she needs to rest. Are there any beds, or…"

"Follow," said a grinding voice behind him. It was Gardenback, the huge statue who'd led them to this place. It raised one huge arm and beckoned as it shuffled into the darkness at the edge of the cavern.

As Ben followed he heard the lance start up again, sizzling and snapping. He turned, and turned back just as quickly to save his eyes, but he'd seen it welding Winter closed, that impossible-to-look-at point of light leaving a glowing red scar on her chest.

CHAPTER THIRTY

ardenback led them to an alcove in the inside of the mountain's hollow shell, on which a shaft of light fell, diffuse and gentle after being refracted through the polished insides of the great machine.

"You are wet," it rumbled, "and cold." It tapped its chest, where its lungs would have been. "Not good for soft things like you. Rest."

The alcove was lined with springy green moss and Ben helped Essa up into it, where she sprawled, half-asleep. He toyed with the idea of giving up the alcove entirely and lying on the stone floor, then decided *screw it* and climbed in next to her, keeping a chivalrous inch of space between them.

Now he wasn't drenched in ice-cold water, Ben realized how hot it was inside the mountain—uncomfortably so, almost like a sauna. At least his shivering had subsided. He turned to thank the huge statue, but it was already lumbering away, its back turned.

"Thanks," said Essa drowsily.

Ben didn't really know what to say. He could feel the warmth of her next to him. He asked, "What happened?"

"To what?" She was only half-listening, her eyelids drooping.

"To Eisenwelt. To the Künstler."

"Oh. The Rust happened. It was the Exile. When it was attacking the Well. Somehow it got into the black iron. Just started...rotting, from the inside out. Like a plague. Oxidizing away. Their whole world."

Ben lifted himself up on one elbow to listen. Essa turned away from him, eyes closed. He could see the curve of her neck where it met her jaw, the skin fluttering in time with her heartbeat. "Their whole world. Künstler sent a delegation to the Library—which they *never* did—to ask us for help.

"And we killed them all. The whole delegation. Right there in the Mandala."

The drowsy, affectless way she said it gave Ben goosebumps.

"Didn't want the Rust to spread. Rot out all the black iron in the Well. So we killed them, and slammed the Door on the Eisenwelt. Only a few dozen Künstler left in the Well after that. Fight just went out of them. They lived alone…tried passing it down…like to Winter…but fewer all the time…less…"

She was asleep. Ben fell back on the moss, felt it absorb his weight, let his knotted muscles relax. The warmth was making his wet jeans steam. There was a tight knot of anxiety behind his breastbone, and although he couldn't remember the last time he'd slept properly, he'd never felt so awake.

The next thing he knew, he was face down on the moss in a puddle of drool and bright sunlight.

Essa was still asleep, in the exact same position he'd left her in, chest rising and falling with slow deep breaths. Ben was ravenously hungry.

Awkwardly, he hopped over her and slid out of the alcove. He rummaged in his bag, found a tin of Cogs army food he'd stashed there. It was even hotter now than when he'd gone to sleep, uncomfortably so, and the tin was warm to the touch. He looked at it doubtfully. He didn't know how long it had to last, or if there was anything else to eat in this world. Lichen, maybe.

Finally hunger won, at which point a new problem presented itself—he had no way to open it. He tried hammering it on the rock floor of the cavern. He tried standing up and hurling it at the wall, but all that did was put a dent in it. Wasn't tinned food supposed to be dangerous with a dent in it? He was too hungry to care. He was hammering on the lid with a pebble when an enormous stone hand plucked it out of his fingers.

He looked up at Gardenback. How could it move so silently, weighing that much? It reminded him of Winter. He was beginning to think that wasn't a coincidence.

The statue punched a hole in the tin with a huge stone thumb and returned it to Ben. His stomach growled and he upended it into his mouth. It was a black gruel, thick with grease, and it had a faintly acrid reek, but it went down and stayed down.

"Thanks," he said finally, wiping his mouth.

The rough statue watched him for a moment and then turned its back on him without saying a word, the ferns growing from its shoulders rustling. Ben shrugged, set the tin down half-full on the floor for Essa and followed. They rounded one of the stone beams as it swooped low to the ground, the polished sphere on the end describing a complicated curve. They were at the stone slab where the statues had laid Winter. It was empty now, oil stains slowly soaking into the rock where she had bled. The black iron tome was gone from the lectern.

"Where's Winter?" he asked. Gardenback gave no indication it had heard, just headed off through the workings of the stone machine. Ben shrugged and followed, pausing as a granite needle like the hand of a clock swept across his path.

Gardenback lumbered through the machine, adjusting the balance of a weight here, clearing debris out of a joint there. It was cooler here in the depths of the machinery, which was a relief, but the sunlight (what little of it that filtered this far into the mountain) had taken on an unpleasant yellow tinge, like it was shining through smoke. He thought of the burning mountain grinding along the plain outside, and wondered how close it was.

A winding stone staircase took them up into the inner workings of the mountain. The steps were statue-sized, and Ben struggled to keep up. High above he could see other statues, both the rough fighters and the slender ones, crossing narrow stone arches through the guts of the machine.

The atmosphere was that of a cathedral or a monastery, and Ben became absorbed in the solemnity of it, the syncopated rhythm of the stone. When Gardenback spoke, it took him a moment to come back to himself.

"Your mate," it repeated.

"She's not my—wait," Ben said. "Are you talking about Essa or Winter? Not that either of them—I mean, they're not…" He trailed off into silence. So he'd established that he couldn't talk to a *rock* without fumbling it. Great.

Gardenback said nothing. Ben reached for something to say, just to fill the silence. "She's—I mean, if you're talking about Essa—she's still asleep. The…duel, with that other Librarian—it really stuffed her up. Do you know about the Exile?"

"Exile," rumbled the statue, slowly, like it was tasting the world. Ben waited, but once again, it added nothing.

Screw it. "Why did you help us?" he asked.

It shrugged. "The mountain approaches the Door and time is short. What else could we do? You were fighting the…Exile. And you brought the child."

"The—you mean Winter?"

"Little iron warrior. Little child. Our child."

This was interesting. Ben said nothing, hoping for more, but there wasn't any. He tried again, not really hoping for a response. "Where is she?"

After the gloom of the cathedral, the cave Gardenback led him to was a blaze of light: he had to stand in the entrance for a moment, blinking, before he could make anything out. They were near the top of the mountain and sunlight poured in through a large opening in the ceiling. The huge crystals growing from every surface of the cave caught the light, shattered and scattered it, bathing everything in a milky glow.

The Book was in the centre of the room, the one thing that didn't reflect light, hulking huge and black on a diamond pedestal. Winter was kneeling in front of it, her head bowed. Ben could see her fragmented reflection in the crystal, her jacket buttoned up with a scar like a weld peeking over the neck.

The statue put a hand on Ben's shoulder. Ben couldn't help flinching, feeling once again the mass and awesome power of it; its touch barely brushed his skin, but if Gardenback let its full weight fall, it would tear Ben's arm off. The hand turned him around, slowly and gently but with no give whatsoever, pointing him at the cave's exit. *Okay, you've seen her, time to piss off.* He got it.

Winter said something, softly, in the harsh clattering language she'd used with the black statue. She didn't turn around. The stone hand lifted.

"I can hardly read it," she said in her hollow voice. She didn't turn from the Book. Her hand reached out to it and then stopped, like she couldn't bring herself to touch it, like she still wasn't sure it was real and couldn't bear to find out it wasn't. "She taught me how to read but I never thought I'd get the chance."

"He said you were their child," said Ben cautiously. Gardenback shifted slightly, stone grating on stone.

"They created the Künstler. This world is where the Künstler learned." Now she did turn to face him. Black tears ran down her cheeks. "We have to help them."

"Help them do what?" said Ben. "Fight? How? You saw how many tattoos the Exile's got. How many of these guys are there?"

"Few," rumbled Gardenback. "The mountains have barely woken. Many sleep still. Their thoughts are few and slow."

"Thoughts?"

"He means himself," said Winter. "Same on the Eisenwelt. The Künstler were the factories' words, their thoughts. Same here."

The statues were thoughts, stone thoughts of massive stone minds. He supposed it wasn't any more a grand or crazy idea than any of the others he'd heard in the last few days—there was the Well itself, for God's sake—but it still made him shiver. Perhaps it was an accident of scale; the idea was small enough to get a fingernail grip on while still being vast enough to shock.

"We have to help," said Winter again.

"The mountains awoke when your Exile came," said Gardenback, "but their first thoughts were caught, brought down by the unseen ones."

"The tattoos?" said Ben. "What are they, anyway?"

"Animals. They lived in caves, crept on stone. Harmless. The Exile bred them, Bound them, twisted them into weapons. They caught the thoughts that travelled over the stone. This silenced the Mountains. They could not speak. To speak, we had to travel *through*."

"The tunnels," said Ben.

The statue nodded, a fine sprinkle of dust puffing out from where its blocky head rested on its neck. "The labour of years, carving paths for the Mountains' thoughts, to allow them to think and speak. But now they *do* speak, in voices that shake the stones. The ones that are left."

"Left?"

"The unseen ones quarry the mountains, to make their Doors." The statue's hand bunched into a fist. "We make it costly. But there are always more. Our scouts have seen the spawning-grounds, egg-pits a mile wide. Always more. And we so few."

"Few? There's hundreds of mountains, I saw them. The Exile only possessed, like, one."

"Most are deep in contemplation. The ones that can be woken…a dozen in this world."

"And the *Exile*," said Winter, and Ben could hear the sudden fury in her voice, the ugly edge to it, like gears grinding—"took one of those. We have to *help*."

"Okay, great," said Ben, "so how?"

"We do not know," said the statue.

"Terrific."

"The mountains' thoughts are slow. And while they are turned to battle"—its massive stone hand tapped a finger on its stone chest—"they cannot craft a plan. And the burning one approaches its Door."

"Aren't you glad it's going?" said Ben. "It'll leave you alone."

"It tells us this. It shouts across the plain that it means no harm. But the mountains say otherwise. They say if it reaches its Door, this world, *all* worlds, will end in darkness."

"Can it do that?"

The statue said nothing.

"All I can do is fight," said Winter. "They have fighters already." She was looking right at him. "They need a plan."

Chapter Thirty-One

Essa was awake when Ben came back, sitting in the mossy alcove with her legs dangling and her head bowed. The circuitry in her arms glittered in a ray of sunlight as they lay in her lap. Beads of sweat shone in her hair. Whisper turned a sluggish figure-eight in the alcove behind her.

"How are you feeling?" asked Ben.

"Just wonderful," Essa said without looking up.

"You did great back there. We wouldn't be here otherwise."

She snorted. "Tell it to Lud. Tell it to Whisper." She held up a handful of glass, then flung it away. It sparkled momentarily as it flew through a beam of the dirty yellow sunlight.

"Is she okay? Whisper, I mean?"

"No. I'm not a duellist, Ben. I had no idea what I was doing. I probably hurt her worse than Gregor did."

"Not Gregor," said Ben. "The Exile. You held your own against the Exile. I think that's worth half a tin of Spam or whatever." He took the tin from the floor beside the alcove and passed it to Essa. She looked at it, but made no move to eat.

"What's Gregor's story, anyway?" asked Ben.

"He backed my research, in the Library. Backed my friend's, too, the one who died. I cheated on her, by the way. With him. And he killed her for her Proof, and stole mine. Then he used them to betray the Well to the Exile, while I just ran away from the whole mess. How's that, Ben?" She looked up at him almost defiantly. "How do you feel about setting fire to your whole life to help me out now?"

"It wasn't much of a life. My parents hate each other and I never had a minute to myself. But I tried like hell to hold it together because I was afraid of what would happen if it didn't, without ever knowing what that would be. So no, I'm not going to lecture you on your...life choices, or whatever. And I don't regret helping you."

Ever since Ben had jumped from the Cogs balloon, giving up his chance to return home, he hadn't had time to think about what that had meant. Now he was talking about it, he found himself probing the idea, gingerly, like you'd probe a broken tooth. He felt something, but he didn't know what it was. Liberation? Maybe. Terror? That was closer. It was part freedom and part freefall, and every freefall had a landing. Usually a sharp one.

"Red Lady," said Essa, but she was smiling a little, "look at the two of us." She slid sideways, giving Ben room to sit next to her. "As for Gregor...my Proof, what I was working on in the Library, was how to grow my own Doors. Very popular problem in the Library, but no one had got anywhere with it. Until the Exile. The Exile cracked it, but whatever it knew, we lost when we ran it out of the Library. Or so we thought. Gregor got me deep access to the Stacks, and we found... traces. I was able to put a Proof together, or rather half a Proof.

"I can grow Doors, to anywhere Wellside or worldside I like, but they take a long time to ripen. As you know."

The Mystery Door in the gym. Whisper working on it for a year, disguised as the dust on the floor. Ben nodded.

"Now the Exile, it can create Doors as quick as it likes, but where they point to is pretty much random chance. All those Doors on the plain—it's been creating them ever since we exiled it, but most of them probably opened a hundred thousand miles upWell of where it wanted. A million. But now it's got what it wanted, a Librarian to channel it. It's all over."

"Maybe not," said Ben. "Maybe we can stop it."

Essa shook her head. "Gregor played us, right from the start. He learned the Exile was back; he sponsored my friend's Proof so he could talk to it; he sponsored mine so he could help it. When I ran, like I always do, he slammed the Door on me so I'd have no choice but to finish my Proof. Which he took and gave to the Exile. He's played me every step of the way."

"Maybe that's something we can use. The Exile's using your research. That gives us an edge. You know how it works, right? So what can we do to stop this?"

Essa ran a hand through her hair. It came off wet with sweat. "Fine. Fine. Give me a moment with Whisper, I'll see what I can do."

At one point, as he'd followed Gardenback on its rounds, Ben had thought he'd heard the sound of water. Now he set out to find it, winding his way through the mountain's brain. He caught the sound, lost it, caught it again, had to backtrack around an impassable nest of obsidian spikes, and finally came up against the towering rock wall of the mountain. High over his head, water insinuated itself into the cavern through cracks in the stone and fell from an overhang high above. Over the centuries, the cascade had hollowed out a knee-deep depression in the floor, full of water.

He'd hoped to cool off, but the waterfall was almost as hot as his blood. The air tasted scorched. Each drop was a stinging slap on his head and shoulders, but he gritted his teeth and stood there, scrubbed at himself ineffectually until he couldn't stand it anymore. He staggered out of the pool, reached out to steady himself, wincing—his shoulder was really stiffening up, not-so-gently reminding him of what he'd put it through in their escape from Deadbeat. He dried himself off as best he could with his filthy T-shirt, then pulled on his jeans. He was already sweating again.

He sat by the water, scooped some up in his hand and drank. It was bitter with minerals, but it woke a raging thirst and soon he was kneeling by the pool, head down, slurping water.

"Nice look," said Essa, sitting beside him.

Ben kept drinking. He'd had a skin of stale water at the Cogs encampment before the attack on Deadbeat, and some water from the canyon stream where the creeps had caught them, and he couldn't remember the last time before that. Finally he lifted his head and sat back. "So what are we going to do?"

Essa laughed bitterly. "My usual solution is to run."

"You can't run your whole life."

"With an infinity of worlds to run to, actually it's surprisingly easy. My biggest mistake was *not* running, when Gregor brought me to the Spires. None of this would be happening otherwise. But I wanted that Proof so badly…. Now there's nowhere to run to."

"Do you think the Exile can do that? Just…turn off the Well?"

"Possibly." Essa sighed. "I've probably done more research on the Exile than anyone in the Library, on what it did to the Well, and I barely scratched the surface. I'd take it seriously."

Ben shrugged. "Maybe it's right, though. Maybe it's saving everything?"

"Gregor thought it was. He wouldn't have gone along if he'd known it would end the Well; he would never be satisfied with only one world to run. And I'm sure the Exile told him it would be fine, maybe it even showed him a Proof…but math was never Gregor's forté. Getting other people to do it for him, now *that* he was good at.

"I don't know *what* the Exile plans to do, that's the thing. I'd feel a lot better about being trapped for eternity with a bunch of stone heads if I did. Assuming the stone heads themselves aren't right, and this is going to save the worlds rather than end them."

"Well," said Ben, "maybe we can find out. Gregor's Ism took your Proof out of Whisper, when you were mingling, or melding—"

"Communing." Essa sat up straighter, the dullness in her eyes receding.

"Right. So when you were fighting with Gregor…that was the Exile inside him, and if it was mixing it up with Whisper…"

Essa had already sent Whisper streaming out of her flask and was surveying the small cloud of red dust, her eyes bright.

"We were duelling," she murmured, hands cycling through those complex mudra, "not Communing. There *could* have been an imprint…but Lady, Ben. Just look at her."

Even Ben could tell Whisper was in a bad way. The eddies flickering through her were sluggish and random-seeming. Compared to her spritely presence when they'd met, she just looked…sad. Bedraggled and pathetic.

"She's not half of what she used to be. No way to get back to the Library, either, so she'll be diminished for the rest of her days. She can barely keep herself together. Even if there's a fragment of the Exile in her, she can't possibly go digging through it for some clue that *might* be there."

Ben nodded. "So maybe we can help her out."

Essa held up her hand, palm out. Whisper drew herself together, although slowly, tentatively, so unlike her earlier alacrity. She fell into Essa's hand, and Essa spread her out on a round flat stone. "Easier for her, the shape she's in," she said. "One fewer dimension to worry about."

Dimples appeared in the flat red surface, grooves that extended themselves into curving characters that drew and redrew themselves, churning too fast for Ben to follow. Essa hunched over them, sorting them with a finger, flicking them this way and that.

"That's part of Whisper. So's that. Now *this* is interesting…"

Essa pointed. "There. There. And there. It could be Gregor's fragment, part of the Thousand Sails, but I've done enough jobs for the Sails in the Stacks that…. You were right." She shook her head in amazement. "We've got a chunk of the Exile to look at. If you told me a week ago I'd be doing this, I'd have called you a liar."

"So what can it tell us?" asked Ben, leaning forward himself to watch the shifting characters, even though they meant nothing to him.

"Right now? Not much. We need to transform it a little, rotate it so Whisper can look at it from the right angle."

Ben was getting it. "Like the transformation back in the cage."

Essa punched his arm. "Yes! Probably the same one, or very similar. Will it work?"

Ben nodded. "I can make it work."

He couldn't make it work.

Since their escape from Gregor, Ben hadn't been able to take his laptop from its bag and look at it. Finally, though, there were no more reasons to put it off, and he slid the laptop out of its case—it didn't look like any water had made it in, but he winced at the nasty dent in one corner, presumably sustained while they'd run from the tattoos, or landed in the underground river.

His finger hovered over the power button, delaying the inevitable as long as he could, then, gingerly, he turned it on.

A second of nothing that made his stomach turn over, then

the optical drive zipped as it looked for a disc and the screen lit up, flooding him with warm relief.

Twenty-four percent, said the battery.

He'd been worried Whisper wouldn't be able to talk to his laptop, but that was no problem either. She remembered, or part of her did, and soon the fragment of the Exile she'd absorbed was cycling on his screen in a familiar hypnotic pattern.

He had the transformation queued up and ready to go, and he ran it right away.

Nothing happened.

He tried again, and again, running the battery down each time. With increasing panic, he looked through the transformation. It seemed fine, but it was choking on part of the pattern.

Nineteen percent, said the battery when he switched the laptop off, tasting bitter failure.

Finding Essa proved easier than he'd thought. *Where will you be?* he'd asked, and she'd replied *Up*; and there was only one way up, that coiling narrow staircase ascending through the mountain, each step sagging in the middle from centuries of colossal stone feet. At the top was a narrow rocky tunnel with bright blue sky at the end. He emerged, and stood squinting in the daylight.

He was standing on a broad stone ledge. Above him, dense foliage spilled over a rocky overhang. The clouds overhead were breaking up again, and the sunlight made everything blaze with colour, the broad leaves shining like emeralds. A wind played on his face, hot and dry enough to make him blink.

Essa was squatting at the edge of the ledge, stacking pebbles on each other in a small pyramid. The ledge curved slightly, dropping away to left and right, and Ben was careful not to slip as he made his way to her. He thought they must be on one of the mountain's jutting eyelids. Behind them, thick vegetation hid the peak from sight. The stone plain with its thousands of Doors spread itself out before them.

"For Lud," said Essa, not looking at him.

Ben looked at the pile of stones. He'd been thinking about Lud himself, or rather he'd been thinking about how he didn't know what to think. Why had Lud done it, saved Winter like that? Or had that even been on its mind? Was it to protect Winter, had it found something worth caring about at last, or was it just a stupid accident? He didn't know, and he would never have the chance to ask.

Essa edged down to where the curve of the ledge steepened dramatically. She reached for another pebble and it skittered away from her fingers. She leaned further out and almost overbalanced. Ben's guts plummeted and he grabbed the back of her robe, pulled her backwards until she could balance on her own. She sat down hard, then turned and grinned at him, showing him the pebble in her hand.

"You'll kill yourself, you idiot," said Ben.

Essa carefully shuffled back to the tiny cairn and laid the pebble on top. "Probably going to do that anyway, if we go up against Gregor and the Exile," she said. She got to her feet and stood next to Ben. They looked down at the little memorial in silence.

"I don't think we are. It didn't work," said Ben. "I couldn't make it work. I'm sorry."

"It doesn't matter," said Essa after a moment, but Ben thought it kind of did, and he tasted that bitterness again. "At least we know. I'm going to make a run for it tonight, head for one of those Doors on the plain. There should be time to get Wellside before the mountain gets here."

Another gust of scorching wind, bringing with it the distant crackle of flame. They couldn't see the Exile from here, but they could see where it had been, a path of scorched stone and charred mountains.

"Then we should have a few hours to take a look at the local worlds. Pick the one we want to spend the rest of our lives in. Are you in?"

Ben nodded slowly. "You think Winter would come?"

"Be serious, Ben."

He nodded. Winter would fight, of course. Winter would throw her life away against the Exile and its slaves, fighting the thing that had killed her world while Ben and Essa ran like hell.

Essa sighed heavily and turned away, looking at the small sad pile of stones. Having nothing else to do, Ben looked at it with her.

After Ben's granddad had died, his family had driven his grandmother out to the grave every few weeks. Ben had never seen what she got out of it. She didn't talk to it, or even leave flowers—she said his granddad would have wanted the flowers in the garden where they belonged. She barely even looked at the headstone, she could hardly see. She could remember him anywhere, so why'd it have to be there? Why mix up her happy memories with—

Ben shot to his feet, one of which slipped on a scorched patch of lichen and shot out from under him. It was Essa's turn to grab him, stop him from rolling right off the mountain.

"What in the name of all the Choir are you doing—"

"I've got it. I think. I don't—I have to go," Ben managed to gasp, and then he was sprinting for the tunnel.

CHAPTER THIRTY-TWO

Another Ism?"

"I don't know about an Ism. But what you separated out from Whisper, you thought it was the Exile? Well, it was, but it was also something else. Just like Whisper mixed herself with the Exile, the Exile mixed itself with…another one."

"And you managed to separate them?"

"I think so. Once I knew what I was looking for, it was trivial." Ben winced. He was nerding out. "Of course, I couldn't have done it without the original transformation you showed me—"

"Just show me what you found." Essa's eyes were intent on the screen.

"Right," said Ben, "here's what you gave me." The pattern cycled on the screen. "Now here it is after I filtered out the…other thing." He switched windows to show another pulsing pattern. Essa watched it, silently gesturing to Whisper. The dust hovered in front of the screen. Diminished as she was, she took a lot longer than it had taken in the cage-cell, the battery running down all the while. Ben could barely restrain himself from asking Essa to hurry her up. Finally, though, she was done, and fell back onto the stone, those Library ideograms drawing themselves inside her again.

"Well," said Essa, leaning over them (Ben quickly dimmed the laptop's screen to save the battery), "for a start, I was right. Gregor, or anyone, channeling the Exile Wellside…it's not remotely sustainable. He'll burn out. Literally. That's why they're bringing the mountain to the Door—once the Exile is in him, he'll have maybe five minutes to get into the Well and do his thing before he's a grease fire.

"And here's what he's going to do." Another set of ideograms took the first set's place in Whisper's red sand. These were different, not the smooth curves of Library notation. They were clusters of angular runes, and to Ben they looked somehow…unpleasant. Wrong. "It's going to open a Door."

"That's it? Just the one Door? Not like last time, with all the overlapping—"

"Just the one. These," tapping the runes, "are the worldside coordinates. Except they're not any world. Any universe. They're to somewhere *else*."

Gooseflesh broke out on Ben's arms at the way she said it, despite the oppressive heat.

"I don't know what would happen then. Presumably the Exile's hoping it'll create a…paradox, an impossibility, and the Well will vanish rather than let that happen. Except…where's the other element you found?"

Ben was already bringing the screen to life, switching windows. The new pattern wasn't circular and flowing like the others. It was angular, harsh. It reminded him more of those alien runes Whisper had displayed.

"Careful, Whisper," Essa said, as the dust hung in front of the screen.

"Will she be all right?"

"She's not all right *now*. But I hope she knows what she's doing."

Whisper took even longer this time, and Ben slapped the laptop shut as soon as she was done. "Well?" he said to Essa.

Essa had only glanced at the symbols churning in Whisper before she sat back heavily. "We're in trouble," she said almost meditatively.

"We are in serious trouble here."

"It's the thing the Exile's afraid of, isn't it?" said Ben. "It really exists?"

"The things in the cracks, for want of a better name? Possibly. We only have the barest understanding of the math behind the Well, but we know the equations don't work, not without something else behind it. Like dark matter, in your universe. Similar principle. The Exile believes they exist, anyway, and it thinks they're a threat to the Well and the worlds.

"*Except*, it got itself…*infected* is the only word I can think of." She tapped those angular patterns. "It thinks it's opening this Door to end the Well, save us from these things, but instead…"

"It's just doing what they want."

Essa nodded. "They lied to the Exile just like the Exile lied to Gregor. This new Door it's going to open…it'll end everything." She sat back. "This puts rather a new complexion on things."

"We're going to have to fight."

"Yes. It's suicide, but yes."

"Winter'll be happy," said Ben, trying and failing to smile.

"Winter'll be *ecstatic*. Doomed last stands against world-destroying enemies is what Künstler do instead of sex."

Ben opened up the laptop again. "Okay. What can I do?"

"We need a Chant. Ideally something to prevent it creating this new Door, but we don't have the time. So we'll have to kill the Exile instead. Specifically, we'll have to kill Gregor when he's channelling it. It'll only be for five minutes, but for those five minutes, he'll be vulnerable. That's our window to take him out. One shot."

"Can you do that?"

"I can now. With your help." She pointed at the screen. "We just need to take the Exile's imprint on Whisper and run another transformation on it. Whisper'll be…out of phase with it, then, I suppose. The Exile will have its defences up, but she can go through them like they weren't there."

"That's it? That's *easy*," Ben said, starting to smile.

"Well, we need to get close enough to take the shot first," said Essa, but she was starting to smile too.

Ben was already at work. He quickly shut down everything nonessential for the battery's sake, every process he could spare starting with the GUI, leaving him with a black screen, a prompt, and a winking cursor. He cracked his knuckles, kind of ostentatiously, then wished he hadn't. He poised his fingers over the keyboard, and the laptop died.

Ben stared at it. "It's not fair," he said.

"Well," said Essa.

"It's not *fair*. There was ten percent left on the battery, I saw it." He resisted the urge to lift and drop the laptop on the cavern's stone floor, and settled for repeatedly hammering the power button. "Come on, come *on*—"

Essa ran a hand through her hair. "Can we do it ourselves?"

Ben stared at her. "Sure. In theory. It's just a bunch of multiplication, when you get down to it. But do you have any idea how many elements we're talking about?"

"Can we?" asked Essa patiently.

"We—" Ben broke off, running the numbers in his head. "God. How long do you think we've got until the mountain gets to the Door? We're really going to have to push it."

"Well then," said Essa, "let's get started."

The lichen was beginning to brown and curl, and the stone underneath was hot enough to sting. He was thirsty all the time, and the only water was almost hot enough to scald. The burning mountain was getting closer.

It was just a matrix transformation, really. In nine dimensions. Thousands of elements. They had to read each one out of the injured, sluggish Whisper, then do the calculations—not with pencil and paper, but chalk on stone. Then Essa had to write each one into Whisper again. All of it with no errors at all. And then, if they got it done before it was all too late, they had to get close enough to Gregor in that five-minute window for Essa and Whisper to fire off their new Chant, and save the world.

Worlds. Plural. It didn't fit inside Ben's head.

The worst part of it was, he didn't even know if this would work. He and Essa had hours of grinding work ahead of them, and at the end of it all, they'd have *one shot* at the Exile, and even if they didn't mess it up, it could all be for nothing.

But now here came the rush again, the world dropping away, nothing but chalk on stone and the numbers flickering through his head.

Essa read them out from Whisper; he worked them out on the stone; he read them back to Essa. They settled into a steady rhythm, almost singing the numbers, a melody like a hammer on an anvil. It *was* like working in a forge, he supposed, only they were forging a weapon made of math and data, axioms and premises.

He thought about all the movies and the books and the games where at the end it came down to one hero with some epic weapon in a final battle. He'd never thought about the guys who'd *made* those weapons, all the effort they'd put in at their forges and whatnot, never knowing the whole time if it would pay off.

Being that guy *sucked*.

As he called out the numbers, Essa used a shard of obsidian to write them in the circle of dust that was Whisper, in the squiggling glyphs of the Library. They disappeared as she wrote them, the sand surging like the surf.

The creep of the patch of sunlight over the moss was the only indication that this hadn't gone on forever, would go on forever. Their voices became hoarse; at first they cleared their throats when that happened, and then they gave up and whispered. So it was quite a shock, enough to make Ben jump a little, when Essa said, full-voiced: "Wait."

"Wait," she said again. She was peering at the glyphs drawing themselves in the sand.

"What's wrong?" said Ben. Essa said nothing. Her brow furrowed.

"Essa. What's wrong? *Essa.*" He couldn't help the tension that crept into his voice; he hated her even raising the possibility that they'd screwed something up, it just made him contemplate the long series of data they'd entered and how many mistakes they might have made. That *he* might have made. It sent his paranoia and OCD into overdrive.

"Essa!"

"Nothing's wrong," she said, "nothing's wrong, it's just—Red Lady. Red Lady's *teeth.*"

Ben relaxed a little, but only a little. "What is it?"

"Feedback from Whisper. She just went through the last batch of numbers we sent her. She's figured something out."

"She's figured it out? How to beat the Exile?" Ben felt a surge of hope, if only that the endless repetition of numbers might come to an end.

"We're not quite that lucky, Ben, no." Essa was pointing at the sand. It was churning like the surface of boiling water, glyphs writing and overwriting themselves too fast for Ben to keep track.

Essa pointed. "That," she said, "is how you make a Door. Fast and accurate. That's a secret that anyone who knows anything about the Well would murder a dozen worlds to have."

"You can understand it?" said Ben.

"Barely. But it works, Ben. I spent years on it, and look at it, it works and it's *beautiful.*" Essa shook her head, her eyes glistening. "You know what this is? Who- or whatever created the Well, this is their language. This is what they were speaking when they punched a hole right through the universes, this is how they did it.

"And this here, this constant, that could be the depth, that could mean there's a bottom—I mean, I'm just brainstorming, but—Lady. I'm dizzy."

"Okay," said Ben. "And this helps us how?"

"It doesn't," said Essa, "but when we get out of this…"

Ben was already back at the wall with his chunk of chalk. "So it's academic."

"I *am* an academic, Ben, and excuse me for having a sense of wonder." She sighed and picked up the shard of obsidian. "Very well then. Shoot."

"Seven-nine-nine."

"Seven-nine-nine." The sand eddied, settled, eddied again.

With a few hours to go, they had to take a break; if they pushed it any further they'd just start screwing up.

Essa collapsed and lay where she fell. By the time Ben had made his way over to her, she was already snoring. He managed to make it to the mossy alcove and closed his eyes.

He skimmed the surface of sleep, numbers chasing each other through his head like shoals of glittering fish. He woke up drenched with sweat, more tired than when he'd started.

He rubbed his eyes. It felt like he had a layer of grit beneath each eyelid. He bent his head back and felt a satisfying *click* in his neck. He wondered if this was how Essa had felt after her duel with Gregor. He wasn't bleeding from the eyes, at least, although he thought it might well be in the cards.

Time for some fresh air. He found the staircase leading to the mountain's eyelid and began to climb, blinking the sleep out of his eyes.

The sky was overcast once more—the clouds formed and broke up here in a never-ending dance—but there was a rent in them a little way off and anaemic sunlight was trickling through, steep-angled and tinged with red. It lit up the mountains around them; he saw that some of them had been defaced, features beaten into senseless jagged rock. The work of the tattoos, he assumed, quarrying stone for all those Doors. Others were untouched but weathered almost to nothing, covered with deep cracks sprouting ragged greenery. One of them had a waterfall running from its ear, cascading and branching into a network of glittering streams that spread over the plain

He looked down at the Doors, thousands of them. How many times had the Exile tried before it'd found the Door to Deadbeat? Ben tried to imagine it—its slave army laboriously raising each door, the Exile doing whatever it did to link it to the Well…then opening each, or waiting for it to be opened—and meeting with failure, over and over again. It would have driven him insane.

Then he saw the shadows flickering above him on the mountain's giant forehead. Carefully, he edged out on the ledge to see what was throwing them.

It was Winter, lit up by the setting sun pouring through another of those rents in the clouds, running through some kind of martial arts drill on the topmost of the narrow ledges that furrowed the mountain's brow. She wasn't alone—Gardenback was with her, and half a dozen other statues, all rough-hewn and faceless. Fighters. They were drilling with Winter; sometimes she led them, sometimes followed, and they were picking up on each other's movements, mirroring them, learning from each other. Then Winter turned, they all did, to face the plain, and the look on her face took his breath away.

He'd thought of Winter as empty, some essential part of her impoverished and made shallow by her singular focus. But now he saw he'd been wrong—she might be narrow but she was deep, and right now, she was giving herself over completely to her art, attaining depths of herself that Ben and Essa and everyone else just didn't have. And now she'd met others with the same depth, and it let them commune with each other, absolutely and perfectly.

He could see the muscles moving under the skin of her back, the dark veins close to the surface, the perfection of every movement, the absolute mastery she had over her body. It was a little heartbreaking, and despite what he knew now about what Winter was, it was sexy as hell.

"She'd snap it off."

Ben twisted around; Essa was sitting behind and above him on the crest of the mountain's eyelid. She had her little leather-bound notebook spread open in her hand and she was sketching, sticking her tongue out as she worked on a detail, occasionally raising her head quick as a bird's to look at Winter and the statues.

Ben felt himself blushing. "How do you know what I was thinking?"

Essa looked at Winter. "Yeah, it was really difficult," she said. She put the pencil down, careful not to let it roll away, and flexed her fingers. "Besides, look at this world. Just one big funeral." She waved at the mountains, faces downcast as if asleep or dead. "And funerals get you horny—sex is how we show death who's boss." She picked up the pencil again.

Ben made his way over to her and looked over her shoulder at the sketch. She held it up for him: Winter was a jumble of light and shade, poised on one foot as she shifted her stance, one dark eye catching the light, the crest of the mountain barely sketched behind her.

"They're big on draftsmanship, in the Library," she said, licking her finger and dabbing at Winter's arm. "Making records for the Stacks, and so forth. I did so much drawing I thought my hand would fall off."

It was probably on account of being out of his mind with fatigue, but Ben decided to go for it. "It's beautiful," he said. "And so are—"

"Ben," she said, not looking up, "we are going to be dead by tomorrow afternoon. You are pretty much certain to get lucky tonight, so don't muck it up for yourself, okay?"

He was saved from having to reply by a sudden sound above them, a ringing blow that made them both jump.

Essa looked up. "Here we go."

The drilling had turned to sparring. Winter faced off against Gardenback, the others spread out across the cliff face watching. As Ben watched, Winter took a skipping step towards the statue, winding up with her fist as she did, and drove it into its midriff with a sound like a jackhammer striking concrete. Chips of stone ricocheted off the mountainside.

Gardenback swung an arm like a club and Winter parried it with her forearm, the impact ringing out over the plain and sending her skidding across the ledge. She dug her heels in and charged, her leg scything out in a low kick, and then they were really going at it, blows and echoes of blows merging into a thunderous clamour. The darkness was gathering and the sparks Winter and the statue struck off each other swarmed in the air like fireflies.

"That could have been me," said Essa quietly. She might not have meant to be heard—Ben only did hear her because of a sudden lull in the sparring above her, as the big statue switched with one of its smaller friends.

"What, an Eisenkünstler?" said Ben.

"No, of course not. I could have been the Library equivalent. Devoted myself to something, I mean. Quit screwing around with abstract stuff, picked an Ism, ran with it, trained *hard*. Gotten really *good* at something."

"Why didn't you?"

"Independence. Beholden to no one, you know? Except I ended up selling out to Gregor anyway. I could have *been* Gregor."

Ben considered. "Well," he said, "you're not. So I'd say you win."

She gave him a lopsided smile. "You're all right, Ben."

Ben was going to say something, but then he remembered what she'd said about not messing things up. So he just kissed her.

Chapter Thirty-Three

Ben's fingers were bleeding. They'd gone numb long since, so he didn't even notice until the numbers he was writing down turned pink. He didn't stop. Every time he stopped, he lost track of where they were and made a mistake, then more mistakes as he sped up to make up for the time they'd lost. Then he'd have to backtrack while Essa waited impatiently, her obsidian shard poised over the sand. He forced himself to keep an even pace while the counter ran down, and all at once they found a rhythm, Ben rapping out numbers, Essa's hand a blur as she repeated them, both of them lost in the rush.

"Three-five-seven."

"Three-five-seven," Essa repeated.

"Four-six-one."

"Four-six-one."

Her hand dipped again, a reflex, anticipating the next numbers, but they didn't come. She looked up. "Ben?"

"We're done," he said. He wiped the sweat from his forehead.

"We're—wait, what? Seriously?"

He nodded. He wasn't able to believe it himself.

They looked at each other, then together they collapsed on their backs on the moss.

"No way of knowing if it worked," said Ben. "Even if Whisper didn't pick up any mistakes. Any number of things could have gone wrong."

"Worth a try," said Essa. "Scared?"

Ben considered. "No. After all that? I'd rather let Gregor pull me apart than admit there was no point going through *that*."

Essa burst out laughing, and rolled on top of him.

Essa wasn't there when Ben woke up. He ran his hand over the depression in the moss where she'd been. The moss was dry and brown. He winced as his bare feet came down on the scorching stone, and quickly slipped his shoes on.

Rubbing his eyes, he wandered beneath the mountain's mind. He saw her, in the distance, sitting there with Whisper whirling around her head, but when he approached her, she shot him an annoyed look. Immediately she softened it with a smile, but one that said plainly *Go away*.

As he retreated, Ben was already starting to worry if he'd screwed things up with her somehow. He could feel that flywheel in his brain revving up, his thoughts getting ready to chase themselves around and around.

Screw it. He was going to be dead in a few hours anyway. He just let it go, and was surprised at how easy it was.

Winter was just outside the crystal cave, in her jacket and leggings and boots, talking quietly with one of the statues—not a fighter but the jet-black faceless one that had led the operation, or ceremony, that had resurrected her. It bowed to her and moved away silently as Ben approached.

"Hi," he said, not knowing what else to say. She nodded slightly and stood there, waiting.

The last time Ben had talked to her was to tell her about their plan. She'd listened without speaking; walked away, presumably to run it by the statues; and the next time he'd seen her, she'd nodded, once, and that was that. It made Ben queasy; people were going to die as a result of this, and it was *his* plan, or partly anyway. But he wanted to say *something*, and this could be his last chance.

He ended up saying, "I'm sorry."

Winter said nothing.

"Essa told me. About the Eisenwelt." He felt like he was wading out into murky water, not knowing if his next step would plunge him in over his head. "She told me what happened."

Winter shrugged. She wasn't looking at him. "I never saw it. She talked about it, though. The one who taught me."

"But I mean…with the Exile…I mean, you must be happy, right? To get the chance to…"

Winter shrugged, the motion nearly lost in her oversized jacket.

"You do what you have to," she said. "One fight at a time. That's all."

"Really?" Ben asked. "That's all you feel?"

She just looked at him.

"It destroyed your *world*. Or your teacher's world, anyway. Don't you feel anything? Besides 'one fight at a time'? Besides clichés?"

Winter considered this. "Clichés work," she said finally, "if they're true. Or maybe they aren't true, I don't care. They work anyway. And they're all the Art leaves you room for."

That just sounded sad to Ben. "Is it worth it?"

"How would I know?" said Winter. Then, abruptly: "I have to go." She turned without waiting for a reply and stepped lightly across the cavern to where Gardenback was approaching.

Ben stayed where he was. From a distance, he saw Winter and the statue talking, her face upraised, open, smiling, and then something crossed it he hadn't seen before. She looked…not vulnerable exactly, but full of wonder and a little bit of fear—treading on eggshells, like she couldn't quite believe this was happening to her—seeing a Book, meeting the stone warriors, all of it. The whole time Ben had known her, she'd seemed, well, unhappy as hell, but also sure of herself, absolutely centred in her hopeless universe. Now she was facing another possibility—that maybe she wouldn't wander for the rest of her life, maybe she'd found a home here—and, maybe for the first time in her life, she was unsure.

The burning mountain had arrived.

They'd watched it approach from the mountain's brow, but the heat had driven Ben and Essa back into the cave. Only Winter still stood there, silhouetted against a sky full of ghastly red light.

"So do we all know what we're doing?" asked Essa.

"Absolutely," said Ben, with a confidence he didn't feel. Winter said nothing.

"Winter, you and the fighters are running interference. You're getting us to the Door, and after that you hang back, okay?"

Winter's silhouette nodded, not looking at her.

"I'm not mucking about here, Winter," said Essa. "Being inside Gregor'll slow the Exile down, but it's not going to let you just stroll up and punch its head off. Stay back and let Ben and me take a shot at it. If we…if it doesn't work out, you can do all the punching you want. All right?"

Winter stood at ease but her fists were clenched and trembling. She was *pissed*, and he expected her at any moment to leap a hundred feet straight down to the plain and start kicking ass.

The temperature was climbing even as they stood there. Far below, dust roiled on the plain around the burning mountain and its dying slaves. Now it was the next mountain over's turn to burst into flames; the wind changed direction as oxygen rushed to fuel the conflagration. Drawing breath was painful.

"All right?" Essa repeated. "Winter?"

A grating noise from behind them; one of the warrior-statues. Winter nodded but she didn't move. She remained there for a moment, gazing down, and then suddenly turned on her heel and strode past them back into the mountain, not sparing Ben or Essa a glance. A dark vein pulsed, metronome-steady, under the pale skin of her temple.

"Screw it," said Essa quietly, "I tried. Lady-braid-my-voice-with-others'-let-it-rise-to-the-vaults," running the words together like a prayer. She breathed deep, blew the air out of her lungs, and turned to follow Winter.

Ben made his way up to the mouth of the cave—he felt the heat tightening the skin on his face—for one last look. Far, far below, in the burning mountain's path, he could see a tiny fleck of black against the grey stone.

Chapter Thirty-Four

The constant grinding noise of the mountain faded as the sled came to a halt. The half-melted visage gazed down at Gregor. He looked up at it, bliss spreading across what was left of his face.

For a moment, all was silence. Then something began to pour from the mountain's ruined face, like a sandstorm or a swarm of locusts. It was neither the red dust of the Library or the white of its agent, but a shifting rainbow of colours like an oil slick on the air.

As the last of it left the mountain, it began to circle, forming a hurricane a hundred feet tall. Lightning crackled inside it, tracing the contours of something inside the maelstrom, something made of many-angled darkness.

"Exile," Gregor whispered, still smiling.

Then he jerked to his feet as the Exile's agent left him, white dust pouring from him and merging with the hurricane. For just a moment he looked up at the Exile with his own mind, and screamed, and screamed. Then the storm fell on him.

It poured into his nose, his eyes, his ears, his screaming mouth, and any humanity Gregor had been holding onto was snuffed out like a match in a cataract. The hurricane contracted, tightened around him—and then, as if a switch had been thrown, it was gone. Gregor's body stood in the centre of a great circle of scoured stone. Dark, distended veins pulsed on his face and scalp. One eye popped, and then the other, and the gore that wept from the socket streaked his face like tears. Outside the circle, the tattoos watched him cautiously.

The heat was gone from the air. The Exile's departure had snuffed out the burning mountain and its half-melted face was dark and cold. A deafening *crack*—the mountain's sudden cooling had opened a crevasse that stretched across its immense face from ear to ear. More appeared, creeping across the stone, and now a chunk of its nose fell, landing in the middle of the swarm of tattoos, who squealed and ran as the mountain's face rained down in pieces.

The Exile paid it no attention at all. It turned, awkwardly, fighting unfamiliar muscles, and began to walk jerkily away from the mountain, towards the Door and the orange light of Deadbeat that spilled from it.

And then it stopped, as a section of the plain a hundred yards away exploded in a shower of debris.

Chapter Thirty-Five

Gardenback's fist hammered into the rockfall that had camouflaged the tunnel's mouth. Ben's ears rang as huge boulders tumbled out onto the plain. Gardenback kicked them aside as it lumbered into the open, picking up speed as it charged towards the Door, Winter crouched on its broad shoulder. The other fighters followed, and Ben and Essa pressed themselves against the tunnel wall as they rushed past like an avalanche.

Ben gripped Essa's hand and screwed up his face, waiting for one of them to clip him and shatter his ribs…and then it was over, all the fighters fanning out around Gardenback in a flying wedge, knocking stone Doors aside like matchsticks as they forged across the plain. Winter now ran with them—ran *on* them, leaping from shoulder to shoulder, making her way to the front.

"Go!" yelled Ben, Essa with him as he rushed out of the tunnel. They sprinted after the statues, stumbling over the rocks, running then sliding down the slope towards the Door.

The statues hit the line of tattoos like a wrecking ball, hardly slowing as they plowed through, fists dripping with blood. It looked to Ben like they would charge forever, but more and more tattoos swarmed over them and all at once their momentum was spent, stranding them a hundred feet from the Door.

On the other side of the melee, Ben saw Gregor watching the

fight. Then he turned his back on it, stepping through the Door; they were side-on to it and it was strange to see, his tall figure disappearing from one side and not reappearing on the other. Winter saw him too. She sprang from Gardenback's shoulder, kicking a tattoo's head in as she leaped through the air.

"Winter, *no!*" screamed Essa.

Winter landed on the lintel of a stone Door, and just as quickly launched herself off, leaping sure-footed from one Door to another, heading after the Exile.

One of the *tireurs* had shot a Wall-goat, and his unit had it over a spit behind a nearby Door. They'd been kind enough to share the wealth with the cavalry, and the greasy chunks of meat were most welcome—the supply train had been one of the casualties of the disastrous attack on Deadbeat, and their actual rations were probably even now raining down on some luckless town downWell. Poinkaré was at the bottom of the siege line, squatting on the walkway and sucking the last of the marrow from a bone while she scanned the Well with a borrowed field glass.

There: the glimmer of Doorlight on brass. And there. And there. Now the red glow of a trio of balloons, miles down but rising. A quarantine line was going up. The Powers, not having any better idea, were cutting the whole thing off, Deadbeat and the remnants of the siege line both. Who knew how many more days they would be stuck here. She sucked extra hard on the bone, getting every last shred of meat before she pitched it off the walkway.

Then she heard the noise. A long, drawn-out sigh, coming from somewhere in the town above them. Ochre dust blurred the outlines of the buildings and began to fall slowly towards the Cogs positions.

Dread closing her throat, Poinkaré reached for her glass. It wasn't the Exile's weapon, though, just random dirt blown in through a Door. The wind from wherever-it-was picked up, becoming an eerie wail, and the dust became a horizontal plume that reached out into the Well.

She glanced across the gap at the bottom of the line, at the small canvas tent within which hunkered Colonel Pevel, currently the ranking officer on what was left of the siege line, after the Dust had smashed Karrère and his entire staff to bits. The last time Poinkaré had seen Pevel, he'd been knocking his head gently against the wall of the tent and muttering to himself while his adjutant had vainly cajoled him to sign a stack of orders. Shock. Poinkaré had considered hauling him out of the tent and shoving him off the walkway, but she rather thought she might be in shock too.

Then, louder, a hollow *bang*, and a shower of splinters and torn netting began to rain from the town. Another, and Poinkaré saw something flicker across a row of buildings, an oily shapeless glow. As it touched the buildings, they exploded one by one like over-filled balloons.

More wood came raining down, and Poinkaré ducked and pressed herself against the Wall. Had she seen something else, just for a moment? Something leaping from roof to roof, just ahead of the oily shimmer?

Houellebek was running along the walkway, wide-eyed. "We're being *hit*—" he was yelling.

Poinkaré shook her head. "I don't think so. I think"—the two sidestepped as a wrist-thick length of cable came coiling past them— "I think someone up there is having a disagreement."

"But who?" asked Houellebek.

Poinkaré looked past him at the other end of the line. It looked like someone had finally got an order out of Pevel, because a young officer bolted out of the tent, juggling semaphore flags and nearly dropping them down Well.

"Well, whoever they are, I think they're about to have a very bad—yes, there you go—" she said as the flags flapped wildly, sending signals down the line.

Open fire, she read. *Small arms only*.

She drew her pistol. "You heard the man," she said to Houellebek as carbines began to crack all around.

The statues had formed a double line by the Door, keeping a path open for Ben and Essa. One fell, dragged down by tattoos, and then another. The others spread out to cover the gaps, but as they thinned out ink-patterned arms reached between them into the open path, clutching.

One of them grazed Ben's shoulder as he and Essa ran past, knocking his bag's strap off his shoulder. He tried to catch it in the crook of his elbow but it slipped off his arm and was gone. He heard the crash as it hit the ground behind him. He didn't look back. He couldn't look back, if he paused for even a second he knew he wouldn't move again, just cower until it was all over.

Ahead of them a statue fell, its head reduced to rubble. They managed to hurdle it without falling but there weren't enough fighters left to close the line and tattoos poured through the gap after them, hissing on their heels. He kept running, gripping Essa's hand, and then they were clear and the Door loomed up ahead of them.

The air scoured Ben's lungs; with every step he took, he was certain that was it, his legs would buckle and he would go down. A hiss behind him, terrifyingly close, and with the last of his strength, he rushed for the Door. Ahead of him Essa stumbled and he planted a hand on her back and pushed her through as their legs went out from under them, and they collapsed in a heap on the platform outside the Door.

After the tropical heat of the plain, the air of the Well was like being dumped into a freezing lake. Ben rolled over and look up, right into the face of a tattoo. Its lips were dyed bright blue and they opened impossibly wide as it leaned forward to chew his throat out. A massive stone hand swept it aside, smashing it over the edge of the platform into the Well, and he was looking up at Gardenback. The statue raised its dripping hand, palm held out in farewell, and it leaned against the great stone Door and pushed it shut.

He blinked back tears. "Are you—are you okay?" he said to Essa.

Essa wasn't listening. She was flipping the cap off Whisper's flask and pulling out a tendril of red dust, her lips moving soundlessly. Ben's stomach lurched. This was it. This was their one shot.

Then they both jumped as an almighty crash shook the air around them. Ben grabbed the handrail as he felt the platform shift, metal screeching. The two of them turned and looked out over Deadbeat.

"…Lady's teeth," Essa said, and Ben could only nod.

Chapter Thirty-Six

Gregor's body stood by the canted steel Door that had once led to Deadbeat's Committee chamber. Its occupant looked out through his empty eyesockets at what was left of Deadbeat.

Half the town lay in ruins, an unrecognisable jumble of wood and rope, slumping dangerously as its remaining support cables sagged under its weight. Now Gregor's body raised an arm and a cloud of oily smoke formed a shimmering tentacle around it, extending a hundred yards straight up into the air. He brought the arm down sharply and the tentacle followed the movement, smashing down onto a heavy cable, parting it and spilling the buildings that had hung from it into the Well.

Just as they fell apart and tumbled into the abyss, a pale flash erupted from one of the buildings, leaping through the air and grabbing onto the severed end of a rope, swinging from it over the void.

Gregor's other arm swept out horizontally and another tentacle lashed Deadbeat, parting the rope and caving in the wall of a building. But the tiny figure had already leapt away and vanished into the warren of the old town. He caught fleeting glimpses of it, vaulting and tic-tacking through the alleys, coming round for another run at him.

Gregor's jaw clenched with such force that it shattered most of his teeth, and he spat out a mouthful of powdered enamel.

The Exile was one of the oldest Isms of any Library. Its mind—if it could even be called a mind—was huge and ancient and strange, and bore not the slightest resemblance to the fleeting psyches of mortals.

Its temporary lodgings in the skull that had formerly belonged to Gregor, however, had imposed certain limitations on it. It had been forced to conform to the shape of the vessel that held it. To something approximating humanity, and human emotion.

Right then, for instance, it was immensely pissed off.

To open the Door that would end the Well, it needed to concentrate. Only a moment would do—but the little iron girl wouldn't give it even that. She simply would not *stop*.

She had burst out of the stone Door right after the Exile had, and she'd very nearly caved Gregor's head in, ruined everything. But at the last moment, the Exile had seen her coming for him, arms outstretched, bent on murder, and it had sent a lance of oily light at her that had almost taken off the top of her skull. She had fled into the depths of Deadbeat, and the Exile had turned to the Door, but the iron girl had come at it again. It had laid waste to half the town as it tried to root her out, without success.

The Exile sent another tentacle whipping across Deadbeat, snapping a dozen rope bridges one after the other. Steel cables groaned as the stress on them built up. The town sagged further into the void. And still the iron girl kept coming.

"*Winter damn it what did I SAY!*" screamed Essa.

"Essa," said Ben, "do it. Now."

"She's going to get herself killed, Ben! I told her, I *told her*—"

"*Essa!*" Ben roared. "She's distracting it. If you're going to do it, do it *now*! Go!"

Essa stared at him for a moment, then nodded. She drew what was left of Whisper out of her flask and swirled her hand, drawing a spiral in dust in the air. The spiral rotated, picking up speed, as Essa's free hand twisted into one shape after another and she muttered commands in those backwards whispers. Whisper spun faster and faster, until Ben was dizzy and had to look away. He glanced up at the Exile, standing there at the highest point of the town.

He saw it smile, and raise its arms.

One of Gregor's eardrums burst, fluid spattering his shoulder and coursing sluggishly down his jaw. The Exile's host was falling apart. If it did not end this soon, then the brains that held it would boil and all would be lost.

Enough of this.

Gregor's body brought its hands together and above it, its tentacles fused into one long trunk that reared up above Deadbeat. It saw the little iron girl, working her way under him, trying to come at him that way. It waited—waited—and then the immense pseudopod came crashing down on the mighty steel cable that anchored half of the town.

In her ten years in *L'Armée du Puits*, Henriette-Marie Poinkaré had seen a lot of spectacular scenes, but only twice had it been enough for her jaw to literally drop. The first time had been at the Battle of Centipede Bridge, when the fire on the *Intrépide* had reached the magazines and the great airship had vanished in an explosion that had taken out the balloons of half a dozen frigates downWell in a nightmarish chain reaction.

The second time was right now.

From this distance, the immense steel cable looked no thicker than a strand of yarn. But when the tentacle crashed down on it and it parted, the noise it made reverberated right through her.

The severed end lashed the air for a moment—and then went slack, and fell.

The Exile's heart sang with vicious triumph as a good third of what was left of Deadbeat fell into the abyss. *Goodbye, little iron girl.*

Now, finally, it turned its attention to the tilted metal Door behind it. Oily smoke poured from Gregor's nostrils and spread itself over the Wall. And the Door began to change.

Ben's heart leaped into his throat. That was it. That had to be it. Winter was gone—

Then he saw her, leaping up the cable as it fell, gaining ground. He lost her through all the debris raining down around her, saw her, lost her again.

Was that it? Was that it? Was—

There.

She stood on the very edge of what was left of Deadbeat, her back straight, small and defiant, the colossal cable far below her, still falling.

Chapter Thirty-Seven

A sizeable chunk of Deadbeat still clung to the cable as it descended, whole rows of terraced houses and networks of boardwalks. When the cable reached its full extension, inertia had its way and they burst into a torrent of wood and stone and steel and glass, raining downWell. The noise was deafening.

But the massive cable hadn't stopped moving yet. It was still anchored at one end, and now it began to swing, sparks raining down as it scraped along the Well. The town's biggest pendulum hung from the end of it, still miraculously intact.

Appalled, Poinkaré watched as the cable smashed into the end of the Cogs' siege line, the pendulum acting as a wrecking ball. Men and crawlers rained into the Well. The cable continued to plow through the line, and she saw it collect Pevel's tent along the way, obliterating it and making Poinkaré the ranking officer on the line.

"Fire," she said, almost without thinking, and beside her Houellebek frantically signaled; but Poinkaré didn't think it'd really matter, because now the cable slowed. Stopped. Started swinging in the other direction, towards Poinkaré and Houellebek as they stared open-mouthed.

Poinkaré recovered first.

"Run," she said.

They did run, like hell, back along the walkway towards their nearest designated safe point, a metal Door opening into a deserted garden shed in a vacant lot on a vacant world. They'd made it halfway when a wrought-iron lamp post skidded down the Well from Deadbeat and demolished ten feet of walkway ahead of them.

Poinkaré looked back and her eyes widened. The cable had been picking up a lot more speed than she'd expected, and it was right on their heels. She grabbed Houellebek as she opened the nearest Door— tall, narrow, white-painted wood—yanked him through and slammed it shut; she barely had the presence of mind to pull her glove off with her teeth and wedge it over the latch to stop it closing fully. Then she and Houellebek leaned against the Door, gasping for breath, and slid down until they were sitting on the floor. Outside they could hear the thundering crash as the cable swept over the Wall where they'd been, muted as all sounds were on the other side of a Door.

"So much for—" she said, and Houellebek said, "*Shhh.*"

She looked around, taking in her surroundings for the first time. The room they were in was illuminated only by a nightlight on a small chest of drawers. By the dim light, Poinkaré could see the painted frogs and bears capering across the walls. A small child sat on a narrow bed in her pyjamas, staring wide-eyed at the two dishevelled figures in shakos who'd emerged from her toy cupboard.

Poinkaré grinned at her and put a finger to her lips. The child nodded solemnly. Poinkaré elbowed Houellebek in the ribs, who cursed under his breath as he hunted through his pockets for sweets.

CHAPTER THIRTY-EIGHT

Whisper, spiraling in front of Essa, had begun to glow as she spun, and Ben could feel the heat coming off her as her glow brightened from red to orange to a blinding white. Would she be okay? Essa was sweating, still muttering.

Above them, whatever the Exile was doing to the Committee's Door was nearly complete. It wasn't even a Door anymore. It was an immense ragged hole, fragments of the Well crumbling from its edges and being sucked to the absolute darkness inside. The Exile raised a hand, and more chunks of the Well began to fall away.

"She's ready," said Essa, through gritted teeth. "I can't hold it, I—"

"Essa, wait," he said, looking up. "Wait."

"I *can't*, Ben—"

"One more second, Essa. Just one more—"

As he spoke, he saw it happen. The Exile turned from the enormous hole, for a final look at the Well.

And it saw Winter, standing there bloodied but alive.

And Winter raised her hand and waved.

The Exile *shrieked*, a howl of untrammeled fury, a terrifying sound that shook Ben to his core. He could barely speak. He managed a single word.

"Now."

CHAPTER THIRTY-NINE

It probably would have worked.

But as Essa screamed and flung her arms wide and Whisper's spiral became a lance, a glowing spear that streaked through the air towards the Exile, burning a bright trail across Ben's retinas, the Cogs' remaining siege guns began to fire.

The first blast knocked them both off their feet, and the lance veered in midair, splashing Gregor in the face instead of slicing right through him. Burning droplets rained down on the Well as Essa's eyes rolled up and she crumpled silently to the ground.

Gregor swayed, and Ben waited for him to go limp, topple into the Well and fall forever. He waited for it to be over.

But Gregor didn't fall. He turned and looked down at Ben. His lips curled in a smile. All the rest of the skin on his head had been seared off, leaving the white gleam of bone. It wasn't fair.

Gregor turned and faced the Door-that-wasn't, preparing to enter. Ben thought he could see something, deep in the darkness. He wanted to look away but couldn't.

Beside him, Essa spat out a syllable like nothing Ben had heard, something that it didn't seem possible had come from a human mouth.

She followed it with another, and then they were pouring from her. The air seemed to grow denser. Ben felt the pressure increase on his eardrums and eyeballs. She raised her arms, fingers twisting into impossible configurations.

Above them, the Well was growing back around the rent the Exile had opened. A Door was growing there, a huge iron gate standing half-open, deep red light shining through.

The Exile was in the middle of stepping through when it changed. It teetered, fighting inertia, looking like it might tumble through anyway—then it managed to rock backwards, plant its feet on the ground.

It looked down at Essa. "You," it said. It raised an arm, and Ben saw that oily shimmer form on the end of it.

Then it glanced sideways, and froze.

Winter was coming for it, vaulting through the wreckage of Deadbeat, building up momentum, her black eyes wide and her mouth frozen in a snarl.

The Exile brought Gregor's arm up, but it was far too late. Winter slammed into it with all her weight, sending them both tumbling backwards, straight through the iron Door.

Essa spoke another syllable, and the gate slammed shut with a hollow boom that rolled through the ruined town. The iron sloughed off it, dissolving like spun sugar in the rain, and now the Door was just a door, plain and grey-blue, EQUIPMENT written on it in peeling paint.

Ben looked down at Essa. "What...?"

"Figured it out," said Essa. It clearly cost her to speak. "How to make a Door. Told you."

Ben grabbed her and held her close. "*Ow*," she said, "easy."

Ben didn't let up. "What about Winter?" he said, but he knew the answer already.

Essa shook her head. "We can't get her back, Ben. She'd bring it back with her. I think she knew that."

Something was climbing up the Well towards them, a brass scorpion with a dishevelled figure in its saddle, its shako askew. Ben waved at it to get its attention.

"Wait," he said, as something else occurred to him. "Won't the Exile just start making more Doors, wherever it is? What's to stop it?"

"I don't think it's going to get the chance," said Essa, "not where I sent it."

Chapter Forty

They landed in red dust that billowed around them.

Winter was on her feet almost instantly, raising a foot to stomp the Exile's head in, but it flung her away with a wave of oily light. It stood up, brushing the red dust off Gregor's robes.

"Red Sand City?" it whispered, savouring the words. "They sent me *home?* They thought *this* would stop me? I—"

It paused. It looked down at the dust.

It wasn't sand.

Slowly, the way you feel in your pocket for something you know isn't there, putting off the moment of revelation, the Exile raised Gregor's head. It said, "*No.*"

Winter was looking too, black tears streaming down her face as she gazed at the city that rose around them. It stood in ruins, the rust eating through the immense blocky buildings and towering chimney stacks, piling in dunes at their feet, but its grandeur still eclipsed anything she'd seen.

"Eisenwelt," she whispered.

"This isn't the end," said Gregor's lips. "All you've done is kill *yourself.* I can find another shell. I can start again. I—" Its voice died as it stared with Gregor's empty eyes at the shadows emerging from the ruined foundries around them.

They were huge, almost buildings in their own right, colossal iron warriors that towered over the ruined body of the Librarian.

"No," whispered the Exile. "No. I rusted you out. I rusted you out and you're all dead."

"It's all about will," said Winter's voice from behind it. "That's the first thing you learn." She fell to her knees. "You hang on until you've done what needs doing."

The circle of Künstler was tightening on the Exile. He lashed out with a shimmering tentacle and an iron woman crumbled to powder, but the rest of them kept coming. Alien panic in its eyes, the Exile abandoned its host. Gregor burst in a shower of blood as it poured into the air, a huge pillar of smoke rising up among the foundries, lightning playing through it.

The Künstler let themselves go too. They fell apart into clouds of rust that swarmed into the Exile, spiralling up and through it, ripping it apart. Lightning crackled continuously, the sound forming a single sustained Tesla-coil note like a long and drawn-out shriek that rose in pitch until Winter's ears bled—

And then the pillar burst, and rained down on the rusted city in a shower of lifeless soot.

Winter looked at her hands. Rust spots were already forming on her skin. She lay back on the dune and closed her eyes.

"Home," she said.

CHAPTER FORTY-ONE

Hi Mum. Hi Dad.

    I'm alive. I'm fine. Really.

    Don't worry about me.

I love you.

Ben.

He clicked SEND, didn't bother to log out. He climbed the stairs out of the basement gaming lounge, then turned right and into the alley beside it.

Essa leaned against the wall, her foot propping open the lounge's fire door. Through it he could feel a cold breeze, and a faint rich smell like earth after rain.

"Feel better?" she asked.

"Not really."

"Told you." She tugged at the band of her eyepatch. "You'll be back one day, Ben, but until then, there's nothing you can say."

He didn't want to talk about it anymore. "How is it?" he asked, looking at the patch. The attack they'd concocted on the Exile, the one that hadn't even worked, had blasted through her with such force that she'd detached a retina. They'd treated it at the Cogs field hospital, after they'd been rescued from Deadbeat; there were Vats microbes crawling around in her eyeball even now, tacking everything down.

"They did a good job," she said. "Henriette-Marie was pretty cool about everything. Considering we'd just dropped a town on her."

It was true, she had been. Although they'd made it easy on her, by leaving out the part about the Exile and the things behind the Well and pretty much everything else. They'd spun a story about hiding in a garbage dump ever since the invasion. They were filthy enough that it was easy to believe.

"So what now?"

"Not the Library," she said. "Not yet." Whisper whirled around her wrist; she held her hand out flat and the dust balanced on her palm, a miniature whirlwind. "She's still not a hundred percent, and I need to talk this over with her properly, what we're going to do with this secret of ours. Until then…I'm going exploring. We can make Doors now, Ben. We can go anywhere, and we won't be anchored to a single Door when we get there. We can see as much of the worlds as we like."

"'We'," he said, "meaning you and Whisper, or…"

She stood on tiptoe and kissed him on the cheek. "What do you think, you dope? Will I need to spell everything out from now on?"

"It wouldn't hurt."

"Idiot," she said, smiling. She held the door open for him. Inside, a length of rope dangled down into nothingness. "Let's see the worlds."

THE END

Acknowledgements

Athena Andreadis and Kate Sullivan at Candlemark & Gleam took a chance on *Wellside* and their editing turned a ramshackle manuscript into a proper story. And if you're reading this, it's probably because Jenny Zemanek's phenomenal cover caught your eye. I can't thank any of them enough.

Thanks to every artist who influenced me and made me want to write in the first place: Yukito Kishiro, Terry Gilliam, Hayao Miyazaki, HR Giger, HP Lovecraft, David Lynch, David Cronenberg, Yukito Kishiro again, and way too many more to include them all here. (Also they taught me that it was okay to be weird.)

Thanks also to everyone at the Canberra Speculative Fiction Guild, who kept me writing, and especially to Leife Shallcross, Ian McHugh, Nicole Murphy and all the others who read an early draft of Wellside (before it was even called that) and whose suggestions made it a much better book.

Last but very far from least, my thanks and all my love to Shauna, who put up with me while I was writing and rewriting, and who it's all for anyway.

About the Author

Robin Shortt was born in Canberra and lives in Vancouver.

You can follow the author online at:

Twitter: @robin_shortt